THE SHIFTER

Hecate's Rebellion Book 1

Jade Hayes

TCA Publishing LLC

CHAPTER 1

L ife sucked.

Penny Dimas leaned on the counter at the diner where she worked, staring out the tinted front windows at the dry and barren Texas landscape, deep in thought. The ground shimmered in the hot sun. Walking home was going to suck even more than walking to work had this morning. She needed a new car. The piece of crap she drove finally gave up the ghost the other day and refused to start. Of course, it waited till the last week of May to do it, when Texas turned into a sweltering, parched, alien planet. Her clean, crisp t-shirt and jeans had been thoroughly drenched in sweat by the time she entered the diner's blessedly cool, air-conditioned interior.

She heaved a hard sigh. What she wouldn't give for something to go her way for once.

At least her grades were good. She aced her finals. Now she had six weeks off before summer classes started. At twenty-six, she was determined to graduate in June next year. It was a long time coming, but there was an end in sight. Finally. She had filled her summer schedule with as many classes as she could take while still hanging on to some semblance of sanity. Her days would be packed and extremely busy, but she would be that much closer to getting her degree. Her parents would be proud of what she was about to accomplish.

Pain lanced Penny's heart. She pressed her lips together and blinked, stemming the tears that threatened whenever she thought about her mom and dad. Her mother had been diagnosed with breast cancer mid-way through Penny's sophomore year of college, and she left school to help her father care for her ailing mother. Nearly two years went by while her mother fought the terrible disease, but ultimately, she couldn't defeat the beast rampaging through her body. Her father followed last year with a heart attack.

But now, Penny was so close to graduating she could almost taste it. She wasn't going to let some pesky obstacle like a broken-down vehicle stop her. Not after everything else that had stood in her way. She was just thankful the car waited until *after* the spring semester ended.

She couldn't fathom how she would get to Austin for school without a car. The little town she lived in wasn't far from the city, but it was far enough that there was no public transportation into Austin. She had six weeks to figure out what she was going to do. Every penny she had went into her bills, so there wasn't really any left over for unexpected events. She was still thanking her lucky stars her parents thought to put money away for her for college.

That still didn't answer what she was going to do about her car, though.

Penny's eyes landed on the auto shop across the street. Maybe she could barter with the owner, Evan Meyers. She knew he hated doing his books for the garage. He might let her work off at least part of the cost of the parts and labor that way.

Heaving another sigh, Penny passed her cleaning rag over the counter, wiping away the non-existent crumbs.

It couldn't get much duller in here. Since the morning rush abated hours earlier, it had been dead quiet. She didn't know why Martin didn't just close up at ten and reopen at four. He said it was because they would lose their lunch customers—all eight of them. The diner wouldn't be busy again until the supper rush started, so here she stood, wiping counters until they gleamed.

She resisted the urge to sigh again.

The bell over the door jingled, and Penny almost jumped out of her shoes. She looked up to see a fiftyish-man dressed in a very expensive suit, carrying an equally expensive brief case, walk inside. Penny couldn't help but stare. She couldn't remember the last time they had a customer after the lunch "rush," and certainly not one dressed like this man.

Mentally slapping herself, she put a smile on her face as the man moved toward the counter.

"Hi. Welcome to Martin's. Would you like a menu?"

The stranger shook his head. "No. I'm actually looking for you, Ms. Dimas."

Penny stood straighter in shock. She knew her eyebrows were even with her hairline. "Me?"

The man smiled and held out his hand. "Davos Katrakis."

Penny shook his hand, eyeing him warily.

"I'm the attorney handling the estate for your Uncle Theo."

Just as quickly as they went up, Penny's eyebrows slammed down into a frown. "Who? I don't have an Uncle Theo."

The attorney opened his briefcase and withdrew a sheaf of papers. He turned the top sheet around for her to see. "Are you not, Penthesilea Aminta Aeolia?"

Penny frowned harder as she looked down at the paper. That was her picture—she saw it on her driver's license every time she opened her wallet. But that was not her name.

"No. My name is Penelope Ann Dimas."

The attorney's eyebrows rose almost comically, and he rocked back on his heels. "Who were your parents? Your real parents?"

This man was making no sense. "Costas and Larissa Dimas."

A look of disbelief and exasperation crossed Mr. Katrakis's face before he closed his eyes and pinched the bridge of his nose.

"They never told you," he muttered under his breath.

"Told me what?" Penny asked, completely confused.

The attorney pulled a sheet out of the stack on the counter and handed it to her. "That you were adopted as an infant. Your biological parents were Ajax and Phoebe Aeolia. They were killed in a car accident just months after your birth. Your father's brother, and your uncle, Theophanes Aeolia, was only seventeen at the time and could not care for you. Family friends, Costas and Larissa Dimas, adopted you and raised you as their own. I had no idea they didn't tell you who you really were." He straightened and ran a hand over his cheek. "Oh my. This must be a shock. I'm sorry, my dear."

Shock was an understatement, Penny thought, reading the adoption decree Katrakis handed her. Those were her parents' names on there, but this couldn't be right. "This really doesn't make any sense. You must have the wrong person." She gestured to the photograph. "One who looks a lot like me, but isn't me. I really don't know those people or Theo-whatever-you-called-him."

Mr. Katrakis sighed and sat down heavily on one of the counter stools. "Theophanes Aeolia. And no, my dear, I'm afraid what I say is the truth. This woman is you. Your uncle kept track of you through-out your life. You really were adopted as a baby. Why they didn't tell you, I don't know. Theophanes—Theo—was your biological father's brother. He died on his estate in South Carolina two weeks ago from a fall. You are his heir, and he left his entire estate to you."

Penny sagged against the counter. "I'm his what? He *what*?" Penny couldn't hold back the shriek.

"Penny?" She turned as her boss, Martin Presley, poked his head up in the serving window. "You all right, girl?"

Whisking a hand over her hair and down her glossy black ponytail, Penny nodded. "I'm fine, Martin."

She was so far from fine!

Martin eyed the man sitting in front of her. "You sure? I can call Dwight."

Penny knew he'd have the town police chief, Dwight Mathias, at the diner in a heartbeat if she said the word.

"No, don't do that. Really. I'm fine, Martin. I just got a little surprised is all," she hastily assured him. As freaked out as she was, she did want to hear what the attorney had to say.

With one more suspicious look at the man at the counter, Martin disappeared back into the kitchen.

Penny turned back to the attorney. "So, let me get this straight. You're saying I'm not who I think I am, and that I've inherited some kind of estate?"

Katrakis nodded. "Your uncle became a rather wealthy man after he finished college. He hit it big on a salvage dive about twenty years ago. Some of it he put back into other dives, and some of it he invested. He's left you a house with some land in South Carolina, as well as the family estate in Greece. All of his business assets have also fallen to you."

Penny gripped the counter until her knuckles turned white. Her mind whirled with all the information Mr. Katrakis threw at her. How could her parents have not told her she was adopted? *Why* wouldn't they have told her, especially considering, if what Mr. Katrakis said was true, they were family friends? And why wouldn't her uncle have been in her life if he knew her adoptive parents?

Unfortunately, all the people with answers were dead.

Disbelief ricocheted through her mind. She had so many questions. While her financial situation certainly seemed to be changing, so did everything else. Life suddenly had bigger complications than how she was going to pay for car repairs so she could get to class in six weeks.

Katrakis withdrew an envelope from his briefcase and handed it to her. "Your uncle left you this. He said it would help explain things." He pulled another sheaf of papers from his briefcase. "This is a copy of the will. I wanted to do this at your parents' bank in Austin, but seeing as you have no idea who you really are, or that Theo even existed, it seems prudent to go over it now."

Penny lent half an ear to the man as he went over the terms of the will. She managed to catch that she was now a very wealthy woman and the owner of a salvage company based out of Charleston, South Carolina. What she was going to do with that, she had no clue.

"That about sums it up, Ms. Dimas," Katrakis said, breaking past the semi-trance she'd been in since the attorney made his pronounce-ment. "I need you to sign these documents, but they need to be wit-nessed and notarized, which unfortunately cannot be done here. For that, I will need you to come to Austin. Would you be able to meet me there this afternoon after your shift ends?"

Penny straightened and drew in a shaky breath, some of the fog falling away at his words. "Um. I don't have a working vehicle right now."

Katrakis nodded in acknowledgement. "I will send a car for you. Would four o'clock work for you to arrive in Austin?"

Still in shock, Penny merely nodded. "That would be fine. I get off in an hour."

"I will send the car to your home then." He showed her the address listed on the sheet with her birth name. "Is this correct?"

Again, Penny nodded, dumbfounded.

"Good." Katrakis gathered all the documents except the envelope and the will and stuffed them back in his briefcase. "I'll leave that copy here for you to read over again if you wish. Once you sign the original, we'll make a copy for you to keep. It was a pleasure to meet you, Ms. Dimas. I will see you at four in Austin."

Penny felt a bit like a broken record, but again, all she could do was nod.

The attorney left as quickly as he came. Penny walked around the counter and practically fell onto a stool. She stared down at the envelope in her hands before ripping it open. There needed to be answers in it. She really, really needed answers because this was just all too weird. She pulled out the single sheet of paper and started reading.

My dear Penny,

If you're reading this letter, then I am dead and have yet to explain all this in person. For that, I am truly sorry. I had hoped to one day ease you into this as my time as the keeper came to a close, but events have occurred that no longer make that possible; contacting you in person would have brought more danger upon you than explaining things posthumously. There are a great many things about you and our family that, for your safety, we have kept hidden from you all these years. I hope one day you can forgive us all for the deception. We did it out of love. No matter what you learn or what happens over the coming days and weeks, please keep an open mind and remember that the world is not as it seems. There are forces at work you will have to come to grips with. These are not the ramblings of a crazy man, as you're probably thinking. Once you take possession of my assets, all will be explained further. There is a safe deposit box at a bank in Charleston that contains answers about your heritage and a guide for your future. Dole out your trust very carefully. There are those who wish to see our family's legacy fall into evil hands. I and your parents—both sets—loved you dearly. May the gods be with you.

-Theo

Penny stared down at the letter, more confused than ever. Evil forces? Family legacy? *Gods*? Seriously, what the hell? None of this made sense and the letter only gave her more questions.

She stuffed the letter back into the envelope, fighting the urge to scream in frustration. She glanced at her watch and groaned. Four o'clock couldn't come soon enough.

CHAPTER 2

S crub brush in hand, Penny scoured the old wash basin she found out back the other day. It was in great shape, if a little dirty, and would look nice filled with flowers on the back deck. Heaven knew she needed a bit of a sanctuary to help her decompress at the end of the day. Theo's business—not to mention the family problems—he left her with had sent her stress levels through the roof in the last four weeks.

Water splashed her bare feet and a fine mist flew around her face as she rinsed the grimy soapsuds from the basin. As she let go of the nozzle trigger, the sound of tires crunching gravel drew her attention. Frowning, she set the hose down and stepped inside, hurrying through the house to the front windows. She pushed aside the curtain to peek outside. Alarm crept along her spine as she watched a silver sedan wind up her driveway.

She had been at Theo's house for two weeks, and this was the first visitor to show up unannounced. All her other visitors called first and were bigwigs from Theo's company or her attorney, Davos.

The curtain fluttered in her fingers. It was probably just people from the salvage company coming to ask her more questions, for which she had few answers. She was learning, but the curve was steep.

She was thankful for her nearly complete accounting degree. It gave her a modicum of business acumen and allowed her to wade her way through all the things involved in running a multi-million dollar salvage operation without drowning.

She couldn't fathom who else could be here to see her if it wasn't someone from the company. She didn't have any friends here; they were all in Texas, including her best friend, Keira. And no one but Davos and a handful of Theo's employees knew the gate code to get onto the property. They weren't supposed to share the code, though, and the car coming closer didn't look familiar.

Penny had deliberately kept the code to a select few. Something about Theo's words in his first letter to her made her cautious. Once she had arrived in Charleston and went to that safe deposit box—well, it was eye opening, to say the least. And scary, because as far as she had discovered so far, all completely true.

As the car reached the fork in the drive, it veered left toward the barn, where it stopped out front. A man the size of a mountain climbed out. She had a feeling he would dwarf her, which was saying something because she was six-foot-one in her bare feet.

His clothes were rather conservative, but the dark jeans and sports coat did nothing to mask the raw power he exuded as he walked up to the barn. His dark hair gleamed as sunlight bounced off the glossy strands. Penny watched muscles flex beneath the sleeves of his jacket as he reached out to tug on the barn door. When it didn't budge, he looked up at the loft door overhead before turning and scanning the property. His gaze paused on her SUV parked in the drive.

Penny cursed. She knew she should have parked in the garage, but after spending an exhaustive morning at Theo's office, pouring over more business files to learn all she could about the operation, she hadn't wanted to walk the extra distance from the garage to her living room. The driveway was closer to the front door and the couch. She needed to get groceries later, anyway.

She now regretted that decision. This hulk of a man knew she was home. If he had nefarious ideas in mind, she doubted she could fight him off.

Deciding to be cautious, she retrieved her uncle's shotgun from its place in the coat closet and propped it next to the door within easy reach. He might be bigger and stronger, but a bullet would still stop him.

When she peeked out of the window again, it was to see him look back and forth between her Jeep and the house, before starting in her direction. Determination flowed off of him like water.

A jolt of awareness speared Penny when the man got close enough for her to see his face. He was almost handsome beyond words. He had a deep tan and a square jaw that looked like it was carved from granite. Dark stubble dusted it, bringing out the angles. His lips, beneath a patrician nose that looked like it was broken at least once in his life, were lush and full. Her eyes trailed down his body, past the breadth of his shoulders and chest. She paused at his waist, where a badge gleamed in the sun next to a matte black gun in a holster on his belt.

He was a cop. Penny wondered what brought him out here. She had her suspicions, especially since he stopped at the barn first, but whether he wanted to uncover the truth or bury it, she could only guess. She found herself hoping for the former.

He reached the house and paused at the base of the porch. After a brief glance around the property, he climbed the steps. She watched as he removed his sunglasses and reached out a hand to push the doorbell.

That jolt of awareness turned into a steady electrical current as she caught a glimpse of his eyes. Even in the shade of the porch, she could tell they were blue, and that they were lit with the same determination she could see etched in the lines of his utterly masculine, utterly handsome face. Intelligence glittered in his deep blue eyes. Penny decided underestimating this man would be extremely dangerous.

Circumstances what they were, she was naturally wary of strangers. She knew she should feel uneasy, having such a large man—cop or not—traipsing around her property, especially an armed one. But there was something about this man that begged her to trust him.

Theo's warning about being cautious echoed through her mind, giving her pause.

She brushed a hand over the shotgun for reassurance that she could defend herself if necessary, and pulled open the inner door, leaving the screen door between them.

"May I help you?"

Startled blue eyes, the color of the Mediterranean, met hers. Penny held in a little smirk of victory that she had surprised him by actually answering the door. She had a feeling it took a lot to startle this man.

He cleared his throat. "I'm Detective Ty Farris with the Charleston County Sheriff's Department. I'm looking for the owner of this estate."

"That would be me."

"You?" Disbelief was clear on his face and in his voice.

Slightly exasperated that he didn't believe her, Penny resisted rolling her eyes. "Yes."

"You're Penthesilea Aeolia?"

She nodded. "Penny, please." She was still trying to wrap her head around her birth name. It had never sounded so good, though, as it did rolling off this man's tongue. It was melodic. "What can I do for you, detective?"

"I'm investigating Theo Davis's death. We have reason to believe it wasn't an accident. I'd like to take another look around the loft where he fell."

Penny jolted at the use of her uncle's alias falling from the detective's lips. Davos had always referred to Theo as Theo Aeolia. It wasn't until after Penny took possession of the estate that she learned Theo changed his surname to Davis. Court papers in his safe deposit box cited threats against him as the reason for the name change. He filed the documents not long after her birth parents died and the Dimas's adopted her.

Coupled with everything else she learned in the last few weeks—as well as some weird occurrences of late—she suspected her parents' accident wasn't an accident. Just like she suspected Theo's death wasn't an accident. She believed he changed his name to hide from the people targeting their family. It worked well for him for a long time, but not well enough or he would still be alive. Truthfully, Penny was relieved this detective was here, and that he believed Theo's death was suspicious.

Theo's warning niggled at the back of her mind again. She cautioned herself that this man could be using suspicion as an excuse to find out about her family and bury the truth—and subsequently her. Letting this detective find out who killed Theo—and who Theo really was—could be dangerous.

To her, if he was on the side of the killer.

To him, if he wasn't.

To everyone, no matter what side he was on.

But Penny desperately needed an ally. She was no detective, and she didn't think she could figure out who killed Theo on her own. Until a month ago, she was a college student, studying accounting. Give her a set of numbers to crunch or a complex equation to solve and she was your girl—but investigate a murder? She hadn't the first clue where to start.

Again, that urge to trust this giant of a man hit her hard as he continued to watch her. Something was insistently whispering at her not to turn him away. That he was tenacious and wouldn't let this go, even if she tried to persuade him it wasn't worth his time. It was something in his eyes and in his stance. The determination she glimpsed spoke volumes. He wanted answers, and he was going to get them.

Penny wanted answers, too. She wanted her life back. Events this past month had her jumping at shadows. First, it was strangers trying to get in to see her at the salvage office, then attempts to break into the house. She was thankful for the security in place here. It had done its job.

It couldn't stop the letters steadily arriving over the last couple of weeks, though. They had her terrified. They not only corroborated all the craziness Theo detailed in his journal and letters to her, but they threatened her if she didn't give them what they wanted. She was handling it as best she could while she tried to figure out who was behind the threats, but she was having little luck. And she most certainly would not give them what they wanted. That would be utterly disastrous.

Taking a leap of faith, and praying to whatever gods watching that she was making the right decision in at least letting him search, Penny grabbed her keys from the hook by the door. She stuffed her feet into her barn boots and pushed open the screen door.

"So, what makes you think Theo's death wasn't an accident?" Penny asked as they made their way across the lawn to the barn. His long legs ate up the ground, and Penny had to lengthen her stride to keep up with him.

"The medical examiner said some of his injuries were suspicious, and the tox screen came back clean. And because I knew Theo. He wasn't careless, and he wouldn't have fallen from the loft window."

That made Penny pause and stare up at him in surprise. "You knew my uncle?"

He nodded. "We were both part of the county dive team. We did some recreational diving together, too."

His gaze turned suspicious as he stared down at her. "And he never mentioned you, or any other family, for that matter. He only ever told me his family was gone, which is why I was very surprised to learn about your existence in his will. What was your relationship with Theo, Ms. Aeolia?"

His tone grated on her nerves. She fisted her hands on her hips and glared up at him before striding toward the barn again. "It's Dimas, and I never knew him. I was adopted as an infant after my parents died in a car accident. I only learned about him—and them—when his lawyer came to see me with the will. I never knew I was adopted, or my birth name, until that point."

They reached the barn, and she unlocked the door with jerky movements. She took a deep breath, trying to get her agitation under control. Getting upset wouldn't help, and he was right to be suspicious of her just showing up on the scene with no warning. If she were in his shoes, she would see herself as a suspect, too.

One perfectly sculpted eyebrow lifted to disappear under the wave of dark hair that fell over his forehead. "Yet, here you are living in his house now. You sure jumped on your inheritance."

"Theo has a large salvage operation here that he left to me as well as this estate. It requires me to be here to make decisions for the business. His entire life was based in South Carolina. I could hardly manage things from half a country away," Penny answered. It was a partial truth. The business did require her attention, but it was the other part of her inheritance that kept her in Charleston.

He hummed a noncommittal answer and headed for the ladder leading to the loft. With an irritated huff, Penny followed. She might understand where he was coming from, but it still bugged her to be a suspect.

"What are you looking for up here, anyway?" she asked as she emerged behind him. Dim sunlight filtered through the cracks around the door and through the dirty windows on either side of the barn. Loose hay dusted the floor boards and bales of it were stacked three high to the side of the door.

"I'm not sure. Something that's out of the ordinary or doesn't belong. It was searched, but not as thoroughly as it could have been. I was given the case after the M.E.'s report came back suggesting some of his wounds weren't caused by the fall." He clicked on a flashlight and started sweeping it across the floor near the door.

"And you're just *now* searching for more clues?" she asked, incredulous. "It's been *six weeks*."

Ty spared her a quick glance. "I wanted to come out here right away, but I had to wait on my captain to give the okay. He thought Theo was likely just drunk and fell out the open window. We found beer cans up here and it was nighttime when he fell. When the toxicology screen came back clean, I finally convinced him something was hinky."

Deciding his explanation made perfect sense, Penny stayed put, not wanting to disturb any potential evidence. "No one else has been up here that I know of. There's plenty of hay downstairs still, so no one has had a reason to come up here." The stable manager, Hector, had a hard time even stepping into the barn now, knowing this was where Theo died. The older gentleman seemed to have been a great friend of her uncle's and was taking his death very hard. She couldn't see him climbing up into the loft unless absolutely necessary. None of the grooms had any reason to be up here, either, since things were still stocked downstairs.

CHAPTER 3

Ty squatted down in front of the haystack, listening to Ms. Dimas prattle on. His partner thought he was on a wild goose chase, but Ty's gut was screaming at him that something foul happened here. He'd known Theo for years. The man was as agile as a cat. Ty had watched him wind his way through the narrowest of passageways in a shipwreck without getting hung up once. Theo was as elegant as they came. Tripping and falling out of an open hay loft while sober just wasn't something Theo would do, even if in the dark.

His light caught on something, and Ty stopped to peer closer. A faint gleam shone from between two of the bales. He edged closer, trying to tell what it was, but it was buried too far back. It wasn't baling wire, though, that much he could tell. He stuck the end of his light in his mouth and pulled out a pair of latex gloves from his pocket.

"Did you find something?" Penny called from her position near the hatch.

Ty grunted around the light as he pulled on the gloves. Taking the light from his mouth, he aimed the beam between the bales and reached in with his free hand. Smooth metal met his fingers. He pulled his hand back to reveal a cuff link with what looked like Greek symbols on it.

"Well?" Penny said from right behind him.

He frowned up at her. "I thought you were waiting over at the hatch." His eyes raked over her long, curvy form, not for the first time, as she leaned over to see what he found.

She had definitely caught his attention in more ways than one. It was rare that he met a woman who didn't look like a dwarf next to him. That this one not only seemed to be a perfect match for his stature, but was beautiful too, hadn't escaped his notice. Her glossy black hair, jade green eyes, olive skin, and curvy body all combined to make one spectacular package. He had to keep reminding himself she was a person of interest in his case, and therefore, off limits.

She rolled her eyes. "I was until you found something. If something sinister really did happen to my uncle, I want to know." She gestured to the item in his hand. "So, what is it?"

He stood and showed her the cuff link. "Do you know if there's another one like it in your uncle's things?"

Ty watched as Penny stared hard at the cuff link, her eyes slightly wide. He narrowed his gaze and studied her expression more closely. She almost looked like she knew what it was and was slightly afraid. "Ms. Dimas? Do you know if there's another one in the house?"

Her gaze snapped to his. "I have no idea, but you're welcome to look in his bedroom. I went in just to look around, but I haven't moved anything out."

Ty stared her down. She wasn't telling him something. He could feel it. "You're sure you've never seen it?"

She shook her head. "I'm sure. I haven't seen another cuff link like that one."

He kept his gaze steady on hers. There was something there in her eyes. She wasn't telling him the whole truth, but he would be damned if he could figure out what she was hiding.

She held his steady stare, almost like she was challenging him to question her statement. She had given him permission to search her uncle's things, though, and he intended to do just that. "All right. Let's head back inside, then. I'd like to see his room."

Penny nodded and turned back to the hatch. Ty quickly bagged the cuff link and followed her down the ladder. He didn't know what he hoped to find in the house, but something to point him in the right direction would be nice. Something about Theo's death didn't sit right. It was more than just the fact Theo wouldn't be so careless that he fell out of an open loft door, or the inconsistent bruises on his body. Theo had been preoccupied and pensive in the weeks prior to his death; his normal, jovial manner almost non-existent. His niece's reaction to the cuff link only cemented the fact that something was off. She knew something she wasn't telling him, and he intended to find out what that was.

He eyed her speculatively as he followed her back to the house. What was she hiding? What was it she feared? And she definitely feared something. He'd seen the brief flash of it in her eyes before she masked it. This whole case was screaming hinky at him now.

Before he could wonder more about the woman with him, they reached the house. Ty's gaze roamed his surroundings, looking for clues as Penny led him upstairs to the master suite. He had been here right after Theo's death, but again, the house wasn't searched thoroughly. They had all thought it was just a terrible accident—strange, yet terrible. Most of his other colleagues still thought it was an accident, despite the coroner's report. Ty's gut shouted otherwise, and he wasn't going to ignore it. Not just because his instincts had saved his ass more than once while part of the SEAL teams, but because it was Theo. His friend deserved justice, if there were any to be had, and

Ty intended to find out exactly what happened so Theo could rest in peace.

Penny held open the door to Theo's bedroom. "You're welcome to look through it all. I'll be downstairs in the living room if you need anything."

Ty thanked her, then crossed the threshold and went to work. He had answers to find.

CHAPTER 4

Penny rested her head in her hands as she sat at the kitchen table with a steaming cup of tea, trying to calm her frantically racing heart. Seeing the symbol on the cuff link brought home that something sinister had indeed happened to Theo. She knew Detective Farris wouldn't find its match upstairs or anywhere else amongst Theo's things. The other one was with Theo's killer.

She took a gulp of her tea. She was so out of her depth here and really wished she had someone with whom she could trust to talk things out. As far as she knew, there was no one besides her uncle's killer and his allies who knew the true situation.

The urge to trust Detective Farris hit again. She believed he could find out the truth. It was a matter of whether he could be trusted to keep it a secret and handle the killer in an unorthodox manner that was the question. Penny didn't know if she had another choice, though, except to trust the detective with the truth. The attempted break-ins and the letters she received made it abundantly clear her life depended on finding the killer and stopping him.

She raised her mug and took another gulp of tea. Life still sucked.

Boots clomping down the hall brought her out of her musings fifteen minutes later. She turned as Detective Farris entered the kitchen.

"Did you find the match?" she asked, already knowing the answer.

"No."

She nodded and turned back to her tea. It was tepid now, but she needed to do something with her mouth lest she blurt out all she knew.

"And you're sure you haven't seen it somewhere?"

Penny shook her head. "Never." She forced herself to meet his gaze steadily. She wasn't lying. She had never seen a cuff link like that one. The symbol, though, was another story.

His eyes narrowed as he tried to ascertain the truth. She had a feeling he knew she was hiding something, but until she had a chance to think and do a little checking into the good detective, she wasn't uttering another word, no matter how much her gut said she could trust him. As soon as he left, she was going to put a call into Davos and have him find out everything he could about Ty Farris. She wanted to make sure there were no secrets in his closet before she decided to trust him with the truth.

"Okay," the detective finally said. "Would it be anywhere else? His office or his car, perhaps?"

"I'm driving his car now and I cleaned it out shortly after I got here. There was nothing in there like that. As far as his offices go, I'll look through them both for you. I can't let you search either without a warrant because of the business papers he has there. You were his friend and you know how he kept the locations of his dives close to the vest."

Ty nodded. "Yeah, secrecy is the name of the game for salvage hunters." He tapped the evidence bag against his palm. "Okay. Can you look through both today or tomorrow and let me know if you find the match?"

Penny nodded. She would search so he couldn't later say she lied, but she didn't expect to find it in either location. The match to that was with whoever killed Theo and currently terrorizing her.

CHAPTER 5

Ty strode to his desk back at the station and tossed the bagged cuff link onto his partner's desk.

Colin Jacobs looked up from his computer, his eyes landing on the evidence bag.

"What's this?" Colin picked it up and examined it.

"Evidence," Ty quipped.

Colin rolled his eyes. "Well, duh. Evidence of what?"

"Murder." Ty settled into his own desk chair.

A frown dipped Colin's brows. "Murder? Whose? Wait." He held up a hand. "Don't tell me this has something to do with you going out to Davis's place this morning."

Ty nodded and folded his hands behind his head. "I found that in the hay loft wedged between some hay bales. Davis's niece says she hasn't seen the match, and I didn't find one in my search of either the barn or his bedroom."

"Come on, Ty. You know that doesn't mean it came from his killer—or that he was even killed."

"No. Call it a gut feeling, though. The niece seemed edgy when I found it. Scared. She eyed that thing like it was a viper about to bite."

That flash of fear he'd seen in her eyes popped into his head again. Yeah. She was definitely scared.

He dropped his hands and picked up a pen, twirling it between his fingers. Every instinct he had was yelling at him that Theo had been murdered. "I'm telling you, something isn't right about all this. Not just because she seems edgy. He changed his name, Col. Why would he do that if he didn't have a reason to hide? There just has to be more to this than what we know."

Colin tossed the evidence bag onto Ty's desk. "Well, you're going to have to come up with more than a cuff link that could very well belong to Mr. Davis to get the captain to sign off on a full-blown investigation. You're lucky he let you search again at all."

"I know, but now at least I have a place to start."

Colin turned back to his computer. "I still think you're chasing ghosts, but I've also learned not to discount your gut feelings. They've saved my ass more than once. Let me know if you need help."

"You know it." Ty turned to his own computer. Now, to find out more about the beautiful Penny Dimas.

CHAPTER 6

T rue to her word, Penny searched her uncle's home office and found nothing out of the ordinary. Just before she drove over to her uncle's business office, she called Davos to have him run a thorough background check on Ty Farris.

Davos picked up on the second ring. Penny greeted him warmly.

"Penny. What a pleasant surprise." The smile she could hear in Davos's voice brought one to her face. The man was delightful.

"Hi, Davos. I have a favor to ask."

"Anything."

Penny fiddled with the latest letter she received that day, fueling her resolve to bring the detective in on her troubles.

"Can you run a thorough background check on the detective running the investigation into Theo's death? A man named Ty Farris."

There was a pause on the line.

"I'm getting the feeling there was more to Theo than I knew. He asked me to do the same thing just weeks before he died."

Penny's eyebrows rocketed skyward. That was not what she had expected to hear.

"He did? Did he say why?"

"Something about making sure he could trust the man as much as he thought he could. He hinted he needed legal advice. I told him I was happy to help in any way I could, but he said I didn't practice the right kind of law."

Penny chewed on her lip, her mind buzzing with reasons Theo would need legal advice on criminal law.

"My guess was he suspected some kind of criminal activity with one of his salvage operations, but he wouldn't elaborate. Although, it's possible it has something to do with why he changed his name so many years ago. He didn't tell me what that was about. Just left a letter for me to open upon his death, stating his real name and that I needed to contact you, his only living relative and heir."

Penny made a noncommittal sound and changed the subject. "What did you find out about Detective Farris?"

"He's clean as a whistle, from what I could tell. I even hired a private investigator to follow him around a bit—a good one too, because following a police detective—especially one who is a former SEAL, is not easy. The man works, goes home, does a bit of charity work and some sports on his days off. His mother died when he was just a child, but he visits his father fairly regularly. His finances are solid and come solely from his job and some wise investments. The investigator couldn't find anything that even hinted at anything nefarious."

Penny closed her eyes in relief. It was good to know her instincts about him were right.

"Theo had me look into Farris's partner, Colin Jacobs, too. He was as clean as Farris. Why are you asking me this, anyway? Is everything all right?"

Penny did some quick backpedaling. She didn't want to alarm Davos. He was her only ally, even if she couldn't tell him everything. "Everything is fine. Detective Farris is poking around Theo's death. I just wanted to make sure he was on the up and up and that he would give the case its due diligence."

"I think he will, my dear. He and his partner have a very high closure rate on their cases, and both men seem to be exemplary policemen on the job and off."

Thanking him, she bid him goodbye and ended the call with a sigh of relief.

Davos's assurances went a long way toward calming her fears about trusting Detective Farris. She wanted Theo's killer brought to justice, but by tracking him down, she was sure to stir the pot and put herself in more danger. After all, she was the only thing standing between them and what they wanted now. It was a frightening prospect, but if she ever wanted any kind of life, she needed the detective's help.

CHAPTER 7

Penny shut the interior door from the garage and leaned against it. Her search of the business office had been no more successful than her search of the house. Not that she expected otherwise.

Now she was just tired. The large whirlpool tub in the master bathroom was calling her name, along with a glass of wine. Her back ached from kneeling to look under furniture and through boxes. The warm water with the tub jets sounded heavenly.

Quickly putting away the groceries she stopped for on her way home, she crossed to the enormous stainless-steel refrigerator, where she pulled out a bottle of her favorite white wine. Grabbing a wineglass from the cupboard, she tucked her phone in her pocket and headed for the stairs, determined to relax in a jacuzzi full of warm water and bubbles.

While the water filled the tub, Penny poured herself a glass of wine and took a hearty gulp. She already felt more relaxed in the rapidly warming air of the bathroom.

She turned on her phone's music app and set it in the speaker dock on the ledge by the tub. A generous squirt of her favorite vanilla bubble bath got the water foaming, its delicious aroma filling the room. She piled her hair high on her head to keep it out of the bubbles and stripped off her clothes.

A sigh of bliss slipped past her lips as she eased into the hot water and settled against the padded backrest. She may not have been able to bring herself to move into Theo's bedroom, but his bathroom was another story entirely. As soon as she saw the giant two-person jacuzzi bathtub that dominated the room, she immediately moved her toiletries in and never looked back.

Sipping her wine and listening to the music playing from her phone, Penny let her thoughts drift. She really needed to call Detective Farris and give him an update. She didn't think it was wise to do so from the bathtub, however. The man sparked her blood. She could only imagine her reaction to his deep, rich voice filling her senses as she soaked naked in a hot bubble bath.

Penny idly wondered if he would fit in the tub with her. It was a big tub, but he was enormous.

She studied the opposite side, where another backrest sat un-used. Would his shoulders even fit there? She was pretty sure his legs wouldn't. Her toes brushed the opposite side, and he probably had at least six inches on her.

She would love to see him try, though. Images of that broad chest and those thick biceps slicked with water made her face flush. Penny grabbed her wineglass and took another gulp. She needed to reign in her thoughts.

Her phone trilled from its spot in the speaker dock next to the tub; an unknown local number flashed on the screen. Wiping her hand on a towel, she swiped to accept the call and put it on speaker.

"Hello?"

"Ms. Dimas, it's Ty Farris. I'm sorry to call so late, but I just wanted to touch base with you before I called it a day. Any luck in your search for the other cuff link?"

Penny felt her blood heat as his deep voice washed over her. She'd been right about it being a bad idea to talk to him while she was in the bath. She clenched her legs to stem the warmth flooding her belly and tried to concentrate on answering him.

"No," she croaked. Good lord, was that her voice? She grabbed her wineglass and took a hearty gulp. "No," she said, trying again, relieved to hear her voice sounding much more normal. "I didn't find it."

Her conversation with Davos played through her mind once again.

"He and his partner seem to be exemplary policemen on and off the job..."

Taking a deep breath, Penny decided to just bite the bullet. "But I may have something relevant to the investigation. Can you meet me—" she cut off abruptly as a noise from downstairs had her sitting up, splashing water all over the floor.

The detective's voice sounded loud as it echoed through the bathroom. He called her name as she listened for what she heard from downstairs.

"Hang on, detective. I thought I heard something," she said, climbing from the tub. She grabbed a towel and tried to wrap it around herself as quickly as she could.

"Ms. Dimas? Penny? What's going on? What was that noise?" His voice got progressively louder with each question as she failed to answer.

"Ssshhh!" She hastily took him off of speakerphone. Creeping forward, she reached the bathroom door and slowly opened it.

"Did you just shush me?" he asked. Thankfully, he had lowered his voice.

"Yes," she hissed. "I'm trying to listen." She nearly made it to the bedroom door when a loud thud sounded from downstairs. She froze for half a second before she ran as quietly as she could across the room to the walk-in closet.

"There's someone here," she whispered frantically. Penny thrust aside a bunch of Theo's suits and stepped behind them. Right now, she wished she had moved into Theo's room after all. She had several long sundresses that would be better suited for hiding. Her legs were showing.

"I'm on my way. Get some place safe." Penny could hear him moving even as he spoke.

"You didn't happen to notice any weapons in Theo's closet when you searched, did you?" She looked around, trying to find a better place to hide amongst all the clothing. Maybe if she threw a bunch of the stuff on the floor, she could bury herself under it.

Immediately, she dismissed that idea. One good kick from the intruder and he would know she was there.

"Why are you in Theo's closet?"

Penny yanked a sweatshirt off of a hanger and pulled it over her head, then grabbed a pair of baggy sweatpants from the shelf and quickly tugged them up over her hips. She let the towel drop to the floor.

"I was in the bathtub in the master bathroom when you called."

There was a long pause and what sounded like a soft, strangled groan before he spoke again. "Okay. There weren't any weapons in the closet, but there was a handgun in his bedside table. It was loaded."

Penny stopped piling clothing and cracked open the closet door, listening intently. Not hearing anything, she scurried across to the table closest to her. She yanked it open, only to find an old phone charger and some handkerchiefs. "Seriously?" she muttered, pushing it closed. "It couldn't be in the one closest to the closet?" She launched herself across the massive, four-poster, king-size bed and pulled open the drawer on the second table. The sound of footsteps coming up the stairs had her grabbing the gun and lowering herself over the edge of the bed. She wiggled under it on her belly. She could just see the bottom of the door from her position.

As she struggled to get her breathing under control, she heard a car door slam on the other end of the phone line and then Ty call for backup.

"Are you safe, Penny?"

"As safe as I can be," she barely breathed. "I'm under the bed now. I heard someone coming up the stairs." She checked the gun, finding it ready to fire, and thumbed off the safety.

There was a pause as she heard him listening to his radio. She could hear the garbled, tinny voice of the dispatcher in the background.

"There was a patrol already in your area, Penny. He should be there in about two minutes."

Penny closed her eyes and prayed. Oh, how her life had become complicated in the last month. Hiding under a bed with a handgun as some madman tromped through her house, looking for her family's secrets—a family she hadn't even known about—was not something she ever imagined doing. It was all so unreal.

The door down the hall—the one to her room—opened. She listened intently for more footsteps coming closer to Theo's room. All she heard was the sound of things hitting the floor as the intruders ransacked her room.

"What's happening, Penny?"

"It sounds like they're searching my room. I can hear stuff falling and feet moving," she whispered.

"There's more than one person?" Ty asked.

"I think so. It sounded like two sets of boots coming up the stairs."

She heard him relay that information to dispatch, along with the gate code to the property. Idly, she realized that was how he got onto the estate earlier. She should have realized the police would know the code.

More footsteps sounded in the hallway. Penny instinctively shrank back as the door to Theo's room opened. Two sets of black boots filled the doorway.

"Check the closet," one man said.

Penny watched a set of feet peel away and head for the closet. She was suddenly intensely glad she hadn't stayed in there. She wasn't sure being under the bed was much better, though. The other set of boots took several steps in her direction.

The welcome sound of a siren reached Penny's ears as the boots came to a halt just feet from the bed.

"Shit! The cops are coming. Let's go!" He ran for the door. The second set of boots beat a hasty retreat from the closet at his partner's exclamation and both men ran out of the room.

"They're leaving," Penny whispered into the phone. "They heard the siren and are leaving."

Her body sagged in relief. The gun felt heavy in her hand. She put the safety back on before she laid it on the floor in front of her, but didn't let go. She let her head drop until her forehead rested on the plush carpet, inhaling deeply to calm her nerves now that the adrenaline was leaving her.

"Stay where you are until the deputy or I reach you, do you understand?" Ty said. "I'm five minutes away. Dispatch notified the responding officer where you are, but he'll have to check the rest of the house first. You stay put."

Penny nodded, then realized he couldn't see her. "Okay."

The front door banged open. Penny heard the sheriff's deputy identify himself.

"He's here," she relayed to Ty. "I just heard him come in."

"Good. You're safe. Just relax. I'm going to stay on the line just in case."

"Okay."

Penny waited for what seemed like an eternity before she heard boots coming up the stairs again. As they reached the landing, Penny heard Ty shout from downstairs and through the phone. The deputy shouted back that the first floor was clear. More footsteps echoed up the stairs before two sets of booted feet—leather and much nicer than the black combat boots the intruders wore—appeared in Theo's doorway once again.

"Penny?"

At Ty's quiet inquiry, Penny scrambled out from under the bed, tugging at the hem of the sweatshirt to untwist it from her torso.

"Are you okay, ma'am?" the deputy asked.

Penny nodded shakily. Her eyes drank in Ty Farris's appearance, and she took strength from his physical strength. With his imposing bulk standing sentry, she felt calmer and much safer, even if he looked little like a cop at the moment. He must have come from home. His jeans looked old, if their faded color and the holes over his knees were any indication. The gray t-shirt molded across his chest looked buttery soft. Only the gun holster and badge hooked to his belt gave any clue to his profession.

"Go check the other rooms up here. I've got her," Ty said to the deputy.

The deputy hurried out, and Ty walked toward her. Penny looked down as he tugged the pistol from her hand. She was shocked to realize she forgot she still held it when she scrambled from beneath the bed.

He checked to see if the safety was on before leaning around her to return it to the bedside table.

Penny sat down hard on the mattress when he urged her to sit. He squatted in front of her and took her hands.

"You sure you're okay?" he asked. "You're shaking like a leaf."

Taking stock of herself, she realized she was indeed shaking. Most of it was from the adrenaline crash. But she was still unnerved by the ordeal. If the deputy had been just a few seconds later—she didn't even want to think about that.

Penny nodded and turned her hands so she was gripping his. "I'm fine. Just shaken."

He stared at her for several moments, assessing the truth of her statement. "Did you get a look at the intruders?"

Penny shook her head. "Just their feet. They both had on black combat boots and black tactical pants."

He raised an eyebrow at that. "Did they say anything? Indicate what it was they were looking for?"

Again, she shook her head. "Only one spoke, and it was to tell the other to search the closet, and then to yell that the cops were coming. After that, they ran out."

He stared at her again for several moments. She got the feeling he was trying to tell if she was lying. She had that feeling in the barn earlier, too. She was lying then, but she wasn't now. Except she knew what they were after.

Penny opened her mouth to spill everything when the sheriff's deputy walked back in, declaring the house all clear. She snapped her mouth closed and took a deep breath. Spilling her family's secrets while there was another person in the house would have been terrible. She could not risk someone else finding out and telling others about the "loony" rantings of Theo's niece. It would not do her or the rest of the world any good if she was labeled a crazy woman.

Ty turned to the deputy. "Check the grounds, but I suspect the intruders are long gone. I'll have Ms. Dimas check to see if anything is missing and close out the report."

The deputy nodded and headed out just as Ty's words sank in.

Missing...

Oh, God! The key!

Penny stood, nearly knocking Ty on his butt.

"Ms. Dimas? What the—" Penny barely heard him as she brushed past him and flew out of the room.

"Penny? Wait! Where are you going?"

Penny didn't bother to answer. She ran down the stairs and went straight to the kitchen and into the pantry.

She stopped at the sight. Flour, sugar, oats, and every other kind of powder and grain littered the tile floor; the boxes smashed and ripped. Dented cans laid haphazardly on top of it all. It was a right mess. She looked up at the tallest shelf, now empty, praying the intruders hadn't reached all the way to the back.

Ty came to a halt behind her. "What's going on? Why are you so all-fired to see if they ransacked the pantry?"

She didn't answer. She couldn't. Not until she knew. Pushing past him once again, she walked into the mudroom off the kitchen and grabbed the step ladder.

It had to be there still. It just had to be. They wouldn't have come upstairs if they found it. Right?

She set the ladder in front of the shelves and climbed. Even with the added height, she couldn't see over the top shelf. But she could reach. When she hid the key, this was the safest place she could think of. She figured if she needed a ladder to reach it, most people would, too. Detective Farris might be the only person she knew who could reach it without at least a step stool.

Her hand ran over the smooth board. *Where was it?* She was almost frantic when her fingers ran over the bump taped to the very back of the shelf along the wall. Her shoulders drooped in relief, and she pulled the key free from the tape.

She brought her hand down and held the tiny key in front of Ty Farris's face. "This is why."

CHAPTER 8

Ty stared at the tiny safe deposit box key Penny held inches from his face. "A key? I'm guessing what it goes to is what you're really worried about?"

Penny nodded, and Ty helped her down from the ladder. "Does this have anything to do with Theo's death?"

Again, she nodded. "I lied to you earlier when you asked about the cuff link." She held up her hand when his eyebrows slammed down in a frown, stemming the words that wanted to break free. "Not about the cuff link itself. I can guarantee the other one is nowhere in this house. Not unless the killer left it somewhere. I lied about the symbol on it. I know what that is and what it stands for."

Ty frowned even harder, processing the information. He knew she was hiding something.

"So, you know who killed your uncle? Why the hell didn't you say something?"

She took a deep breath and blew it out, pushing her hair back. "I don't know *who* killed him. But I do know why. Look, I don't want to talk about this here. I don't know who could be listening. Especially since someone was just in the house."

Ty looked around incredulously. She couldn't be serious. "You think the house is bugged?"

She nodded. "It's possible."

"Lady, you are off your rocker. Why would anyone want to bug Theo's house?"

She grabbed his hand and started pulling him back upstairs, not answering his question.

"Where are we going?" This situation was rapidly spiraling out of his control. He needed answers, and she still refused to give them to him.

"My room. I need to change."

Ty's eyes roamed her backside, ascending the stairs in front of him, even as he told himself to focus on the case. The woman had some seriously distracting curves. While the sweat suit was baggy, it did little to hide her shape—and it dipped just a little lower than it should over her hips. He wouldn't mind if she stayed in this outfit.

A mental slap brought him back to the matter at hand. What the hell was wrong with him? This woman was the victim of a crime. The niece of a homicide victim. No matter how beautiful or intriguing he found her, he needed to forget thoughts like those and focus on the case. Being distracted was how people got hurt.

She led him directly to her bedroom and immediately tested his resolve. "If I'm going to show you why all this is happening, I am not leaving the house without at least some underwear on."

Biting back a groan as the memory of their phone conversation earlier pinged through his brain, Ty followed her into the bedroom. She grabbed a couple items off the floor and stepped into the bathroom. He had to hand it to her. She didn't seem all that fazed by the state of her room. The entire floor was covered in clothing, books, and broken knick-knacks. The would-be burglars had left nothing in the drawers or on the shelves. *Everything* was on the floor, and she had just walked over it like it wasn't even there. Whatever that key kept safe had her total attention.

In what had to be the fastest clothing change on record, Penny emerged from the bathroom in jeans and a t-shirt.

"Come on." She flew by him again. "Let's do this before I chicken out."

Ty frowned, wondering what she meant by that. He followed her as she first stopped to drain the bathtub, and then as she headed downstairs. He was so confused and felt like all control had slipped from his grasp. She was like a locomotive, running full steam ahead with no brakes, leaving him in the dust.

It was time to catch up and take back the reins on his investigation. He grabbed her hand as she went to pick up her purse and car keys from where they had been dumped unceremoniously by the interior garage door.

"Hang on, sugar."

The look of impatience on her face was enough to make him smile.

"While I appreciate you're finally ready to tell me some things you should have this morning, how do you propose to do that when it's nearly eleven o'clock and all the banks are closed? Why don't I help you make sure the house is secure and get you to a hotel? We can finish this in the morning."

She was shaking her head before he even finished. "No. Now that I've decided to trust you, you need to know this." She held up that little key again. "And this key, and my name, mean I have the bank manager at my beck and call."

Ty didn't quite know what to say to that. He knew Theo had clout, but that it carried over to his never-before-known-about niece said something about what was in that box. Had Theo found some cache of sunken treasure Ty didn't know about? It was entirely possible. Salvage hunters tended not to tell others about their finds until it was all scooped up. Opportunists trying to steal a piece of the treasure for themselves were a real problem. Maybe Theo had stashed some rare and priceless find in that box.

Penny made for the door again, but his hand on her arm stopped her. "Wait. This is insane. Getting into Theo's safe deposit box can wait until morning. Dragging the poor bank manager out of his bed for some treasure Theo stashed away is asinine. It's not going anywhere. The best thing we can do tonight is put your house back in order and make sure everything is secure."

She rolled her eyes at him, then just stared at him, clearly annoyed.

Ty glared back, just as annoyed. She could pitch a fit all she wanted. This was one lead that wasn't going anywhere. It made little sense to open the box tonight.

"You don't understand," she argued. "I'm not worried about what's in the box. Now that they've made their move, we've run out of time. They won't stop until they have what they want, which is me dead, and the artifact in their hands."

Ty snapped his fingers and pointed at her. "So, this *is* about some treasure Theo found. I knew his death wasn't an accident." He narrowed his eyes at her, suspicions flaring. "What do you know about who killed him? Were you involved?" He would lock her up so fast, her head would spin, and then he'd throw the damn book at her. He didn't care who she was, or what kind of connections she had. He would nail her to the damn wall.

"No," she was quick to reply. "I had nothing to do with Theo's death. I told you already I didn't even know about him until the lawyer came to see me. And it's not just 'some treasure' in the box. Theo didn't find it. He inherited it, just like I did." She huffed and grabbed his arm, trying to tug him toward the garage.

Ty planted his boots and refused to move. "I'm not going anywhere until you answer my questions. What do you know about Theo's murder?"

Penny sighed, and he watched some of the fight leave her. "I'll tell you, but not here." She glanced around once more.

Ty resisted the urge to roll his eyes. He forgot she thought the house had ears.

"So, where do you suggest we go?"

She pointed at the door leading into the garage.

"You want to talk in the garage?" He frowned.

She nodded.

He looked heavenward, praying for patience.

"Fine," he finally acquiesced. He wanted answers. "But you will tell me everything, or I will take you down to the station and we'll do it there. Understand?"

She nodded once more and spun, opening the door and hurrying through. Ty followed her in, flipping the light switch as he did.

"Talk." He crossed his arms and blocked the door, giving her his best cop glare. He was done messing around now.

"Lock the door, please."

Without taking his eyes off her, he reached behind him and flipped the deadbolt.

"Talk," he demanded again, harshly, his voice rumbling low through the cavernous space.

She took a deep breath, wringing her hands. "You won't believe anything I say without proof, so you're going to get that first. Everything that's going on—with Theo, with me—is not as it seems. If you're going to help me, you need to know everything."

Before Ty could ask what the hell she was talking about, a shimmer, almost like a mirage, surrounded her. Suddenly, he wasn't looking at Penny anymore, but a sleek black cat with jade green eyes.

"Holy shit!" Ty leaped back. Stumbling, he slammed into the door, making it rattle in its frame.

The shimmer surrounded the cat, and Penny reappeared.

Ty blinked hard, trying to make sense of what he'd seen. "What the hell just happened? What are you? Some kind of master magician?" Ty's eyes darted around the garage, searching. "Is that why you insisted we talk out here? You have a bunch of mirrors or some shit set up, so you can perform your little illusion? Where'd you hide the cat?"

Penny sighed. "There are no mirrors or cats, detective. That was all me. I told you nothing is as it seems."

Ty frowned fiercely. "No. That is impossible." She couldn't be saying what he thought she was. It just wasn't possible.

Penny shook her head. "It's not, if you're part goddess."

His eyebrows shot to his hairline as his disbelief soared. "You really expect me to believe that? You're bloody insane." He reached out to grab her arm, intending to haul her out to his truck and down to the station, only to have it *disappear* from his grasp.

A songbird fluttered in front of his face where Penny stood only moments before.

Ty slowly dropped his hand and just stared, eyes wide. His breath left him in a huff of disbelief. He had felt her change beneath his fingers.

But it couldn't be real! People didn't shape shift, and goddesses didn't exist.

Did they?

CHAPTER 9

P enny watched the emotions cross the detective's face. His anger gave way to disbelief, before a sort of incredulous acceptance settled on his handsome face. Only then did she shift back to human form.

She'd been practicing her shifting for weeks now, ever since she read Theo's explanation of who she was, where their family came from, and the abilities she possessed in his second letter to her. It had triggered a memory from when she was a child. She had been three. One day, she watched the family dog tree a squirrel and wondered what the world would look like from up there.

Headstrong as ever, Penny walked right up to the tree and wished she was a squirrel too. The next thing she knew, she'd shifted into the fuzzy little rodent and scampered right up the tree trunk, peering down at her family below.

Her mother was horrified and told Penny to come down immediately. Penny had seen nothing wrong with what she did, and it wasn't until her dad threatened to get a ladder and come up after her that Penny came down, switching back to her little girl self.

The next day, a nice lady came over to visit, and she brought a tea for Penny to drink. It was disgusting, but her mother demanded she finish it.

Penny wondered now what had been in that tea, and how her parents knew who to contact. She had never shifted again until she read about the ability in Theo's letter.

"Are you ready to listen to me now?" she asked the detective softly.

He just nodded, looking a little shell-shocked.

"I'm not crazy, and I'm also not some supernatural being. I'm just an ordinary woman from Texas, with an extraordinary ability thanks to my heritage."

He continued to just stare at her, waiting for her to explain further.

Penny sighed. "How much Greek mythology do you know?"

Ty looked taken aback at her question. "Greek mythology? A smattering, I guess. Enough to know the symbol on that cuff link is Greek. My dad's a historian at the University of Charleston. He teaches Greek and Roman mythology. I was going to take it to him tomorrow to see if he could tell me what it was."

"No!" Penny practically shouted. She clutched his arm. "You absolutely cannot share the details of this investigation with anyone. Not even your partner. Not yet. Maybe not ever."

He laughed incredulously. "You're kidding, right?"

She shook her head.

"You can't be serious. I'm a detective. With the sheriff's department. Not some two-bit private investigator who can do as he pleases. Theo's death is an active investigation. I can't report something just because you ask me not to."

"Do you really think they'll believe a word of any of this?" she asked softly.

Ty frowned, his brow puckering as he thought about that. "Fine. But it's still murder we're talking about here. I can't just ignore that."

A hard glint appeared in her eyes. "Trust me, detective, I know exactly what we're talking about. You don't, so perhaps you should give me the benefit of the doubt. Once you know the whole story, it'll all make sense, and you'll understand why we alone have to deal with this."

His eyes hardened. "Okay, enlighten me," he bit out.

Penny could tell he didn't like being in the dark. It was bothering him to be at a disadvantage here. She intended to use that to her benefit. He wanted answers? Well, he was going to have to cooperate with her first.

"I'll tell you more on the way to the bank."

This time, he didn't protest when she headed for the car. He just muttered a terse, "I'll drive," and then steered her out the side door to where his pickup was parked haphazardly in front of the garage.

CHAPTER 10

Ty tried to reengage his brain as they climbed into his truck. Even with what she just shared with him, he was sorely tempted to skip the bank and drive straight to the station. He needed time to process her revelations. It went against everything he believed, but he couldn't deny she had indeed changed into an animal right before his eyes—twice. It was only that weird juju and his need for more answers that kept him heading toward the bank.

"Talk," he demanded once more as he pulled through the estate's gates and onto the main road.

He rolled his eyes at himself. He sounded like a broken record. All the weirdness had short-circuited his brain.

She turned slightly in her seat so she faced him. "That symbol on the cuff link is the symbol for the Ancient Greek city-state of Mycenae. According to the journals Theo left, my family comes from Thessaly and has been—at odds with a Mycenaean family since ancient times."

Ty thought for sure his eyebrows were going to be permanently stuck to his hairline by the end of the night. Every time she told him something else, the whole thing got more ludicrous. "You're telling me someone killed your uncle over a what—forty-*century* feud?"

She nodded. "It's a little more complicated than just a feud, but yes. I told you it was far-fetched."

He scoffed and stared out the window. That was an understatement. It was utterly ridiculous to think Theo had been killed because two families hated each other dating back almost four thousand years. No one held a grudge that long. That was the Hatfields and McCoys to the extreme. And then some. She really seemed to believe it, though.

"You said there's more to it than just a feud." Ty wanted her to elaborate. "And where does your little trick fit into all this?"

"It goes back to the Trojan War."

Before he could respond, or she could continue, head lights suddenly came up behind them. The car's brights were on, flooding his truck with light and bouncing off the mirrors. Ty squinted against the glare.

"Ty?" Penny's voice wavered slightly as she eyed the vehicle rapidly coming up on them.

"I know. Hang on." He gripped the wheel harder and ran a map of the area through his head. They would be in the suburbs soon. If he could outrun their pursuers until then, he could lose them in the maze of residential streets. Until they hit those areas, though, there weren't many places to turn and get away.

Seeming to realize where they were as well, the car behind them sped up until it was nearly on their bumper. Ty could tell it was an SUV nearly as large as his truck. He pressed the accelerator, pushing the truck to go faster. If they rammed him, it would be an even match.

The truck growled as he pushed it to its limits. Just as he reached for his radio to call for backup, a sickening *thwack* hit the back windshield, and it spider-webbed. A second *thwack* hit and the glass shattered. Penny screamed, and Ty started swerving as more shots pinged off the back of the truck. The bastards had decided to shoot at them rather than ram them.

"Take my gun and shoot back!" Ty yelled, desperately trying to maintain control of the truck as he swerved hard back and forth to make them a harder target to hit. It was only a matter of time before a shot hit a tire.

Penny lifted the gun from the holster on his right hip and pointed it out the back. The blast of the weapon firing was deafening in the close confines of the truck, but Ty paid it little heed. They were only a mile from the first suburb. He reached for the radio again.

Penny quit firing to put her hand over his.

"No! No cops."

"They're shooting at us!" No matter what secrets she held, they needed backup.

"And what will we tell them when they ask why the people in the SUV shot at us? I will not say one damn word and will deny all knowledge of what they want. You can't tell them anything, because you don't know anything other than they want to kill me." She stared him down. "You have to trust me, Ty. The fate of the world depends on it."

He spared her an unbelieving look. "You hold the fate of the world? You? You seriously expect me to believe that?" He shook his head. "Whatever is in the box is not worth all of this."

Another shot pinged off the tailgate. Penny fired back. The SUV backed off again. Ty growled and pushed the truck harder, trying to put some distance between them and their pursuers.

"I'm sorry you feel that way, but we don't have another choice. Arresting me will just bring you more problems and possibly get me killed."

Ty growled again and smacked his palm on the steering wheel. "What the hell are you involved in?"

Before Penny could answer, their pursuers opened fire again, this time hitting a tire. Ty fought for control, but he could feel the truck tipping past the point of no return.

CHAPTER 11

Ty felt like he was flying. The truck rolled end over end as it went off the embankment. Penny's hand landed on his, gripping it tight. A tingle raced through him and suddenly, he wasn't inside the car anymore. He opened his eyes to see the ground beneath him. He flinched and tried to wrap his arms around his head to protect himself from the impact before he realized he *wasn't falling*. He was floating. Upside down. And there weren't arms covering his head, but feathers. And something was holding him by the feet.

Before he had time to fully process what was happening, he was swooping toward the ground in a controlled descent. Whatever had hold of him let go just before his head hit the ground. Instinctively, he tucked and rolled, coming to a rest on his back, arms—make that wings—akimbo. He stared hard at the feathered appendages attached to his body. He was dreaming. He had hit his head in the crash and was unconscious. This was all just a crazy-ass dream, he told himself.

An owl, feathers an unusual burnished gold that glowed in the moonlight, hopped next to him. Intelligent jade green eyes stared at him from the owl's face. Before he could do more than marvel at its beauty, a shimmer surrounded the owl, and suddenly he was staring at Penny again.

He scrambled back—on his hands this time and not on wings.

"Holy shit," he breathed. "Penny, what the hell is going on?" He looked away and struggled to stand. "This is a dream," he murmured to himself, staring at the ground. "Just a really weird, fucked up dream." He had *not* just been an owl.

A hand on his forearm stopped his muttering.

"It's not a dream, Ty. If you give me a chance, I can explain."

Ty looked up to see Penny standing in front of him, tears shimmering in her pretty green eyes.

He looked around the field they landed in, his eyes bouncing from one spot to another. The same tall grass surrounded them as far as he could see. "Where are we?" He needed to know so he could get the hell away from this woman. She had turned him into a frickin' owl!

"I flew us inland a few miles before you realized what was happening and started to struggle. I was afraid I'd drop you, so I landed us here. We're far enough away from the accident that no one from that SUV will be able to find us." She sank down into the grass.

His knees gave way as a semblance of reality slowly started to sink in. He sank to his butt in the grass next to her. This was completely crazy.

He turned to Penny. "Explain," he demanded. "How can you shape shift? How can you make *me* shape shift?"

"First of all, I want to say I know exactly how you feel right now. A month ago, I knew nothing about any of this. It still all seems a bit fantastical, and I've been wishing it was ever since I read Theo's letters and journal."

Ty nodded. No lie there. Even after all he just experienced, he was still struggling to accept it as truth.

She took a deep breath and continued. "Have you ever heard of the Greek goddess Thetis?"

Brow scrunched in thought, Ty waded his way through all the Greek history his father drilled into his head as a kid. "She was a sea nymph, right? And Achilles's mother?"

Penny nodded, a small smile curving her lips. "Yes. She was also the daughter of Poseidon, and she could shape shift."

Ty's eyes widened at the implication. His brain had put the pieces together, but believing what it was telling him was hard to swallow. It was just unfathomable. "That's not possible. The Greek gods are just myths."

Penny wrapped her hand over his. "No, Ty. They're not. My family are direct descendants of Thetis. Apparently, her abilities have been passed down to her descendants. Until this past month, I only ever shifted once before in my life, and I was a child then. I had actually forgotten all about it."

"How did I shift, then? I'm not related to you."

She shook her head. "Likely, my emotions amplified the ability, and I was able to transfer it to you. I just grabbed you and prayed as we started to roll. I wasn't even sure I could change you, but I knew if I didn't try, you were going to get seriously hurt."

Ty swallowed hard. That was a sobering thought. He was grateful she had the foresight to do something.

He cleared his throat. "What does this have to do with Theo and whatever's in that deposit box?"

Penny pulled her hands back and folded them in her lap. He missed her touch immediately, which was plain crazy. This entire situation was nuts. His mind reeled, and not just from the bump he got when the truck rolled.

"I really wanted to sit you down, explain who Theo really was, and show you his journal. Ease you into this. Show you the artifact."

"Artifact? You mentioned that earlier. What is it? And what do you mean 'who he really was?'" Ty interrupted.

Penny sighed. "His real name was Theophanes Aeolia. He was my father, Ajax's, younger brother."

"Why did he change his name? That's been bugging me since I read his will."

"To hide the artifact. And me," she stated matter-of-factly. She pushed back the hair that had come loose from the topknot on her head. "Do you know who Hippolyta is?"

Wonder Woman popped into his head, and he frowned. "The Amazon from the comic books? Wonder Woman's grandmother or whatever she is?"

Penny nodded. "She's been fictionalized, but she was real, too. Her father was Ares, and he gave her a golden girdle—a belt."

He nodded. He remembered this story from his youth now. "It was supposed to make her unbeatable in battle."

Penny nodded encouragingly. "Yes. Exactly. And it worked very well. But she was arrogant and didn't always wear it. She died because of that. The belt, and the title of queen of the Amazons, went to her sister, Penthesilea, after Hippolyta's death."

"Your namesake."

"Right. During the time of the Trojan conflict, Penthesilea—who fought later in the war—met Achilles, and they fell in love. Now, I know ancient scribes all had her and Achilles dying in battle, which is true. What they don't mention is that Penthesilea and Achilles had a child, a son, Aelon. Penthesilea hid him with her sisters before she went into battle. When she died, they sent him to his grandmother, Thetis, to be raised. She kept him safe, and he grew into adulthood."

"What does that have to do with Hippolyta's belt?"

"The belt allows the wearer to wield enormous power. If you can't be beaten while wearing it, it stands to reason there's nothing you couldn't do, which is why someone wants it. According to the journal, my family, as descendants of Penthesilea and Achilles, were tasked with protecting the belt and keeping it from those who would use it to take over the world."

Ty rocked up on his heels and rubbed a hand along his jaw. This was all just a little unbelievable. A magic belt? World domination because of an accessory? Shape shifting? "Okay, so you're basically telling me that belt can change the world if it falls into the wrong hands?"

Penny nodded.

Ty rubbed his jaw again.

What. The. Hell?

What the *hell* did he stumble into? He never would have guessed Theo was some sort of secret protector of the world. Or that a damn belt could bring about the end of the world as they knew it.

"So, who's after it? Did Theo mention that?"

The sag in Penny's shoulders told him all he needed to know. "No. I have no idea who wants it. Only that it's likely someone related to Atreus. His nephew, Eurystheus, had it briefly after he commanded Hercules to get it as part of his ten labors. When Eurystheus and his heirs died in the pursuit of Hercules and his sons, the belt fell to Atreus. Aelon and his aunts—the other Amazons—reunited because they all felt it was too dangerous for the belt to remain in Atreus's hands. He was an awful man and only out for power any way he could get it.

"Theo's journal states that a small band of Penthesilea's ancestor's—including Aelon—stole into Mycenae and took the belt from Atreus one night. They hid it, and they have kept it hidden for centuries. I think Theo died because someone finally found out who he really was and where he was. And I'm not entirely sure my parents' deaths were an accident. Theo wrote in his letter to me that my father was the belt's protector before he died."

"So if you die, too, without an heir or someone to whom you've willed your assets, it'll revert to the state," Ty mused.

Penny nodded. "And become fair game for whoever bids on the items at auction." She rose to her knees and grabbed his hands again. "I know this is bizarre and very hard to believe, but you have to trust me. I'm not crazy, and it is imperative we keep that belt safe. If Atreus's heir gets his hands on it, a lot of people are going to die."

"Why me? You said you decided to trust me? Why?"

She shrugged and pulled her hand away. "Because I felt I could. The moment I saw you when I opened the door, I had a feeling I could trust you."

He looked at her, incredulous. "So you went on blind faith? How do you know I'm not part of the conspiracy to get the belt?"

"I don't for sure, but Davos said you and your partner are both upstanding cops with no skeletons in your closets, from what his investigators could tell."

Ty held up a hand, incensed. "Wait a second. You had us investigated? Who's Davos and how the hell could he know what kinds of skeletons we had in a day?"

Penny looked away sheepishly. "I admit, I did call him about running background on you. I desperately needed an ally in all this. Not even Davos—Theo's attorney and now mine—knows the whole truth. He knows something is going on, but to keep him safe, I can't tell him anything. He's innocent in all of this, and I want to keep him that way. The background check was actually done weeks ago. Theo asked him to run it on you and your partner."

Ty's eyes bugged out. Theo had him investigated. That was something he would never have expected. "Why did he do that?"

Her expression turned soft. "Because he needed an ally, too. He knew someone was after him, and I think he was going to tell you about all this and have you discreetly look into who it was, but he was killed first."

Ty stood and started pacing. His heart ached. Why couldn't Theo have said something sooner? He could still be alive. Anger flared, hot and bright, at the faceless enemy that had murdered his friend. Ty wanted to catch the bastard and make sure he rotted in jail.

It was still hard to wrap his head around the reasons behind Theo's death, but it supported Penny's freaky ability. It also meant that if this was all true, then there really were killers after Penny, she was part goddess, and she held the fate of the world in her hands.

And she had chosen him as her protector. So had her uncle, it seemed, only he had done so too late.

Determination like none he ever felt before flowed over Ty. He would keep this woman safe and see that the artifact stayed out of enemy hands. Theo had been a good friend. He owed it to him for deciding to trust him with such a secret.

He spun back to Penny, where she stood watching him. Plans flew through his mind. "Okay. We need to let my partner in on this. You can trust him just like you trust me. Colin can run interference for me with the brass and anyone else who comes snooping around. Besides, now that my truck is a mangled hunk of metal on the side of the road with no bodies to be found, I can't let him think the worst. He'll launch an investigation and won't stop until he finds us. It's just better to let him in on it all now. He'll handle the truck and anything else we need. But you're going to have to tell him what you told me."

He pulled out his phone. "I'm going to ask him to meet us at the bank. He'll have an easier time accepting all this if you show him what's in the box." For that matter, Ty needed to see it, so he could reassure himself he wasn't crazy. Or dreaming.

He thumbed open the speed dial on his phone.

"How are we going to get to the bank?" Penny asked as he dialed. "Even if we were still near the truck, as you said, it's a mangled hunk of metal now."

Ty looked up as he put the phone to his ear, a devilish grin slashing across his face. "That's easy. We fly."

CHAPTER 12

"That was terrifying." Penny shifted them back to human and looked around the parking lot where they just landed. It was completely deserted, thank goodness. Rolling her shoulders, she glanced at Ty, who grinned at her.

Penny shook her head. "You actually enjoyed that."

He shrugged, still grinning. "What can I say? I'm an adrenaline junkie. It was like skydiving, only we moved sideways instead of down."

She just shook her head once more. She would be perfectly happy never to do that again. They had quickly discovered that while she could transfer the shape shifting ability without heightened emotion, the transference didn't last without Penny touching him. Within moments of letting him go, he was human again. As a result, she flew them here, dangling Ty from her claws. She'd been terrified the entire time she would drop him. Even in animal form, he was bigger than she was. It took all her strength to keep hold of him. Elated didn't even begin to describe how she felt to set him down when they reached the city.

"Whatever. Let's go find your partner."

Ty laughed, but followed her as she stormed off toward the bank.

It didn't take them long to walk the block to the bank, where the manager met them at the door. Colin Jacobs, Ty's partner, stood next to him.

"Thanks for meeting us, Col," Ty said.

"Sure. You were just cryptic enough on the phone to pique my interest. What the hell's going on, anyway? And what happened to your head, man?"

"We'll explain in a minute." Penny answered before Ty had a chance. She shot a meaningful look at the manager as they followed him inside. The man didn't need to know anything except that she wanted to access her box. Both detectives nodded at her silent warning.

Penny tapped her foot impatiently as the manager opened the outer door of her box and withdrew the metal firebox inside. She thanked him softly for his assistance and took the box from him. Eyeing her speculatively, he left them alone, the door closing quietly behind him.

She looked up at Colin as she inserted her key in the box's top. "Before I open this, I'm going to tell you the same thing I told your partner. Keep an open mind. It's all going to seem really crazy, but I promise it's all very real. And you can't tell anyone about any of this."

Colin cast a quizzical look at Ty.

"Just go with it."

At Colin's small nod, Penny turned the key and lifted the lid. She reached in and pulled out the belt.

Ty stepped forward and peered closer. "It doesn't look very impressive, but then at the same time, it does."

Penny wholeheartedly agreed. She fingered the long, golden belt. It was unpretentious—only about an inch wide—with a simple clasp on the ends and the symbol for Ares etched into the gold. It really didn't look fancy, but when you looked closely, it was truly a work of art.

Flexible as leather, but made entirely of metal, it was a perfect accessory for a demigod and warrior queen.

"You brought me out here at midnight for a belt?" Disbelief laced Colin's voice.

"Not just a belt." Penny pulled the journal from the box and handed it to Ty. He sat down at the table and immediately flipped it open, starting to read. Penny looked up at Colin and told him the same story she told Ty in the field. By the time she finished, he was sitting too, staring at the belt in her hands.

"This is unbelievable," Colin murmured.

Ty barked out a laugh. "Wait till you see her shift."

"Shift?"

Penny gritted her teeth. She'd been hoping to leave that part out again. It wasn't something she wanted to broadcast. It was terrifying to think it might get back to the wrong person, and not only would she lose the belt, but she would become a science experiment gone wrong.

But Colin needed to know everything just to be safe. She concentrated on a dog and felt the familiar tingle race along her spine. In seconds, she was four feet shorter and staring up at the men at the table.

Colin leaped back, falling from his chair. He landed in a heap on the floor before quickly bouncing up to a crouch. "Holy shit, man!" He looked at Ty, eyes frantic. "What the hell just happened?"

Penny quickly changed back.

If possible, Colin's eyes got wider. Ty just shook his head in wonder.

"How did she do that?" he asked Ty. His gaze swung back to Penny. "How did you do that?"

"Because I'm a descendant of Thetis. It was her ability, and it's apparently inherited."

He stood up and stared at her.

Penny felt for the man. It was still shocking to her, and she'd had a month to come to grips with the entire crazy situation.

"She can transfer it too."

Colin's eyebrows drew together quizzically. "What do you mean?"

"I can turn you, too. It's how Ty and I got here. How we got out of his truck when it rolled."

Colin reared back as if she'd slapped him and turned to his partner. "Wait. You crashed your truck? *That's* why you have that goose egg on your head? Where were you? How did you crash?"

Ty filled him in quickly on the night's events.

"And you—flew—out of the truck? As an owl?"

Penny nodded. "I have to maintain the contact, though. If I let go, he was human again within a minute. It made the trip here harrowing to say the least."

"Nah." Ty grinned. "I had faith."

Penny rolled her eyes. She was glad one of them did. She was still a basket case, thinking about the flight here. When he shifted human mid-air, before they figured out she had to maintain contact, she nearly had a heart attack. The whole way to the bank, she was terrified she would drop him and it would happen all over again.

She was also amazed he was taking this so well. Something, somewhere in his life, taught him to roll with the punches. And she was grateful. Not having to fight him on things was making this so much easier. She finally felt like she had a chance at discovering who killed Theo and was now after her. It was such a weight off her shoulders to know she wasn't alone anymore.

The flip of pages drew her attention to the journal and the man reading it. "It's fascinating, isn't it?"

He looked up, wonder in his eyes, and nodded. "I wish I could show this to my dad and tell him your story. He would be over the moon to know it was all real. He practically lives and breathes ancient history. Even my name is related to it."

"Ty is ancient?" Colin asked skeptically.

"My full name, Tyreece. It means child of the Titans. My dad has a thing about the Titans and their offspring, especially Hercules for some reason. He said the man was more of a hero than anyone knew. Something about what Hercules and his son, Hyllus, did for a tribe of Amazons. I don't remember the entire thing. It was just some story he told me one day. He said it was one his dad told him who heard it from his grandfather and so on." Ty shrugged. "Oral history at its finest."

Penny's eyes widened as pieces of Ty's story triggered a memory of something in Theo's journal. She rushed around the table and grabbed the book out of Ty's hands.

"What?" Ty asked, watching her flip through pages. Colin came around to stand behind her as she paged through the book.

She held up a finger. It couldn't be. There was no way the story Theo wrote about, and the one Ty heard from his father could be the same thing. It was just entirely too coincidental.

Penny's frantic search came to a halt at the picture of Hercules and Hyllus standing on the shore next to several women and one man. Her stomach dropped.

No way!

She turned to look at Ty. "Do you believe in fate, Ty?" She placed the journal back on the table in front of him and pointed to the drawing.

His brow wrinkled in confusion as he looked at the page.

"What is that?" Colin asked.

"That," Penny said, tapping the page, "is Hercules and his son, Hyllus, standing on a beach in Thessaly with a tribe of Amazons—Hippolyta and Penthesilea's sisters and nieces—and Penthesilea's son, Aelon. My ancestors. Hercules brought Aelon and the tribe to the Thessaly region of Greece so they could hide. Hyllus hid them there so Atreus couldn't find them and kill them. Hercules and Hyllus knew if Atreus discovered the belt's true owners—Hippolyta's sisters and descendants—were alive and searching for the belt, he would stop at nothing to destroy them all."

"Whoa," Colin muttered from above.

Ty rested his elbows on the table and cradled his head in his hands, staring at the journal. "This is unbelievable."

"Do you know where the story originated?" Penny's mind whirled at the same time her heart soared. To her, this was confirmation that trusting Ty Farris was the right move. The implications were also incredible. She may have more allies in this fight than she thought.

He shook his head and turned his vivid blue eyes on her. "No. He just mentioned that it was a story passed down through the family. There's always been an interest in my family in ancient history. One of my so many greats-grandfather was an explorer and spent some time in the Mediterranean area. I couldn't tell you much more than that, though. While I liked the history, it didn't fascinate me the way it did my dad. I've forgotten a lot of the details of the stories he told me as a kid."

"How trustworthy is your father?" Penny asked. She didn't like it—more people meant more chances something would leak—but they may have to bring him in on this. He might have valuable information that could lead them to Atreus's descendants. "Can he keep it a secret and not try to publish any of this?"

Ty nodded immediately. "If I asked, yes, absolutely."

Penny scooped up the journal and thrust it at Ty, decision made. "Hide this under your clothes."

She threaded the belt through the loops on her jeans and buckled the clasp. A power like she'd never known blasted outward from the belt until it radiated all over her body. Her hands fairly vibrated with the energy.

"Wow. That's a rush." She took a deep breath to steady herself and embraced the belt's power. It flowed over her like liquid gold. No wonder Atreus's descendants wanted it. The power it contained was incredible.

Penny flipped the lid closed on the safe deposit box and locked it. Urging the men to follow, Penny headed for the door. "You're going to get your wish to tell your dad, Ty. But we're taking Colin's car. I am not flying your ass anywhere again anytime soon," she tossed over her shoulder.

"Your girl's kinda badass," Penny heard Colin mutter to Ty as they walked out.

"I'm beginning to see that."

Penny couldn't help but smile at Ty's reply. Right now, she felt pretty badass.

Jack Farris was an older, slightly shorter version of his son. He also wore the same dumbfounded and wondrous look Ty wore only hours earlier. Ty had directed Colin to his father's house, where they were all now seated on comfortable leather sofas and chairs in Jack's study. Jack held Theo's journal and reverently turned page after page, committing every word and image to memory, Penny was sure.

"Dad, do you know where the story came from? The one about Hyllus and the Amazons?"

Jack turned to the image Penny, Ty, and Colin looked at earlier in the bank. His fingers gently traced the photocopied drawing glued to the journal page. "Not really. It's just a story that's been passed down through our family. My father told it to me and his father told it to him. I think his father told it to him. It's actually what really sparked my interest in ancient history as a child. I devoured everything I could find on the Greeks and later the Romans. I never could find the story written anywhere, though. Until now, I just thought it was a nice story. I only told it to you because of its significance to me. In making me want to learn about the Greeks," he said, looking at Ty.

Jack looked back down at the picture. "To think it's real—" he drew in a deep breath and looked at them all. "I can't fathom how it came to be part of our family's history."

A speculative light entered Ty's eyes. "Could that ancestor of ours who did the digs in southern Europe and northern Africa have heard it there?"

Jack tipped his head thoughtfully. "It's certainly possible. I think I still have his old journals." He stood and walked to the floor to ceiling bookshelves lining the wall behind his desk. He bent low and pulled several thin volumes from a shelf.

He handed all but one journal to his son. Penny took the one Ty offered her, as did Colin.

"I haven't read these in years. Probably since I was your age or younger, Ty. But I don't remember anything in them that seems pertinent to any of this." He sat back down and began thumbing through his journal. "Like I said, though, it's been almost thirty years."

Penny skimmed her own journal. Hers seemed to all be from Italy.

Ty's phone trilling broke the steady swish of turning pages.

"It's dispatch. Someone probably found my truck." He swiped to accept the call.

"Farris." He listened intently, but Penny could tell he was plotting what story he was going to spin about his vehicle. His eyes took on a hard and a bit faraway look as his brain whirled.

"Sorry about that. Colin and I must have gotten our wires crossed about who was going to call it in, so no one else stopped," he told the dispatcher. "I was on the phone with him, filling him in on a case when a deer ran out in front of me and I flipped the truck. He came out to get me and took a report. I've got a tow truck coming tomorrow morning to get it out of the ditch. I thought he was going to call it into dispatch. He must have thought I was going to call it in." He listened again. "No, I'm fine. A bit of a bump on the head, but nothing serious. It looked a lot worse than it was. Seatbelts and air bags are amazing."

Penny smiled when he looked at her and rolled his eyes. "Yes, ma'am. I'm sure you'll see a report on it in the morning." His head bobbed. "Thank you, ma'am. Good night."

Ty ended the call and turned to his partner. "You're going to have to file a report on my truck tomorrow morning and call a tow truck."

Colin grinned. "I gathered that. Thanks for the extra work, partner."

Ty grinned back. "Not a problem."

"Wait a second," Jack said, breaking in. "You rolled your truck?" His eyes roamed over his son. "Is that what that mark on your head is from?"

Penny dropped her head into her hands. Here they went again. She headed Ty off at the pass. "Jack, you remember how I said I was a descendant of Thetis?"

He nodded.

"Do you remember what her god power was?"

His look turned introspective as he thought about it. "She could shape shift."

Penny nodded and waited for him to connect the dots. When he did, the look on his face was comical. It was a mixture of disbelief and little boy excitement. His eyes ping-ponged between her, Ty, and Colin. "You can do that?" he asked in wonder.

She nodded again.

Jack left his chair and sank to his knees in front of her. "Will you show me? You don't have to, but it would be amazing to see. I've spent my entire life studying something I thought was pure myth. To see it so real in front of me would be remarkable."

Penny smiled. She liked Ty's dad immensely. He truly appreciated what they brought him. Just as she knew she could trust Ty, she knew she could trust Jack too. "Okay."

His smile was its own reward.

"Step back a little."

He quickly complied.

"Do the owl again," Ty said, his voice quiet. "You were beautiful as the owl."

A blush stained Penny's cheeks, and an odd thrill swept through her at his words. With a small smile, she nodded. Taking a deep breath, Penny pictured an owl and let the now familiar tingle run along her spine.

"Oh my," Jack breathed. "Ty was right. You're gorgeous. Oh, that's magnificent."

Penny changed back and smiled at Jack's awed expression. Colin, she noted, looked less shell-shocked this time around.

"Oh, my dear, that was wonderful. Thank you for showing me." Jack laid a hand on her knee.

"Would you like to try it?" Penny didn't know why she offered it, but something about Jack said he would appreciate the experience.

His eyes widened. "What? How?"

She laid her hand over his and explained how she and Ty escaped the truck and then made their way to the bank. By the time she finished her tale, his eyes were as wide as saucers and he was nodding.

"Yes. Please. I'd love to experience it."

She glanced at Colin. "Would you like to try it?"

He shook his head, a grin spreading across his handsome face. "Nope. I like the way I look."

Penny grinned back and turned her attention to Jack. She slid off her seat to kneel in front of him. "Take my hand."

He placed his palm in hers and Penny let the change roll over them both.

If an owl could smile, she had a feeling Jack would be grinning from ear to ear. He held out one brown and white speckled wing and inspected it, then the other, before hopping from foot to foot.

Penny changed them back, and then couldn't hold in the laugh at his expression. He looked like a kid at Christmas who got the best present of his life.

"That was incredible!" Jack spun to look at his son. "Did you see that? Holy crow! I had wings!"

They all laughed at Jack's enthusiasm.

"You really carried my son out of that truck?" Jack asked once they settled back into their seats.

Penny shrugged. "When the truck flipped, I just grabbed him and thought 'free' and we flew out the back window. I wasn't sure it would work, but I knew I had to try. I just wished I could have gotten him free before he hit his head on the window." She smiled ruefully. "Although, it made it easier to get him away from the scene, since he was a little dazed at first. He started struggling once he realized something weird was going on."

Jack grasped her hand and squeezed. "Thank you, my dear. For saving my son."

Penny nodded and furiously blinked away tears, the enormity of what could have been hitting her. "You're most welcome."

They spent the next hour going over the journals. Jack and Ty's ancestor visited the right regions but made no mention of any finds that would support the origin of the story. To say Penny was disappointed they hadn't uncovered more information was an understatement. She'd hoped to find something that pointed her to the identity of Atreus's heir.

"I'm sorry we didn't find more, my dear." Jack stacked the journals on his desk.

Penny patted his hand. "It's okay, Jack. I figured we were probably chasing ghosts, but it was worth it to look."

Colin stood. "I'm going to head out and try to catch a couple hours sleep before I have to falsify a police report to save your ass, Farris." He punched his partner on the arm.

Ty gave a fake pout and rubbed his bicep, then grinned. "Thanks, Col. I appreciate it."

"Yeah, yeah," Colin said with a wave. "Y'all need me to drop you somewhere on my way home?"

Ty shook his head before Penny could speak. "Dad, if you don't mind, Penny and I are going to stay here tonight."

Penny frowned. She had not agreed to that. Cognizant of the danger coming at her, the last thing Penny wanted to do was to put Jack in harm's way. She would rather stay at some hotel among the anonymity of strangers. "Ty—"

He cut her off. "We're safe here," he said, accurately reading her thoughts. "We've already been here a couple hours, and I don't think your pursuers would think to look here for us. Let's get some sleep. We'll figure out our next move in the morning."

He was right, she knew, but it didn't stop her from worrying.

She sighed, wishing she could just go home and forget the entire day. She craved the familiarity of Theo's big house to help calm her enough so she could sleep. She'd only been living in the house a couple weeks, but it already felt more like a real home than her house in Texas. Since her adoptive parents died, that place felt like a mere shell. At Theo's, she felt the connection to her past, and it was comforting.

Plus, she wanted her bed. Her mattress was one she brought with her from Texas. It was as soft as a cloud and oh so comfortable. She could really use some comfort right about now.

But it was safer here at Jack's, so she would make do. If today was any indication, it might be awhile before she saw her bed again, anyway.

She looked at Ty and nodded. "Okay. So long as tomorrow involves getting me more clothes—either from my house or new—I'm okay with staying here."

"Awesome." Colin clapped his hands together. "I'm out of here, then. Ty, you let me know if you need anything. I'll run interference with the captain and tell him you're off chasing leads."

"Sounds good." Ty patted his partner's shoulder. "Just don't mention Theo. Pick a different case. Penny's right. We can't tell anyone about this."

Colin's mouth quirked up in a sardonic smile. "No one would believe it, anyway." He paused in front of her on his way out of the study. "Take care of my partner."

Penny nodded and laid a hand on his forearm. "I will. Thank you for trusting me."

With a quick nod, he left, leaving her with father and son.

Jack broke the silence. "Ty, your room is always made up. Penny, let me show you to the guest room and bath."

Ty stepped forward. "I'll show her, dad. You don't need to traipse up the stairs and then down again. Head off to bed."

Jack started to protest, but a huge yawn overtook him. It ended on a chuckle. "All right. I guess I'll take you up on that."

He patted Penny softly on the shoulder as he passed her. "Good night, my dear. Son."

Ty and Penny both murmured good night and were left alone in the study.

Penny shifted her feet nervously, suddenly very aware of Ty filling the space in the room. Even though there were fewer people now, it seemed smaller. It was harder to ignore his masculinity and overwhelming size when it was just him. She glanced around the room, trying to appear nonchalant, even as her insides quivered in awareness. He was just so—*male*.

Clearing his throat, Ty started for the door. "Let's go to bed. I don't know about you, but a mattress sounds heavenly right about now." A slight pause in his step was the only indication that he realized how his words sounded.

Penny's face flushed as, unbidden, images of the two of them together on said mattress flooded her mind. She mentally slapped herself. Now was not the time to be fantasizing about anyone, particularly Ty Farris, no matter how attractive she found him. She needed him to help her solve the mystery of who murdered her uncle and who was now after her, not to slake her libido. She only hoped sleep and some time to decompress would set her head to rights.

But, as she wordlessly followed him from the study, his broad, muscular back filling her line of vision, she had a feeling convincing herself of that was going to be easier said than done.

CHAPTER 13

"You find anything?" Colin asked as they sat once again at Jack's, this time in the kitchen eating burgers from a mom-and-pop burger joint just down the road. Ty swiped at the sauce on his mouth that leaked out of the burger as he bit into it and shook his head.

He and Penny spent the entire day going through Theo's personal papers, looking for some clue as to the identity of Atreus's heir. Ty even put his dad on research duty and tasked him with looking up anything and everything he could find about Mycenae and Atreus, hoping to track his descendants. It was a long shot, but they needed some kind of clue.

"Nothing in Theo's papers. Dad, did you find anything?"

Jack shook his head. "Not really. You're sure it's Atreus's line that's after you and the belt?"

Penny nodded. "According to what Theo left and what our family has been led to believe, yes."

Jack frowned. "There's no record of Atreus or any of his descendants holding any sort of animosity toward the Amazons. They had enough of their own problems, what with Atreus killing his half-brother and the rampant cannibalism in his family—they were all just a little bit cuckoo." He twirled a finger near his ear.

A deep frown marred Penny's face. "If it's not Atreus's line, then who else knows about the belt and wants it badly enough to kill my family?"

Jack shook his head. "I don't know, my dear."

"Could the original Atreus descendant have been a woman?" Colin interjected.

Everyone stopped and stared at him.

"What? I'm just asking. I know women back then weren't given the same credit or due diligence in the history texts. Is it possible?"

They all watched as Jack pursed his lips and thought it through.

"It's definitely possible, and it would explain why there's so little knowledge of who it is. Even if it's a man now, tracing a *woman's* lineage from that time period would be much, much harder."

Penny felt a thrill at their first real lead. It had been an exhausting day, and it was nice to finally have something to latch on to. Some place to go. "So how do we go about finding her and then tracing her lineage?"

"I fear the answers to that are not in any textbook. If they are anywhere, they would be in Greece. But after nearly four thousand years, your hopes of finding anything are very slim," Jack stated.

Like a lightbulb, an idea pinged through Penny's head. "My uncle's house."

Ty frowned. "We searched it already, Pen. There's nothing there."

She waved her hand at him impatiently. "Not that house. His house in Greece. When Davos explained my inheritance to me, he said Theo also maintained the family estate *in Greece*."

Three sets of eyes widened at her statement.

"I didn't think much of it at the time. I was reeling from the fact my identity was not what I'd known my entire life and that I was now responsible for a multi-million dollar salvage operation. A house across the ocean was the least of my concerns, especially since the will mentioned it had a caretaker."

Her mind whirled with the possibilities. There could be answers to all their questions at the estate in Greece. "I need to go there and have a look around. It seems like the most logical place to find answers."

"I'm going with you," Ty immediately replied.

She started to argue, but he cut her off.

"There's a killer after you. There's no way you're getting on a plane without me, so don't even bother arguing." He crossed his arms over his massive chest. Penny swallowed hard, trying not to stare at the bulging muscles.

"What about your job, son?"

Ty turned to grin at his partner. "How much time off do I have saved?"

Colin rolled his eyes and balled up his napkin, tossing it onto the table. "An eternity. You never take a day off."

Ty turned to Penny and Jack. "See? Not a problem. Our case load is slim right now, and we don't have any court appearances scheduled for a couple weeks. I should be able to get away with little fuss."

Penny opened and closed her mouth like a guppy. Well, that went from nothing to wild in no time flat. "I guess we're going to Greece, then."

She wasn't sure it was wise for her peace of mind to go off the grid alone with Ty Farris. Covertly, she ran her gaze over his muscular physique once more. But her need for answers trumped her wayward hormones soundly. Like it or not, she needed Ty. He had the investigative skills to actually uncover something, if there was indeed anything to find over there.

Life still sucked, but at least now it was interesting.

CHAPTER 14

Penny stepped off the boat and stared up at the cliff. A winding staircase carved into the rock face led to a sprawling house, the roof just visible, perched atop the bluff.

"There are stairs now?" Ty groaned.

Penny felt his pain. This trip was like a never-ending journey. Once they decided to come to Greece, they left on the first flight they could get. Eighteen hours later, they touched down in Athens. A private plane shuttled them to Skiathos, where the estate's caretaker met them with a small cabin cruiser to take them to the house on the next island, Skopelos.

"Come on." She thrust his backpack at him. "We get to the top and we can sleep."

That thought nearly made her giddy. A proper bed. With sheets and a real, full-size pillow. She ached to stretch out and just melt into the heavenly goodness. She was so tired.

With a burst of energy, Penny shrugged on her backpack and snapped up the handle on her suitcase. Squaring her shoulders, she started the long, arduous journey to the top.

About halfway up, her energy flagged. Suddenly, her pack felt like it weighed a hundred pounds, and she struggled to lift each foot onto the next step.

When the path flattened out slightly on a natural ledge, Penny stopped to catch her breath. Twenty-four hours of traveling had taken its toll.

But it was worth it for this view. The deep blue waters of the Aegean Sea stretched endlessly before her, glittering like a giant sapphire in the sun. Soon, it would turn silver as the sun sank lower in the sky. It was absolutely breathtaking.

It was also very remote. No boats dotted the water, no landmasses rose on the horizon. Nothing but vast, open water greeted her for as far as she could see. Penny could understand now why Hercules and Hyllus picked this place to hide Aelon and his aunts. Isolated wasn't a strong enough word for it.

Penny turned to the estate's caretaker, Xander Dragos. The man had halted with her when she paused to take a break. "Do you haul supplies to the house from this path?"

He smiled and shook his head. "No. We dock in Skopelos Town and bring them by road. I know you wanted your arrival to be as quiet as possible, so I brought you this way."

Penny appreciated his stealth, if not the path up the cliff face. As far as Atreus's descendants knew, she was still in South Carolina. She wanted to keep it that way as long as possible. She would gladly walk this staircase and one even taller if it meant keeping her time in Greece a secret from those after her and Hippolyta's belt.

Taking one more deep breath, she started her trek up the steps once again. Ty hadn't paused on his way up and was nearing the top of the cliff. Penny bit back a smile at the knowledge that once he reached the top, he would likely stand there, tapping a foot as he waited on her.

He could wait.

Finally cresting the hill several minutes later, Penny took in the house sprawled in front of her. It seemed to meld into the landscape. It was the same gray tone as the rocky ground beneath their feet. Only its terra cotta tile roof kept it from looking like a cave rising out of the hill. The design was simple, yet exquisite all at the same time.

Ty stood next to the locked gate, suitcase at his feet and arms crossed once again over his massive chest. The breeze rippled through his thick, dark hair, while the sun made his tanned skin gleam like bronze. He looked for all the world like a statue of a Greek god come to life.

Penny swallowed hard. She was in deep trouble.

Oblivious to Penny's dilemma, Xander produced a key and unlocked the wrought-iron gate set into the stone wall surrounding the house. He held the gate for Penny and Ty to pass through, then locked it behind them before leading them to the porch. There, he unlocked the front door. Once inside, he held the key ring out to Penny.

She frowned at the man. "I don't want to take your keys, Xander. I don't know if we'll see you before we leave, and I want you to be able to do your job once we're gone."

He shook his head. "These are yours, *despoinída*. I have another set."

"Oh." Penny took the keys and slipped them into her pocket. She should have realized that. Just another casualty of her sleep-deprived brain. "Okay. Thank you."

After a quick tour of the living area, Xander let himself out with a promise to check on them tomorrow. Ty locked the door behind him and leaned against it.

"I don't know about you, but I could eat a horse and then sleep for a week." Weariness gave his voice a raspy quality.

Penny nodded and turned toward the kitchen. Xander and his wife had thoroughly stocked the fridge and pantry. She quickly threw together some sandwiches while Ty went to check out the security system mounted on the wall by the front door.

He walked back into the kitchen just as she finished the last sandwich. "The system is on and all looks well. I want to double check the window locks yet, but decided food took precedence. We can check when we head to bed."

Penny nodded as she slid two of the three sandwiches onto a plate and put it in front of him.

He took a hearty bite, moaning in delight. Penny covered her smile with a bite of her own sandwich. It was nice being around someone who took pleasure in something as simple as a sandwich after a long day.

They ate quickly, fatigue weighing heavily on their bodies. Penny barely noticed her surroundings as she wolfed down her food. She was sure that tomorrow she would be impressed with the bright space with its modern appliances and colorful artwork, but right now she just couldn't muster the interest. All she wanted was to crawl into bed and let oblivion take over her brain for a few hours.

Ty seemed to be on the same page. He finished his food, heavy-lidded, before following her out of the kitchen. Shadows fell, long and dark, through the living room windows as the sun dipped lower. With all the traveling and the time difference, Penny wasn't quite sure what day it was anymore. She was too tired to do the math.

Grabbing the handle on her suitcase, she looped her backpack over her shoulder and headed down the hall in search of a bed. She couldn't wait to sink into a soft mattress. She wasn't even sure she'd get undressed first.

The first door Penny poked her head into was an office.

"Check the window lock," Ty said as he walked past her to the next door. He pushed it open. "Bathroom." He moved into the room to check the window.

Penny did the same in the office, then crossed the hallway and opened the door there. The sight of the king-size bed clad in a mint green comforter nearly made her swoon.

"I found a bedroom," she called down the hall to Ty.

He opened the last door and stopped.

She frowned as he just stared into the room. "What?"

He turned to look at her. "Well, I guess we're sharing. This one is full of dive equipment and other miscellaneous stuff."

"What?"

Slightly more awake at his words, Penny strode down the hall, throwing open doors. All of them were in use, but not as bedrooms. Of the four rooms in the hall besides the bathroom, only one actually had a bed. There was the office she found first. Another was obviously a library; shelves lined the walls, filled with books. A table sat near the window with a straight-back chair in front of it, while two very comfortable looking oversize chairs sat grouped in the center of the room. The third room, where Ty stood, was indeed filled with dive equipment and stacks of boxes, as well as other sports paraphernalia.

Penny stared, wide-eyed, at the mess. "How does he only have one bed? Doesn't he ever have guests?" She supposed she shouldn't be so surprised. The house in Charleston only had one extra bed before she brought hers in. That house had six bedrooms. One of them was completely empty. Penny had a feeling Theo bought the place for the barn and for the security the stone-walled property offered and not for its size.

Ty moved out into the hall. "I don't know, but I'm not going to dwell on it. I'm too tired. Let's just get some sleep." He walked back to the master bedroom, the wheels on his rolling suitcase clacking on the tile floor.

Penny stared at his back, trying to wrap her head around the idea of sharing a bed with the giant police detective. All her tired brain could process was that she was very glad it was a king-size bed. She didn't think there would be room for them both without being plastered together if it were any smaller.

That thought brought a rush of heat coursing through her body. Ty Farris was gorgeous. Hands down, full-stop. He was what women's fantasies were made of. Even in her extreme sleep-deprived state, her body hummed with the anticipation of being so close to him. She just prayed once they were actually in bed, her brain would take over and shut her body down so she could finally get some decent rest.

Squaring her shoulders, Penny rolled her suitcase back down the hall to the one and only bed in the house. Her body would just have to get the message, because she was exhausted.

CHAPTER 15

Ty woke to brilliant sunshine shining in his face. The sheer white curtains hanging over the window did very little to mute the bright light. With a wince, he tried to roll, only to find something holding him down. He squinted against the sunshine and looked down.

Make that someone. Penny's dark head was pillowed on his chest, her arm flung across him and one leg tossed over his thighs. She was plastered to him like a fly to honey.

As the softness of her body registered in his sleep-fogged brain, he found he didn't really mind her using him as a body pillow. She snored softly, still deeply asleep. From the angle of the sun, it was still early, so Ty turned his head from the window and closed his eyes, savoring the ability to lie in bed for once. Having a beautiful woman draped over him didn't hurt, either.

Gently, he reached down and tangled his fingers in the silky black hair tickling his bare chest. He didn't want to wake her, but he couldn't resist touching her at the moment. She truly was a beautiful woman, and she intrigued him to no end. Even with the danger following them, he wanted to get to know her. To find out if her mouth was as soft as it looked. He hoped their relationship didn't end with the apprehension of the killer they chased.

Realizing he needed to rein in his thoughts, Ty forced his mind onto what they needed to do today. They really needed to find a clue about who was after Penny and the belt. Hell, he'd settle for a clue where to look to find a clue at this point. He wanted to question the caretaker. The man might know nothing about Theo and Penny's ancestry or their abilities, but he might know where Theo had visited on his trips here.

They needed to search the house, too. He hoped there was a secret nook or something that they'd find all the answers in. He doubted they would find anything as glaringly obvious as a name, though. Theo would have told Penny who to look out for in his letters if he knew who Atreus's heir was. But a place where they might find someone connected to Atreus—that was a possibility.

Penny stirred beneath Ty's hand. She stretched, and his contented feeling fled, replaced by a surging arousal. He bit back a groan as she came awake and ran her hand down the length of his torso. The rest of his body awakened with her and he bent his free leg to hide his reaction to her touch.

Abruptly, she lifted her head. "I'm sorry," she said, coming awake quickly. A blush stained her cheeks as she scooted to her side of the bed and sat up, clutching the sheet to her chest.

He grinned at her as he sat up next to her. "No worries, sugar."

She ducked her head and peeked up at him through her lashes. For some reason, he found it extraordinarily attractive. He silently cursed his traitorous body as it hardened further. He battled to keep his smile in place and hoped it hadn't suddenly turned into a grimace. He clenched his jaw tight to keep a rein on his sudden desire to drag her beneath him.

"Why don't you use the bathroom in here? I'll take the one in the hall," he ground out.

Penny nodded and scrambled off the bed. She didn't even bother rummaging through her suitcase for clothes. She just dragged the whole thing with her into the bathroom.

Once she disappeared, Ty flopped back onto the bed and scrubbed his face with his hands. She was temptation personified. He was going to need an iron will to make it through the next few days without pouncing on her every time she was near.

With a groan, Ty rolled out of bed and headed for a cold shower.

CHAPTER 16

While Ty finished dressing, Penny busied herself by making them coffee. She could still feel the flame in her cheeks from earlier and tried valiantly to tamp down the embarrassment. She still couldn't believe she'd thrown herself over him like some kind of human blanket. Apparently, her unconscious mind had no qualms about acting on her attraction to the man. Now was not the time for that sort of thing. There was someone trying to kill her. The hot cop should be the last thing on her mind—awake or not—she silently berated herself.

Disgusted with her traitorous subconscious, she dug a yogurt out of the fridge, grumbling about her stupid hormones. A startled yelp flew past her lips when she swung around to see Ty standing in the doorway to the kitchen. She set the yogurt down carefully on the counter and pressed a hand over her racing heart.

"Don't sneak up on me like that!"

He smiled sheepishly as he plucked a banana off the bunch. "Sorry. Wasn't trying to."

Penny eyed him with playful suspicion before picking up her yogurt again and digging a spoon out of the drawer.

"So, what's our plan for today?" She peeled the foil lid off the yogurt container and took a bite.

Ty swallowed a hunk of banana before responding. "I want to talk to your caretaker. See if he knows where all Theo would go when he was here. I also want to look through this house and see what there is to find. The boat, too. There's got to be a clue somewhere that points to a more specific location than just Mycenae. We'll never be able to find one family in a city that size without knowing more."

Penny pulled the spoon from between her lips. It was a sound plan and echoed basically what she was thinking. "I'll call Xander as soon as we finish breakfast and have him stop over."

Ty nodded, swallowing the last of his banana. He moved to the fridge and grabbed his own container of yogurt. "Good. While we wait, we can start searching."

***

Penny slammed the nightstand drawer shut and sat down on the bed with a huff. She had really hoped to find something in here. Everywhere else had been a bust. Their talk with Xander didn't reveal any clues, either. The man said he kept the boat fueled at the dock at the base of the cliffs and that was the extent of what he knew. Theo never invited him on any of his excursions, and he had never asked Xander to take him anywhere besides Skiathos. Penny and Ty had thanked the caretaker and sent him on his way, all while trying hard not to let their disappointment show.

Their search of Theo's home office likewise yielded no clues. They found a well-worn map of Mycenae and its surroundings, but Theo didn't mark anything of interest on the map. She got the feeling from the many creases and the softness of the paper he'd been systematically searching the city with little result.

Penny looked around the room, hoping she missed a place to search. From what Ty said about Theo, and what she'd learned about the man herself from reading his journals, he kept things close to the vest. She'd been sure if there was something to find, it would be somewhere intimate and personal. His bedroom was a wash, though.

Wash...

Penny stood as the thought slammed into her. Her head whipped toward the master bathroom. She practically flew into the room and fell on her knees in front of the sink. She flung the doors open. A few bottles of cleaners and a box of trash bags greeted her. After a quick search found nothing behind the bottles, she stood and turned to the linen cupboard standing sentry in the corner. Penny yanked open the door and began pulling things out. It was full to the brim with towels and sheets. Her frustration mounted as she cleared each shelf and found nothing. She yanked the last towel out of the cupboard and flung it over her shoulder with an irritated huff.

"You know, I'm all for you throwing towels at me, but I'd prefer it to be after you've whipped it off your body."

Penny jumped, startled at the sudden intrusion, and looked over her shoulder to see Ty pulling the towel off his head.

"Sorry." It took a moment for his words to register, but once they did, thoughts of his hard chest beneath her hands earlier inundated her brain. Penny's face flushed white hot. She turned back to the cabinet to hide her reaction.

Ty crossed the tile floor to stop beside her. She glanced up at him through her lashes. He cocked an eyebrow at her, silently asking what she was doing, tearing through the linen cabinet.

Firmly shutting the door on the lascivious thoughts running through her head, she slumped against the cabinet. Weakly, she waved her hand at it.

"I was hoping he hid it in here. I know it's the last place I would look if I were searching for something." She huffed, her jaw clenched. "But it's freaking empty, just like every other drawer, nook, and cranny in this bloody house!" She slammed her fist down on the cupboard shelf, incensed they couldn't find even a single clue.

Something rattled from behind the cabinet and Penny froze. Her eyes cut to Ty, whose gaze was caught on the shelf.

"Did you hear that?"

He nodded and moved closer, peering inside the cabinet. He struck the shelf, and again they heard the rattle. It was coming from *behind* the back of the cabinet. Ty motioned for her to stand back. She moved out of his way.

He pulled on the cabinet, but it was firmly anchored to the wall. He reached for the shelves and started yanking them out, piling them haphazardly to the side. "I need a crowbar or a flathead screwdriver. Something to wedge into the crack and pry out the back."

Penny scurried out of the bathroom and went to what they had affectionately termed the junk room. She remembered seeing a toolbox when they were searching earlier. Tossing aside a couple of scuba tanks and several coils of rope, Penny found the toolbox. She grabbed several sizes of flathead screwdrivers and ran back to the bathroom.

"Here." She thrust them at Ty, who was peering into the cabinet at the back panel.

He took them from her and quickly wedged one into the crack. The panel wobbled a bit. He jabbed another one along the side and jimmied from two directions until he had it far enough out he could get his fingers around the edge.

Penny stood back and watched Ty put his muscular physique to use. He wrenched the wood until it cracked, then worked a section of it free, tossing it onto the pile of shelves before tearing into what remained.

Halfway down, he stopped. "There's a niche built into the wall with a shelf. I see a strongbox." He reached one long arm into the hole in the back of the cabinet and pulled out a small metal box.

He turned it over in his hands. "It looks old."

Penny stared in dismay at the lock. "I don't suppose there was a key in there as well, was there?"

Ty shook his head, a smile quirking one corner of his mouth. "Nope, but this will work." He held up the screwdriver. Like the wood before it, the metal lid gave way to the screwdriver wedged in the crack. Ty bent the lid enough to get the screwdriver into the lock mechanism and popped it open. Penny peered into the box.

A sheaf of old papers sat in the bottom. She took them out and quickly leafed through them.

"They're all in Greek." She looked up at Ty. "Do you think your dad could translate them for us?"

Ty nodded. "We just need to send them over a secure email."

"I have a secure account," Penny informed him. He was right. They didn't dare send anything someone could intercept.

Ty quirked a brow in question.

"Davos insisted. He said Theo drilled it into his head from the very beginning that all communication done via email had to be done over secure servers." She shrugged. "Until I learned more about the secrets he kept, I just figured it had to do with his business."

Ty nodded and pulled out one document that was several sheets taped together. He carefully spread it out so they could look at it more fully.

"This looks like a family tree. One that dates back centuries." The lines connecting words on the page looked like a lineage tree, but like all the other documents, it was written in Greek. "I wish I'd paid more attention now when Dad tried to teach me Greek."

Penny gathered the rest of the papers and headed out of the room to the hall. She started toward the library. "Let's get pictures and get them sent off to Jack. The sooner we do, the sooner we'll know what they say and *hopefully* have some answers."

CHAPTER 17

The warm water of the Aegean lapped against Penny's feet as she stood on the beach at the base of the cliff and stared out to sea. A hot, dry summer breeze caressed her skin and lifted her hair. She was taking a much-needed break from worrying about who was trying to kill her. She was in Greece, dammit. It was a place she never dreamed she would see in person, and she was going to appreciate its beauty while she had the chance.

Peeling off her swimsuit cover to expose her purple bikini, she dropped the cover-up in the sand and walked into the warm, blue waters of the Aegean.

As the sea closed around her, Penny let out a long sigh. She had always loved the water—found it soothing. It made sense now why she had such an affinity for it.

Thoughts of her ancestry triggered questions about the strength and limits of her abilities. Penny smiled to herself. What the hell. It couldn't hurt to test them.

She pictured a fish, sleek and colorful. The now familiar tingle ran up her spine and suddenly she was underwater, breathing through gills. Penny stared around herself in wonder. Life under the sea through a fish's eyes was so much more brilliant than she had ever experienced while in human form. If she'd been able to in that moment, she would have laughed in delight. As it was, she flipped her little fins and tail and swam around near shore, taking in the life teeming just below the surface. Sea anemones clung to the lava rock that made up the island and its coasts. Small, colorful fish darted around and in and out of openings in the rock.

Movement in the sand caught her attention. She turned to see a stingray rise off the sea floor and glide toward her. Panic seized her momentarily as she realized in her current form, she was food for the ray. But as it came closer, it slowed and seemed to just look at her. Penny faced it, watching. It fluttered a few feet away before swimming forward to brush past her and head back to the bottom.

After several more minutes of meandering around the rocks and sea floor, noise from the shore caught her attention. Swimming to the surface, Penny shifted to her human form and popped her head above water, her back to the shore. She'd swum out several yards to where it was deep enough she couldn't touch. More noise drew her attention, and she spun toward the beach to see Ty standing at the water's edge.

She made quick work of swimming to shore. As she rose out of the water, two things registered about his expression. One, he liked the sight of her in her swimsuit, and two, he was angry and a little perplexed.

"What the hell, Penny?" His voice was a low growl. "I came down here to find your cover-up sitting in the sand and you nowhere in sight." He clutched the offending garment in his large fist.

Penny strode toward him and took the terrycloth cover-up he held, using it to wipe some of the water from her skin. "I went for a swim."

"An underwater one that you shouldn't have survived?" he asked, incredulous. "I was a SEAL and even I can't hold my breath that long."

She grinned up at him. "I was a fish."

One eyebrow whisked upward. "A fish?" He pinched the bridge of his nose before fisting his hands on his hips. "Next time, tell me if you plan on doing something like that. I thought you'd drowned."

Any humor Penny felt instantly fled at the look of worry and concern on his handsome face. She laid a hand on his arm. "I'm sorry, Ty. It was a spur-of-the-moment thing. Once I realized I could be a fish and breathe underwater, I got caught up in the wonder of the moment."

He sighed and wrapped an arm around her, tugging her close. Penny's heart galloped in her chest at the feel of his long, muscled body pressed against her. Tingles, different from those she just felt in the water, but no less exciting, raced along her spine.

"Just tell me the next time you want to do something like that," he ordered softly. His free hand wrapped itself in her hair and tugged, holding her head tipped toward him. Delicious heat skated through Penny's body as he trapped her in his arms. She stared into the eyes that looked like they'd been dipped from the Aegean behind her. Eyes that told her she wasn't the only one feeling the heat. He bent and brushed his lips over hers, his warm breath mingling with hers.

The terrycloth cover-up slipped unnoticed from her fingers. Eager to take part, Penny threaded the fingers of one hand through his hair and gripped his bicep with the other. Sensation washed over her when Ty pressed his mouth more firmly to hers and splayed the hand at her waist over her back, pressing her even closer. Penny sank into his embrace, opening to him. His tongue danced along the rim of her mouth and darted inside for a taste. She heard a whimper, only to belatedly realize it came from her. She didn't care. Kissing Tyreece Farris differed completely from kissing any other man. She knew her experience with men was limited, but none who had come before him had ever reduced her to a whimpering pile of need with just one kiss.

Just when Penny was ready to climb him like a tree to get as close as possible, Ty slowly pulled back and ended their kiss. He rested his forehead against hers, breathing hard.

Ty cursed softly. "I should not have done that."

Hurt lanced through Penny's chest at his words. It didn't matter that she agreed a relationship between them right now was a bad idea. He didn't need to put it into words.

He took a step back, and Penny felt bereft without the contact of his body on hers.

"Come on." He took her hand. "Dad emailed us back, and he wants us to call him."

"Well, why didn't you say so in the first place?" Her desire for answers pushed back her raging hormones and warring emotions. She turned and headed for the stairs, Ty on her heels.

"I'm sorry. I was a little distracted by the thought you *drowned*." Sarcasm dripped off of every word. "And then by something else." His eyes took on the same molten quality they had just before he kissed her.

Penny turned her head briefly and stuck her tongue out at him. It was childish, she knew, but if she didn't do something to lighten the moment, she might end up right back in his arms. Answers from Jack be damned.

He grinned at her. "You know, I can think of some other uses for that tongue."

Heat flushed her cheeks. It took all of her willpower not to get sucked back in. Ty was magnetic, and she didn't quite know how to handle a man like him. She really didn't have time to figure out how, either. They had a killer to catch before he caught them.

CHAPTER 18

Ty sat crowded next to Penny at the table in the library, waiting for Jack to accept their call. Penny's secure email server also hosted video chat. Unfortunately, the range on the laptop's camera meant he had to sit very close to her. While she'd changed out of her bikini, Ty couldn't help but remember the curves it revealed and the feel of them pressed against him as she kissed him senseless. And those legs. She had the longest, silkiest legs he'd ever seen on a woman. Even now, his fingers itched to trace their lines.

He reached out to fiddle with the pen and paper next to the laptop so he didn't reach over and do something stupid. They needed to concentrate, and he really didn't want his dad to see them making out.

He glanced over at her, eyes tracing the line of her mouth. He wanted to feel it again. And on places other than his own lips.

Ty put a firm lid on over those thoughts. Damn, but she was distracting. Being anywhere near her was wreaking havoc on his ability to focus. He needed to catch Theo's killer, but he couldn't do that if all he could think about was how her mouth felt on his, or how her long, pretty fingers had gripped his hair as they kissed.

Ty nearly wept in relief when the computer came to life, saving him from his thoughts. Jack's face appeared as he accepted their call, filling the screen.

"Hi, Dad."

"Son. Penny." Jack sat rather rigid in front of his web cam, a pensive expression on his face.

Ty sat up straighter, instantly on alert. "What? What's wrong?"

Jack hesitated a moment before shaking his head. "Nothing. Things finally make sense."

Ty looked at Penny, hoping she understood what was going on. Her frown mirrored his own, though.

He turned back to his dad. "Then why do you look like someone killed your cat?"

Jack held up a hand. "I'll get to that. But first, Colin was right. It's a woman's lineage. It's one or more of Iphigenia's descendants who are after you, Penny." He perched a pair of reading glasses on his nose and held up a sheaf of papers. "These give a brief account of attacks, skirmishes, and other encounters your ancestors have had over the years with her descendants."

Penny's frown deepened. "Why would my ancestors hide that information from future generations? That doesn't make any sense."

Jack held up a finger and flipped to the last few pages of the sheaf he held. "But it does when you read this. This—journal page, for lack of a better term—was written by Nikolas Aeolia, your great-great-grand-father. According to Nikolas, over the centuries, your ancestors believed it was a descendant of Atreus who was after the belt. All documents your family had about the belt and those who were after it—except the one you possess—were lost in a series of fires, wars, and natural disasters. Time perverted the oral history passed down amongst your ancestors until the only thing known about the enemy was that it was Atreus's descendants. No family name and no location."

He shifted in his seat. "Now, the world wars changed all that. With the advent of new technology and the chaos created by the fighting, your family managed to uncover from whom they were hiding for centuries. It was not Atreus who demanded the belt's return. It was his granddaughter, Iphigenia.

"Nikolas managed to turn a servant working for the Artemenko family—her descendants—and got a treasure trove of information about with whom they were dealing. Apparently, the head of the family at the time was a tyrant and a cruel, cruel man. Once Nikolas spirited the servant away, she told him everything she knew. What he learned was the Artemenko family was large and ruthless and closing in on the Aeolias. The servant said her employer, while he had not discovered the Aeolia family name, had figured out they were on an island in the Aegean. They just didn't know which one."

He set the papers down. "At that point, Nikolas packed up the family and moved to America, but not before hiding all this information behind a false back in that cabinet. In the last paragraph, he mentions he did it to protect his son, Alexis, and his unborn grandchild. Alexis was determined to find the Artemenko family and eliminate the threat, but Nikolas knew after talking to the servant, the Artemenkos had far more resources and numbers than the Aeolias. He was afraid his son would die and perhaps lead the Artemenkos to Nikolas and Alexis's wife, and get their hands on the belt."

Jack lifted a hand and touched the edges of the papers before pulling his hand back into his lap. "The pages state Nikolas refused to tell his son anything about the Artemenkos, including the name of the family, and convinced Alexis to go west to America. According to the journal, it was Nikolas's intention to one day tell his grandchildren about the pages he had hidden away at the family estate in Greece, but from what I could tell from the quick census lookup I did, he died within a few years after they reached the United States and never got the chance."

Penny sat back in her chair, her mind reeling around the information Jack just gave them. They finally had a name to start with. But what to do with that name was the question. If the Artemenko family still had all the resources it did nearly a hundred years ago, did she even stand a chance?

"Did the papers state where the Artemenko family was based?" Ty asked.

Jack nodded. "The Ukraine."

"Ukraine?" Surprise and shock colored Penny's tone. That was a bit of a leap from Greece.

"It's where Artemis took Iphigenia when she was supposed to be sacrificed by her father for his sins. Artemis accepted a lamb in her place and hid Iphigenia away. I'm guessing Iphigenia took offense to her father, using her as a sacrifice to absolve himself, and wanted a way to get revenge. I'm also surmising she felt a debt to Artemis, and that's where the family name—Artemenko—came from. A lot of this started because of the Trojan War. It's possible she saw the loss of the golden belt as the catalyst for all her family's troubles, including her father's sins and his decision to sacrifice her. It could be, she decided that getting the belt back was the only way for true revenge and ultimate power."

"And it's a quest she passed on to her descendants," Ty concluded. "Great."

Jack nodded. He furrowed his brow, though, and leaned closer to the camera. "Ty." He removed his reading glasses. "There's more."

Ty frowned at his father's visage on the screen. "Does this have to do with that pinched look on your face?"

Again, Jack nodded. He shuffled through the documents until he came to the family tree. "It's not bad, but it is a little hard to swallow. It has to do with this." He tilted his head at the long document.

"What is it?" Penny asked.

"Hercules's family tree up until the 1930s."

Ty frowned. "Hercules?"

Penny mentally echoed the statement. That was not what she had been expecting to hear.

Jack pointed to the surname on several of the lines. "See this?"

Penny and Ty nodded.

"It says 'Farris' in Greek."

CHAPTER 19

Penny stared at the image on the screen, her eyes wide. Shock left her dazed. Jack had rewritten the family tree in English and now held it up for Ty and Penny to see. Sure enough, translated at the top, it said "Descendants of Hercules." Every male name down the line for the last seven hundred years had the surname Farris.

"This name here," Jack pointed at one at the very bottom, "is my grandfather, Peter." He moved up a line. "This one is my great-grandfather, James." He set the paper down. "I did an ancestry search, and it's correct as far back as I could get without having to pull actual records."

"How can this be?" Ty swiped a hand down his face.

Penny glanced at him to see disbelief shining from his eyes.

"How are we descendants of one of the most fabled men in history and we don't even know it?"

Jack shrugged. "I don't know. But I do know you meeting Penny when you did was not a coincidence. Nor is your name, your size, or the story passed down through our family about Hercules. I'm a firm believer in the Fates now, son. Whatever's happening, you are meant to be part of it."

Penny looked between Ty and Jack, unbelieving. It made a strange sort of sense, though. If things were coming to a head between her and the Artemenkos, it was only fitting that the same family who helped them safeguard the belt in the first place should be the one to help her defend it when it was most threatened.

It also helped her feel like she had a chance in this fight. She had an ally now who was also part god.

Penny studied Ty surreptitiously, seeing his physique through a new lens. And maybe one who was just a little bit more indestructible than an ordinary man.

"I don't suppose you found out where exactly the Artemenkos are in Ukraine, did you?" Ty asked his dad.

Jack shook his head. "No. But based on Iphigenia's history, I'd say they're somewhere on the Crimean Peninsula. Tauris—where Artemis took her—is modern day Sevastopol."

Well, at least that gave them a place to start, Penny thought. How they were going to get into Sevastopol was another matter, though. Travel to Russia was already difficult for Americans and it was doubly difficult when you were talking about regions under conflict.

"Can you email translations of what you just told us?" Ty asked.

Jack nodded.

"All right. Thanks, Dad. If we come up with anything else, we'll be in touch."

Jack leaned forward again. "Sounds good. Be careful, son. This is a dangerous game."

Ty nodded, his face stoic and serious. "I know, and we will. Talk to you soon."

Jack bid them goodbye and severed the connection.

Ty turned to her. "Things just got a hell of a lot more interesting." He sat back in his chair and looked at the ceiling.

Penny could see the wheels turning in his mind as he went over what Jack told them.

"So, you're being hunted by the descendants of Iphigenia, who was pissed that daddy-dearest, Agamemnon, wanted to sacrifice her to the gods. And I'm the many greats-grandson of Hercules." He scoffed and shook his head. "And I thought you turning me into an owl and flying me out of my truck was weird."

Penny couldn't help but smile at his tone. Disbelief mixed with some awe. "I know how you feel." She laid a hand on his thigh. Thick muscles flexed beneath her fingers.

He put his hand over hers and looked down. His steady gaze landed on her face. He was quiet a moment before he replied. "I believe you're about the only one who does."

Suddenly, he smiled, and Penny's breath caught at the twinkle that appeared in his blue, blue eyes.

"Does this mean I can do weird, magical stuff like you?"

A laugh burst past Penny's lips. "Hercules was only half-god, but maybe. You've certainly got the 'strong' part down." She flicked his bulging bicep with her free hand.

He laughed with her. "I guess we'll find out if I have super-strength if the need ever arises. I don't think I've ever pushed my strength to the very edge before. Not even during my SEAL days."

Unbidden, images of him ripping apart the bathroom cabinet flashed through her head. That had been quite the display of strength. She didn't know many people who could have ripped the wood apart the way he did. Maybe there was something about Hercules's god powers being passed down after all. With all the other facts stacking up, leading her to think they were at the final showdown with the Artemenkos, it wouldn't surprise her to learn Ty had Hercules's strength.

She drew in a deep breath and withdrew her hand from his leg, its bulging muscles a distraction she did not need at the moment. "So, what's our plan now? Russia's not the easiest place for us to travel."

Ty sat up and started typing on the laptop. "We may not have to go there. The Crimea has been in turmoil for the last several years, so I'm wondering if the Artemenkos are even still there. They may have fled to escape the conflict."

"How do we find out?"

He pulled up another video chat line. "Colin."

Penny frowned. She was lost. "How does he factor into this? Are you going to send him there? He won't have any better luck getting in than we will, and it'll take him longer to get there."

One side of Ty's mouth quirked up, and he slanted her a look. "He doesn't have to. Colin's got resources I could only dream of. He was Army Special Forces. His unit did a lot more intelligence gathering than my SEAL team. I'm hoping he'll be willing to use a few of his resources to get us some answers."

Ty clicked the button on the screen, requesting a video chat with his partner. In seconds, Colin's face filled the screen.

"Hey, man, what's up? How's Greece?"

Ty grinned. "Interesting." He quickly explained what they found and what Jack told them.

Colin let out a low whistle. "So, you're magic too, huh? This just keeps getting weirder."

"No kidding." Ty ran a hand through his hair. "I need a favor from you, though."

"Name it."

"You have a hacker buddy from your days in the Special Forces, right?"

"Yeah," Colin said, his voice suddenly a lot softer. Penny watched as he glanced around to make sure no one was listening. "Why?"

"We need some info we can't get without some deep digging."

The hesitation was clear on Colin's face. Penny jumped in. "Please, Colin. We wouldn't ask if it wasn't important. Getting into Russia is too time consuming. It could turn out to be a wasted endeavor anyway if the Artemenkos fled Crimea to escape the conflict."

Colin sighed and ran a hand over his jaw. He pressed his lips together briefly before finally nodding. "All right. I'll see what I can do."

Ty nodded, and Penny wilted in relief.

"Thanks, Col. I owe you."

Colin's grin was swift. "That's two, now."

A matching smile spread across Ty's face. "Yeah, yeah. Probably won't be the last either."

They clicked off.

Ty's bright blue gaze found hers. "Now we wait."

CHAPTER 20

"I can't believe I let you talk me into this," Ty muttered as he climbed behind her. "Don't you get enough of stairs at the estate?"

Penny laughed and looked over her shoulder at the mountain of a man steadily climbing stairs behind her. "You sure have something against steps."

"Only old crumbly ones that drop off into the sea." He craned his neck to peer over the edge. It plummeted into the Aegean after a ten-foot ledge.

Penny laughed again, feeling freer than she had in a long time. It felt great to leave her worries behind for a few hours. They had decided to venture out and explore a bit while Colin's hacker friend tried to locate the Artemenko family.

Right now, they were climbing the long and winding rock staircase that led to the chapel used in the film *Mamma Mia*.

"There's a railing, you big baby. Just climb. We're almost there."

"Did you seriously just call me a baby?" He sent a mock glare her way. "What are we? Twelve?"

"I'm not the one whining about some steep stairs." She raced up the last few steps, still laughing.

"Oh, no you don't! Get back here." Ty half yelled, half laughed, hot on her heels. He caught up to her just as they cleared the last step. His arm circled her waist, and he swept her toward the trees near the fence that rimmed the little area atop the cliff where the chapel sat.

Penny's feet barely touched the ground as he whirled her behind a tree and pushed her up against it. Her heart hammered in her chest, both from the exertion of the climb and the feel of Ty's body on hers once again. Her laughter faded as the feel of him, an immovable block of muscle and bone, fully registered. They were plastered together from chest to knee. He surrounded her.

Penny inhaled deeply, filling her head with a mix of his scent and the fresh, salty air coming off the sea.

He felt as good as she remembered. She had been longing for this since their kiss on the beach ended yesterday. She hadn't even gotten the satisfaction of feeling him against her while they slept last night. When it came time to turn in, Ty had matter-of-factly informed her he would bunk on the sofa in the living room.

Penny couldn't to argue with his logic. They'd both been strung tight after that kiss. Sharing a bed likely would have led to the inevitable conclusion, and neither of them were ready for that yet. They definitely didn't need the distraction a relationship would bring.

But now, squished between the unyielding surface of the tree and Ty's long, muscular frame, Penny was having a hard time remembering that. Apparently, he was too.

"I've been staring at your delectable ass all the way up that damn staircase. I can't take it anymore," he growled at her.

He lifted her up the tree, aligning her mouth with his. His thigh parted hers and she came to rest on the long length of corded muscle. Penny bit back a moan at the contact just as his mouth covered hers. She raked her hands into his hair and held on for dear life as heat burst to life inside her. The kiss on the beach had only fanned the fire that smoldered since he arrived on her doorstep, looking for answers about Theo. Now, it threatened to consume them. It was both heady and terrifying in its swiftness.

His mouth left hers to trail along her jaw to the spot behind her ear that made her whole body shiver. He fisted a hand in her ponytail, tipping her head back to give him unfettered access to her neck. She ran her fingers through the silk of his hair and along the tops of his shoulders, muscles bunching beneath her fingertips. She wanted to feel them without the cotton shroud of his shirt.

Voices filtered through the need rampaging through her brain, breaking through the fog of desire long enough for her to realize this was madness.

"Ty." Her voice was little more than a rasp.

He answered her with a grunt as he licked the hollow at the base of her throat. His hands grasped her hips, holding her against his thigh. Penny about rocketed into the stratosphere at the pleasure that speared through her from the pressure. What was it she wanted to say? She swallowed hard, trying to remember.

A laugh from the other side of the tree brought her back to earth again.

"Ty. This isn't the best place for this," she whispered, desperate. Desperate for what, she wasn't quite sure. Desperate to be somewhere the lady behind the tree wouldn't walk around to their side and find them like this. Desperate to take this to its natural conclusion. Mostly just desperate for him.

He moved back up to that spot by her ear again.

"I know."

His roughened voice was a soft whisper, tickling her and making her shiver again. She rocked against the denim-clad thigh between her legs once more and bit her lip to keep from moaning aloud. As it was, a whimper escaped.

His mouth covered hers again, but he withdrew his leg from between hers. She slowly slid down, her body skimming along his, until her feet touched the ground.

They broke apart, their breaths coming in short, heavy gasps. He pressed one more soft kiss to her lips before moving back.

"Come on. Let's take in the view. I need a minute before we mingle with the other tourists."

Penny couldn't help but look down at the bulge his jeans couldn't hide. A blush stole over her cheeks. She nodded and peeked up at him through her lashes, fire still burning in her eyes.

He groaned and pushed her ahead to the railing. "Don't look at me like that or we're going to shock that lady and her friend into next Tuesday."

Penny laughed as she leaned against the railing, taking in the view. The idea of continuing what they started against the tree held merit, but Penny was definitely not into exhibitionism.

Content to let the fire simmer and just enjoy Greece with this man in the midst of the turmoil that was her life, Penny lifted her face to the gentle sea breeze.

CHAPTER 21

Ty watched, transfixed, at the sight of the woman next to him. Right here, in the brilliant sunshine with the breeze blowing strands of her ponytail around her face, Ty could see the goddess in her. The power of her heritage and the beauty that came with being a descendant of the gods shone from within. She took his breath away.

"What?" she asked, casting him a soft smile.

He shook his head and laid a hand on her back, running it around her side until it wrapped her waist. "You're beautiful." He tucked her against him and pressed a kiss to her temple. Contentment washed over him as she laid her head against his chest and wrapped her arms around him. He could get used to this.

He wanted to get used to this, Ty realized with a jolt. He didn't know how it happened, but this woman meant something to him. And in a very short amount of time. He'd known her days, but the thought of going back to a life without her felt foreign. Something drew him to her. Every fiber in his being wanted to be around Penny. To enjoy and cherish her. It was bizarre, but felt strangely right.

Even so, she was a distraction he didn't need if he was going to stop the Artemenkos. No centuries-old grudge was going to rob them of a future because he couldn't get a handle on this attraction.

Ty wasn't sure how long they stood at the rail, looking out to sea. He didn't particularly care. Long enough for the women on the other side of the tree—as well as a few newcomers—to come up to the rail and take pictures before wandering back toward the chapel. Life faded away for Ty with Penny in his arms. And for a time, he was able to shove all their troubles to the back of his mind and just be in the moment.

His cell, dinging with an incoming text, brought the world flooding back. He pulled the phone from his pocket and sighed when he looked at the screen. It was from his partner, asking Ty to call. He turned it so Penny could see. "Seems Colin has something for us."

She nodded and dropped her arms.

He quickly grabbed her hand, refusing to let all contact between them cease. He texted Colin back with his free hand, telling him they needed a bit since they weren't at the house.

Thrusting the phone back into his pocket, he looked down at Penny. The slump to her shoulders echoed his mood. He wasn't ready for the quiet interlude to end, either.

"We're going to catch them." Ty's voice rang with conviction. "Then we can figure this out and have all the quiet moments we want."

Penny nodded and pressed a quick kiss to his cheek. Ty took her hand again and led them back down the rocky staircase.

CHAPTER 22

For the second time in two days, Penny found herself in front of the laptop, talking to Ty's partner, Colin. This time, the jovial face was gone, replaced by one of concern.

Ty cursed as soon as Colin's face popped up on the monitor. Penny echoed the sentiment.

"What?" Ty asked immediately. "What did you find out?"

Colin took a deep breath. "Well, your theory they left the peninsula was right. But your timing was wrong." He rubbed his forehead above his eyebrow. "Or at least it was partly wrong. Charisse—my hacker friend—found their estate in the Ukraine. It's only had a skeleton crew for nearly the last thirty years. When the fighting broke out a few years ago, they abandoned it completely. Took everything of value from the property and locked it up tight."

Penny frowned. Thirty years? A sinking feeling took up residence in her stomach. "Colin. Where was the rest of the family?"

Colin drew in a deep breath and stared at her for several moments. "Texas," he finally stated.

Penny sucked in a breath through her teeth, the sinking feeling suddenly worse.

"More specifically, Austin, Texas."

Tears welled in Penny's eyes and she felt Ty's hand on her thigh, offering support. "They found us, didn't they? Way back then? That's why my parents died. Why I ended up with family friends and not with Theo. It wasn't an accident."

Colin nodded, deep sympathy shining from his eyes even over the webcam. "It looks that way, Penny. I'm so sorry. It looks like Theo went to ground after your parents died and sent you to live with your adoptive family to protect you. I got a copy of the police report from the accident, but it's incredibly thin." He waved a file folder at the webcam. "There are holes here you could stick a two-by-four through." He tossed it onto his desk with a snort of disgust.

Penny sniffed away the tears. Her blood boiled as the reality of what had been done to her family fully sank in. Tears wouldn't help her, and they wouldn't bring her family back. Her anger, though—her anger would help her focus. She wanted to nail the Artemenkos to the wall.

"Where are they now? Are they still there?"

Colin nodded. "Charisse thinks so. They dropped off the map shortly after immigrating. There are no records anywhere of them after that. Somehow, they have managed to stay off the radar."

Penny's mind whirled. It seemed impossible they'd been so close for so long.

"We need to go back to the states." She looked at Ty as his gaze swung her way. "There's nothing here for us anymore. We found what we needed to find. The rest of the answers are in Texas, it seems."

Ty stared at her steadily for several moments. Penny stared right back. She was right, and they both knew it.

Finally, he nodded. "Okay. Texas it is."

CHAPTER 23

The boat motored into port on Skiathos the next morning as they began their long journey back to the U.S. By the time they ended their video chat with Colin and packed their bags, evening had descended upon them. Not wanting to cross the Aegean in the dark, as well as go nearly two days with little sleep, they decided to wait until morning to head back to the states.

Although, truthfully, Ty wasn't sure he wouldn't have slept better on the plane. That couch, while comfortable to sit on, was entirely too short for his gigantic frame. But there was no way he was sharing the bed with Penny. They were entirely too close to passing the point of no return after that searing kiss on the chapel grounds. Sleeping in the same bed would have pushed his self-control to the brink. He might want a relationship with her, but that didn't mean they were ready to start one. And the timing was certainly terrible. So, Ty retreated to the too short sofa for another night.

Stifling a yawn, he pushed his sunglasses further up his nose to keep the bright Greek sunshine at bay. He got ready to jump onto the dock as Xander steered the boat into its slip. When it slowed and hit the bumpers, Ty leaped over the side to tie the craft to its moorings.

Boat secure, he hopped back on board to help Penny with their luggage. Using his long reach, he lifted their heavier suitcases over the boat's side to set them on the dock before looping both backpacks over his shoulder and disembarking.

Xander came down from the pilot's house to bid them farewell.

"I hope you come back when you find what it is you've been looking for."

Ty saw the knowing light in the caretaker's eyes. While Xander Dragos may not have known anything about Theo's activities, he was an observant man. He'd figured out something was amiss with the master—and now mistress—of the estate.

Penny turned her bright smile on the man. "Thank you, Xander. For everything. I hope I get to come back for many more visits in the future."

Xander returned her smile. "I'm sure you will. And do not worry about anything here. I will take good care of the house." His words were for Penny, but his eyes caught Ty's and spoke volumes. Xander would keep an eye out for anything strange.

She laid a hand on his arm. "I know you will. Thank you, again."

Ty nodded his understanding and thanks to the man and helped Penny disembark. They headed for the marina's exit, where there was supposed to be a car waiting for them.

He just wished it was taking them to the airport. Because Skiathos was a central distribution point for the islands in this part of the Aegean, charter flights were scarce. They had to wait until late after-noon to get a flight over to Athens so they could catch a commercial flight back to the U.S. As a result, they were playing tourist again.

It chafed that he wasn't doing more. Ty was not a fan of being idle, especially in the middle of a case. He was a man of action, as evidenced by his choice of career. This forced downtime was going to be torture. Especially since he had a feeling Penny wanted to go shopping.

Ty suppressed a shudder. He would have preferred to stay at the estate until it was time to catch a flight to Athens, but Penny wanted to explore Skiathos before they left. He envisioned a lot of benches and cups of coffee in his future today.

A soft sigh pulled Ty out of his head. He glanced over to see a serene expression on Penny's face as she tipped it to the sun.

"It's such a beautiful day."

He agreed. Although it was only late morning and already scorching hot, the humidity was relatively low and a soft breeze blew, taking the edge off of the heat. Just a few thin, high clouds marred the otherwise blue sky. If they had to have downtime, Skiathos wasn't the worst place they could be.

"So, what do you want to do all day?" he asked.

Her grin said it all.

Ty grimaced. "Just find me a comfortable place to hang out."

Penny laughed and looped her free hand through his elbow. "I'm sure we can find you a nice place where you can soak up some sun."

Exiting the marina, the town car Xander hired for them sat at the curb, a man in a suit standing next to it with a sign proclaiming Penny's name. Quickly stowing their luggage in the trunk, they hopped into the car with instructions for the driver to take them to the shopping district.

Skiathos was as beautiful as Skopelos, but more populous. It was also more of a tourist attraction. People milled in the streets, guide maps and shopping bags clutched in their hands. Many of them looked like they'd come straight from one of the island's many beaches.

The driver dropped them off in the heart of town and told them to call when they were ready to be picked up again. Ty fleetingly thought about waiting with the man to save himself from the endless shopping that was sure to come. But then he took one look at Penny's relaxed face and decided he would gladly spend every day for the rest of his life following her through store after store if it made her this happy.

He took her hand and led her down the sidewalk.

"So, where to first?"

She studied the stores around them, before pointing at one several doors down. "There. The artisan décor place. I have that giant house in Charleston that could use some color. Even you have to admit, Theo wasn't much of a decorator."

That was an understatement. The house was barren except for artifacts Theo had picked up over the years. Of those, he had quite the impressive display.

Pulling open the door to the store, Ty waved Penny inside. He followed her in and was immediately surrounded by a decorator's mecca. Handmade pottery lined an entire wall. All shapes and sizes of bowls, plates, cups, and vases adorned the shelves. Colorful rugs and blankets hung from racks or sat rolled against the wall. Glass cases filled with custom jewelry formed an L-shape counter.

Penny made a beeline for the pottery. Ty pulled up an empty section of wall and watched her shop. It was interesting to see her be normal for a change. They'd been on the run and under pressure since they met. It was nice to see the real, more carefree Penny come out to play.

The shopkeeper, a woman in her mid-forties, wandered over while he watched.

She smiled at him and offered him the large mug she carried.

The enticing aroma of rich coffee reached his nose. Ah, his first cup of their outing. It'd be better if it was beer. Or had a shot of whiskey in it. After the last few days, he could definitely use it.

Still, he wouldn't turn down coffee. Not after the restless night he had.

He accepted the cup from the woman. "Thank you."

She nodded. "You are welcome. You are not the first husband I have had come in here trailing his wife."

That made Ty grin. He supposed he did look like a bored husband. He wasn't going to correct the woman on his marital status, though. Arguing would just make her more likely to remember him. He wanted them to be forgettable in case anyone came around asking questions.

Well, as forgettable as a six-foot-eight man and a six-foot-one woman could be. Ty went nowhere without someone noticing him.

The woman's eyes traveled to Penny, who examined a traditional Greek vase. The color reminded him of her eyes.

"Your wife, she has good taste," the shopkeeper remarked in thickly accented English.

Taking a sip of his coffee, he peered over the rim of the cup at Penny. She put the vase down and picked up a serving bowl.

"She's shopping to decorate the new house."

"Does she have a particular style in mind?"

Ty arched an eyebrow and smiled. "Not mine," he said, making her laugh. "She likes color. I'm more of a leather and tan kind of person." That much, at least, was true. He'd noticed everything Penny owned was a different color of the rainbow. Ty was perfectly happy in his apartment, with its beige walls and oversize leather furniture. If Ty and Penny ever moved in together, he would need to get used to seeing color everywhere he looked.

"Well, then anything Greek should suit her wonderfully. We celebrate color in all parts of our lives."

He took another sip of the wonderful coffee. "She has certainly been enjoying Greece. It's beautiful here."

The woman smiled brilliantly. "It is like no other place on Earth." She patted his arm. "Enjoy your coffee. I am going to go see if your wife needs any help."

The woman wandered over to Penny to offer her assistance. Ty leaned back against the wall again, content to watch his "wife" shop.

A week ago, that was a word he never would have thought about in relation to any woman with whom he was involved. Now, though, it held a vast amount of appeal. Penny had gotten under his skin quickly. She was an incredible woman. The type he'd always envisioned for himself. Tall, fun, sexy, smart, courageous—she was everything he ever thought he wanted, but so much more. She was also soft and feminine. Quiet and bookish, even a little naïve at times. He liked that she let him play protector even though he had a feeling she would do just fine protecting herself. Anyone who could do what she could, had a leg up on danger. It didn't matter, though. He wanted to be the man who protected her all the time. Not just for now.

But he had a killer to catch first.

CHAPTER 24

After Penny bought enough stuff to fill another suitcase, and they ate a late lunch at an outdoor café, they decided to do a bit of sightseeing before heading to the airport. The most famous landmark on Skiathos—other than the town itself—was the castle on the northern point.

Penny googled it on their way there, wanting to know more about it. She discovered it was built in the mid-fourteenth century by the Byzantines as a defense against Turkish pirates. It remained the main settlement on the island for over four hundred years.

The car rolled to a stop, and she could just make out the castle through the windshield. Perched atop a high hill, it was surrounded by cliffs on three sides and a manmade wall to the south.

Penny climbed out of the car and couldn't stop the laugh that broke free when she got her first full look at the historical site. There was a long winding path, ending in a rocky staircase that rose up the cliff side to the castle on top.

A groan from behind her only made her laugh harder.

"No. Nope. You can admire the ruins from afar." He pointed at the castle. "We have a trans-Atlantic flight ahead of us. I am not climbing up there."

His disgruntled expression was that of a little boy told to clean his room if he wanted dessert.

Penny laughed again and hugged him quick. "Relax. I'm not keen on walking up that hill, either." She took his hand, tugging him back toward the car. "Come on. Let's just take a driving tour of the island. We only have about an hour until we need to be at the airport, anyway."

She slid back inside the car, pulling Ty in beside her. As the driver hopped in and started the engine, Ty tucked her up against his side and placed a gentle kiss on top of her head.

Contentment washed over her. For the last few hours, she'd been able to pretend nothing was amiss and just enjoy being with Ty. He had been such a good sport as she hauled him from store to store. Shopping for fun was something she hadn't done much of in the last several years. There was something that came up to suck away all her spending money, whether it be tuition, car repairs, or medical bills. It was nice to do more than window shop and doubly nice to have someone by her side, even if he did lounge against the wall or on a bench most of the time. She felt normal, which was something sorely lacking in her life of late.

She looked up at the man next to her, thankful fate brought him into her life. Things could be very different if he wasn't around. Her intruders the other night likely would have found her and killed her. In hindsight, she should have shifted and pretended to be the family pet, but the fear overwhelmed her, clouding her thinking.

Ty was her rock in the storm, offering guidance and protection. His presence allowed her to regain control and put a plan into motion to get her life back. In the process, she might have discovered more than she ever dreamed.

The "L" word—love—rattled around her brain. She'd known the man a handful of days, but she already didn't remember life without him. He filled in all the holes like they were never there. It wasn't hard to envision them together well into the future.

But, boy, that was a scary prospect. Love. Forever. She wasn't a stranger to relationships, but no one held a candle to Ty Farris or what she felt for him. Things with him were deeper and had happened faster than she ever thought possible. It was a bit like being caught in a tornado—sudden and disorienting. She just hoped that when she landed, things would be clear.

"Hey." Ty's quiet voice broke into her thoughts. He tipped her face toward him with a finger under her chin. "You okay? Your smile faded and you got really quiet."

Penny nodded and offered him a soft smile. "I'm fine. Just thinking about things."

"None of that, now. We were supposed to put all of that behind us for the afternoon."

"I know. I was actually thinking more about us."

He frowned, curious. "What about us?"

Penny turned in her seat so she faced him. "Like how fast things have—developed—between us. We only met a few days ago, but I feel like it's been months. I know you, but then again, I don't. I don't know hardly anything about you other than you were a SEAL, now you're a cop, and you've got an awesome dad."

Ty's mouth quirked. "Don't forget great-grandson of Hercules."

She punched him in the arm lightly, a smile blooming on her own face. "I'm serious. I'm sitting here contemplating what kind of relationship we're going to have when all of this is over and I don't even know if you've ever been married or your mother's name. I don't even know how old you are!"

He smoothed a hand down her ponytail, bringing it to rest on her nape. His touch had the same calming effect it always did, and Penny's anxiety ratcheted down a notch.

"Hey. It's okay. All of those are things that don't really matter. It's all just filler." His other hand came up to cup the side of her head. His thumb traced her cheekbone as he talked. "I care about you. More than any other woman I've ever known." A sardonic smile flitted at the corners of his mouth. "And no, I've never been married. Or engaged. My life has been about my career until I met you. I haven't been a monk, but women—dating—haven't been my priority."

Eyes locked, Penny's heart beat faster at the intensity she saw in his gaze. She knew he was attracted to her—their kiss at the chapel wiped away any doubts about that—but she did doubt she was what he wanted in a partner. Other than her shape shifting abilities, she was ordinary. Men didn't flock to her like they did to some women. As a result, she felt a little overwhelmed by his attention and wasn't sure it was real. If ever there was a man who would be suited to the arm of a supermodel, it was Ty. He exuded masculinity and confidence, not to mention he was absolutely gorgeous. Men like him simply weren't interested in a too tall, quiet woman like her.

But seeing the emotions shining in his eyes now, Penny's doubts fled. Whatever was happening, whatever it was she felt for this man, he felt it too.

Penny leaned in until her forehead rested against his. "I still want to know how old you are."

His laugh was quick. He pulled back a bit to look into her eyes. "I'm thirty-four. And my mother's name was Anna. She died when I was three. In childbirth. My sister didn't make it either."

"Oh, Ty." Penny's heart clenched at his confession. "That's terrible. And your poor dad."

Ty sat back and twined his fingers with hers. "Yeah. I know he misses her. He never remarried. Always said there wasn't anyone else out there for him. I don't really remember her. I have pictures, but no real memories of my time with her."

"That's so sad." She stroked the side of his face. "I might have lost both of my parents—my adoptive parents, I mean—but I have my memories of them to look back on and remember all the fun we had. I wouldn't trade that for anything."

He covered her hand with his where it rested on his cheek. "I'm glad your childhood was a good one. It could have been so terribly different if the Dimas's hadn't taken you in."

Penny had similar thoughts after she learned of her family's history. She would always be grateful to her parents for taking in an orphaned infant, even though she was in mortal peril. They had scoffed at the danger in order to give Penny a chance at a normal life. Many people wouldn't have been so selfless.

Feeling emboldened by their conversation and the look in his eyes, she reached up and pressed a soft kiss to his lips. He returned the kiss. She pulled away before it could turn deeper. "Even with all the tragedy in our young lives, we were both lucky," she said. "We both had parents who cared. They're the ones who made us who we are today."

Ty wrapped his arms around her in a tight hug, pressing another kiss to the top of her head. "You are remarkable. I don't know anyone who could have handled all of this better than you."

She leaned back to look at him again. "It helps having a rock to lean on."

He framed her face in his hands, gazing down at her intently. Penny stared right back. He was right. All the other stuff was filler. What mattered was this. The connection they shared. It was real, and it wasn't going away.

As his mouth landed on hers, Penny vowed to do her part to make sure they got a chance to let their connection flourish. She just hoped fate had the same plan.

CHAPTER 25

Penny felt a bizarre sense of déjà vu as she pulled up to her old house just outside Austin, Texas. Similarly to when they arrived in Greece, she and Ty were both bone tired and just wanted to sleep. She was now very glad she couldn't part with her childhood home when she left Texas for South Carolina.

And like the house in Greece, it only had one bed since she'd moved hers to Theo's estate.

She slid a sideways glance at Ty as they climbed out of their rental car. Sleeping was going to be interesting. Either she was going to end up on the couch—because there was no way a man of Ty's size and stature would fit on her parents' sofa—or they would be scrunched in the queen-size bed in the master bedroom. At least at Theo's, the bed was king-size. No matter what, sleep would be elusive.

Penny had one foot on the first porch step when the front door flew open. A pint-size woman with curly dark hair squealed and burst through the doorway, enveloping her in a hug before Penny could do much more than blink.

"Hi, Keira." Penny laughed and returned her friend's embrace. "It's so good to see you."

Keira pulled back, a grin splitting her face. "Same here."

"Thanks for getting things ready for us and for letting us in." Penny climbed the porch steps beside her friend.

"Oh, not a problem. I'm just excited you're back, even if it is temporary." Keira looked back at Ty, who tromped up the steps behind them. "So, who's the hunk?" she whispered.

Penny laughed. She had missed Keira's frankness. "Let's get inside and I'll introduce you."

The three of them filed through the front door. Penny turned just as Ty dropped all their things inside the door with a thud.

"I don't know how you accumulated so much crap in the few days we were in Greece." He shook his hands to get the blood flowing.

She just grinned at him. She didn't regret any of it. If they lived through this, she would have some beautiful memories lining her mantle.

As well as a few in her heart.

Ty smiled back at her, his eyes telling her he understood exactly where her thoughts went.

"Greece?" Keira interrupted, bewildered. "I thought you were in South Carolina."

Penny turned back to her friend. She forgot Keira knew little about their adventures over the last few days. She was too tired for that story, though. "It's a long story, Keira. I promise I'll fill you in tomorrow. Right now, we just need to get some sleep. We've been up nearly a full day now."

Keira's eyes narrowed, like she wanted to argue, but she let it go. "Okay. So long as you promise." She wagged a finger at Penny.

Penny nodded. "Of course."

"Good." Keira punctuated that with a quick nod. "Now, introduce me to the hunk."

Prickles of awareness skittered along Penny's spine as Ty moved to stand beside her. Grasping onto her equilibrium with both hands, Penny introduced them, calling Ty a friend.

"Riiiight." Keira rolled her eyes. "A 'friend.'" She laughed and held up her hands before Penny could protest. "You call him whatever you want. I'm going to call him a hottie and wish you a good night." She waggled her eyebrows, and Penny flushed.

Keira handed Penny the house key as she brushed past. "Don't do anything I wouldn't," she whispered.

Penny couldn't help but roll her eyes and smile. There weren't a lot of things Keira wouldn't do.

Keira's phone rang as she reached the door, and she pulled it from her pocket. "Oh, it's my dad. I better see what he wants. I'll see you guys tomorrow." In a whirl of energy, Keira was out the door, the solid piece of wood slamming shut behind her. Penny could hear her greet her father as she walked down the porch steps.

"Is she always such a bundle of energy?" Ty moved further into the room. He had his cop face in place as he looked around.

Penny nodded and grabbed her carry-on from the stack of luggage. "Pretty much. She's been that way since we were young. Made her a great cheerleader in high school."

Ty grinned at her over his shoulder. "I bet."

Pulling his backpack from the luggage pile as well, Penny thrust it at him. "Come on. I'll show you around quick and then we can get some sleep."

Penny's childhood home was small, but solid and well kept. The front door opened into the living room, with the stairs leading to the second floor directly in front of them. Penny walked further into the living room on their right and moved toward the back of the house.

Down a short hall there was a bathroom, then the kitchen, which doubled as a dining room.

Penny surveyed the small but bright kitchen. It was nice to be back here. The kitchen, especially, reminded her of her mother. Tiny, yet vibrant. Larissa Dimas's personality was reflected in every aspect of the room, from the gleaming white cabinets to the sunny yellow walls and sky blue curtains. Paintings of wildflower fields adorned the walls and brightly colored towels hung off the oven door. Even the small golden maple table tucked into the corner where her family had shared many meals reflected her mother. Sturdy and no-nonsense, it could withstand anything and was always there.

Well, almost anything. A lump formed in Penny's throat as she thought of her mother's courageous battle with cancer. She fought hard to conquer the disease, but ultimately lost. And while Penny knew now that Larissa wasn't her biological mother, she was still Penny's mother at heart. She missed the older woman fiercely. There would always be a hole in her heart from her mother's death.

Not wanting Ty to see her on the brink of tears, Penny opened the fridge and stuck her head inside to see what kind of groceries Keira brought over. Penny asked her to get the basics, but knowing Keira, there could be anything from boring yogurt and eggs to the makings for some new fad kale and spinach smoothie occupying her fridge. Thankfully, boring was all she saw. She didn't think she could handle one of Keira's concoctions with the current state of affairs. She needed as much normal as she could inject into her life at the moment.

Grabbing two bottles of water, Penny closed the door. She handed one to Ty and motioned for him to follow her. Wordlessly, she led him back through the living room and up the stairs to the only room with a bed. She pushed the door open to reveal the master bedroom with its light blue walls, sheer white curtains, and white furniture. A soft gray, lightweight comforter covered the queen-size bed.

This room, too, reflected her mother. It was bright and cheerful, but not as bold as the kitchen. Her dad had been more subdued than his effervescent wife, and Larissa decorated this room to fit them both. Penny cleared away all their personal belongings after her father's death. She left the colors and bedding, but all of their clothes she either donated or packed away. Even though this was now more of a guest room, it still felt strange to be sleeping in here.

"I can sleep downstairs if you want me to." Penny eyed the bed. It had been just right for her parents, but it seemed downright small when she thought of Ty stretching out his long frame on it. His feet were going to hang off the end, even if he slept alone.

Ty merely gave her a look she interpreted to mean *don't be stupid*, and set his backpack on the wingback chair by the window.

"I'm taking a shower to wash off the airplane gunk and then I'm falling asleep as soon as my head hits the pillow." He grabbed the collar of his shirt at the back of his neck and pulled it up and over his head. Penny thought she'd melt into a puddle on the carpet right then and there as he bared his magnificent chest and abs. She had a feeling Hercules couldn't hold a candle to his many greats-grandson in the looks department.

Her eyes finally traveled back to Ty's face, only to see a knowing smile on his handsome face. Despite the grin, desire darkened his eyes to twin midnight blue pools.

Penny swallowed hard. Memories of his mouth on hers and of his hands caressing her body played on a reel in her mind, ratcheting up her arousal until she could barely stand it.

Sex right now was a bad idea, though. Sure, they were attracted to each other, but they were also both tired and stressed. When—*if*—sex between them happened, it needed to be when their emotions weren't in a blender from the danger lurking behind them and when fatigue didn't pull at their minds.

Turning away from the seductive picture in front of her, Penny grasped the handle of her suitcase and headed toward the door. "I'll shower downstairs and sleep on the sofa. You can have the bed."

"Penny." Ty's long arm shot out to gently grasp her bicep.

"Don't, Ty." She chanced a glance back at him, trying her damnedest to keep her eyes on his face and not drop lower to his massive, sculpted chest.

"If I stay, we won't be sleeping. Neither of us needs the distraction that sex—a relationship—will bring. I know there's much more here than just friendship, but exploring it right now just isn't a great idea. I can't deal with what's been going on in my life and you, too. It's all too much for me right now."

Penny sent a silent prayer he would understand she was too emotional to stay with him, as well as too tired to fight their growing attraction. The past month had left her reeling, her emotional state in tatters. Sleeping with Ty when she couldn't filter her emotions and sort through them would only make things worse. She didn't want to mess up what they had—what they *could* have. As attracted as she was to him, he scared the life out of her. Ty Farris had the potential to be more than just another boyfriend. She just didn't have the energy to deal with that in her sleep-deprived state.

Penny felt like a bug under a microscope as he regarded her with those deep blue eyes. When he finally nodded, relief flooded her system.

"Okay. But you stay up here. I'll go downstairs. I've slept in worse places than a too short sofa. I'll throw the cushions on the floor and be fine." He released her and grabbed his backpack. Hefting it over his shoulder, he brushed past her, closing the door behind him. Penny sagged against it as she willed her body back under control. She had a feeling her dreams were going to be full of that perfect chest.

CHAPTER 26

"This is it?" Penny stared out the car window at the nondescript, two-story house. Ty asked Colin to track down the officer named in the report on her biological parents' car accident. They sat outside the officer's house now, unannounced, hoping to catch him off guard so he would reveal something that would lead them to the people behind all of this.

She leaned forward to get a better look at the house. Black shutters framed the windows and a cheerful summer wreath adorned the wooden front door. Neatly trimmed hedges and blooming flowers filled the beds beneath the windows. A late-model, dark blue pickup sat in the driveway. It most decidedly did not look like the home of a dirty cop, Penny thought. It looked like a normal, bucolic family home.

Ty doubled checked the address in the text from Colin. "This is the one." He pushed his door open. "Come on. Let's see what the detective has to say."

Penny followed Ty up the sidewalk to Detective Don Carson's home. Reaching the front door, Penny rang the doorbell before wringing her hands together as they waited. She hoped this detective could shed some light on her parents' accident. She barely slept last night between wondering what he would tell them, and her unfulfilled lust for Ty. Penny didn't hold out much hope, though, that Detective Carson would offer them anything of importance. If it truly wasn't an accident, someone had convinced him to falsify a police report. Penny couldn't see anyone freely admitting to something like that.

The door opened to reveal a man much younger than Penny would have expected. Don Carson, with a trim physique and a full head of silvery hair, didn't look a day over fifty.

"Can I help you?"

Ty flashed his badge. "I'm Detective Ty Farris, Charleston County Sheriff's Department. This is Penny Dimas. We're investigating the death of Theo Aeolia and have reason to believe you may have information that could lead us to his killer. May we come in?"

Penny watched the man visibly pale at Theo's name. He knew something. Now they just had to convince the man to tell them what.

Carson swallowed hard before nodding and opening the door wide enough for them to pass. He led them into the living room and motioned for them to sit. Penny perched on the edge of the cream-colored sofa. Ty settled next to her while Detective Carson took the chair opposite.

"So, what leads you to think I know who killed your victim, detective?"

"Because you are the officer listed on the report of the accident that killed Theo's brother and sister-in-law, Ajax and Phoebe Aeolia." Ty cut right to the quick.

Sweat popped out on Carson's brow, and Penny watched a fine tremor run through the man's hands. He clasped them together in his lap to hide it.

"Who?"

Ty smirked. "Don't play coy, detective. We know someone convinced you to falsify their accident report. That or you were just a horrible police officer. I'm surprised that report made it past your boss's desk." Ty sat forward, forearms resting on his knees, and clasped his hands together. "Look. I'm not here officially. This investigation, while it landed on my desk legitimately, has become wholly unofficial. I'm not at liberty to discuss why, but you should know I'm not after you. I'm after Theo's killers and we—" he glanced at Penny, "think the people who ran the Aeolias off the road twenty-six years ago and convinced you to falsify the accident report are the same ones who murdered Theo. We just want a name."

Carson frowned at them. Penny could see the indecision in his eyes, along with a healthy dose of fear. Something held his tongue even after a quarter-century.

He turned to stare out the French doors that overlooked the backyard. "I can't tell you who it was because I don't know. I got a call asking me to do it with the promise of a significant payment. I did it and then got an envelope full of cash through the mail slot in the door the next day. My mother was very sick and drowning in medical bills, so I took the cash and did what they asked." He looked back at them. "I never heard from them again."

Penny narrowed her eyes as she studied the retired police officer. She might not be an investigator like Ty, but she knew when someone was lying. Detective Carson was holding something back.

"Are you sure you didn't recognize the voice of the person who paid you off, Detective Carson?"

He smiled at her sadly. "You look a lot like her, you know."

Penny sat back, eyes wide at that. Ty deliberately used her adopted name. Carson shouldn't know anything about her. She knew she looked like her mother—she found photo albums in the safe deposit box—but she didn't realize she would be so easily recognizable.

Ty, in contrast, sat forward. "Did you know Phoebe Aeolia?"

Carson shook his head. "No. I saw her picture, though. The newspaper did a write-up of the accident. I'll never forget her face or that of her husband." His voice trailed off as he stared sightlessly out the front window.

Inhaling deeply at the unspoken confirmation that her parents were murdered, Penny found her voice. "Mr. Carson, please. Anything you can tell us will be useful. My life and possibly many others depend on us finding these people and stopping them."

Carson stood abruptly. "I'm sorry, Ms. Dimas. I've already said more than I should have. I think you both should leave now."

Penny opened her mouth to protest, but Ty wrapped his hand around hers and squeezed, quelling the words on her lips. He stood, pulling her up with him.

"Thank you for your time, Mr. Carson. We appreciate it."

Penny frowned at Ty. Why wasn't he pushing the issue? Carson obviously knew more than he was saying. She opened her mouth to protest again, but the look Ty shot her had her snapping her lips shut and frowning further.

Carson ushered them to the door and pulled it open. "I'm sorry you lost your parents so young, Ms. Dimas. I wish I could tell you who contacted me, but I can't." He motioned to a picture on the mantle of himself with two teenagers and a woman who was obviously his wife. "For their sakes. I tried to do the right thing once and nearly lost everything."

Penny nodded, his reticence finally making sense.

"I can tell you that you need to be very careful. The people you're looking for have a long reach and the power to back it up." He stood back so they could exit. "I hope you find your answers. Good day, detective. Miss Dimas."

Penny followed Ty back to the car and climbed inside, waiting until both doors were shut and Ty was pulling away before she commented on the encounter. "He's obviously afraid of whoever paid him to falsify the police report." She chewed on her fingernail thoughtfully. "So, how do we find out what he knows?"

Ty shook his head and heaved a deep sigh. "I don't think we do. Not unless he contacts us. If the threat is still there, he won't say anything. I don't blame him. I'm not sure I would either if my family was on the line."

"Do you think they actually paid him off like he said?"

A frown puckered Ty's brow. "I'm not sure about that one. It sounded like the truth, but he could be the story he's stuck with all these years and doesn't want to change it. I don't think it really matters, though, at this point. The threat to his family is enough to keep him quiet. If he took a bribe, it paid off his mother's medical bills, and that was the end of it. There's no other evidence of dirty money in the way he lives."

Penny slumped in her seat, dejected. She'd hoped to get more out of Detective Carson. "So, where do we go from here? We don't have anything more than we did before."

"Not necessarily," Ty said, his tone thoughtful. "He did give us one clue. Whoever we're looking for is influential around here. That narrows things down a bit."

Penny frowned. "So, someone with money?"

Ty shrugged. "Possibly. More likely, it's someone in a position of authority. Carson said they have a long reach, which leads me to believe it's a family with their fingers in a lot of pies. I'll get Colin to run background checks on those in positions of power. Hopefully, he'll find a connection between several individuals we can follow up on."

His hand closed over hers and he took his eyes off the road long enough to offer her a reassuring smile. "He gave us enough, Penny. We'll get them."

Penny certainly hoped so. She had a bad feeling things were about to come to a head. She would at least like to know who she was fighting.

CHAPTER 27

"All right. Spill."

Penny stepped back as the whirlwind who was her best friend breezed through the doorway.

Keira spun and pinned Penny with a look that said she would be put off no longer. "Who's the hunk you brought with you and why were you in Greece with him? Why were you in Greece at all? I swear, it's like you became a different person when you moved to Charleston. You leave, and now I know nothing about your life anymore." Keira's arms made a journey over her head in exasperation before coming to a rest crossed over her chest. She arched an eyebrow, and Penny fought back a smile. She had certainly missed her friend's gregarious personality.

"Hi, Keira. It's nice to see you too. Won't you come in?" Penny grinned and pushed the door closed.

Keira rolled her eyes and dropped her arms back to her sides. "Okay. I know. I'm being dramatic." She pointed a finger at Penny. "But these are all legit questions. You've been gone nearly a month. Now you're back all secretive-like with an Adonis in tow, who I didn't even know you knew, *and* you took him with you to a foreign country? I mean, what the hell is going on, Penny?"

Penny heaved a sigh, mind working overtime to come up with a plausible lie to tell Keira. She really hated deceiving her friend, even though she knew it was safer for Keira. Lying had never sat well with Penny—lying to someone she loved, even less.

She settled for a half-truth to appease her conscience. "Ty is investigating my Uncle Theo's death. We had reason to believe there might be information about what could have precipitated his murder at Theo's estate in Greece. I told Ty I could go on my own and look, but he insisted on going with me." Penny gave a small smile. "I think he might have been afraid I would disappear with the evidence or something. He didn't really trust me much when we first met."

Keira frowned. "Wait. Murder? You went looking for evidence of Theo's death? I thought it was an accident."

And here's where the lying got tricky. "So did I until I got down to Charleston. There's just a bunch of stuff that doesn't add up and the coroner's report listed injuries inconsistent with a fall. The logical conclusion is he was murdered."

Keira stared at her thoughtfully. "Huh. So what evidence was in Greece?"

"Nothing, as it turned out," Penny lied smoothly. "The police have chalked up his death to something to do with his salvage business. Ty and I went to Greece to look for any records or artifacts Theo might have had there that someone would want to kill over."

"And you found nothing?"

Penny shook her head. "Not really. A few things pointed to my birth parents, which is why we're here, but none of that has panned out either." She itched to blurt out the truth and fervently hoped Keira couldn't tell she was hiding something.

Ty chose that moment to walk up, saving her from having to explain further. She was glad for the distraction. Keira's tenacity was legendary. It made her an awesome attorney, but it was a pain when Penny wanted to pull one over on her.

"Hi. Keira, right?"

Keira nodded and took the hand he extended to her. "Hello, detective."

"Ty, please. It's good to see you again. I know Penny thanked you last night for getting the house ready for us on such short notice, but I want you to know we really appreciate it. We both enjoyed being able to relax once we got here yesterday."

Keira waved off his comment. "It was nothing. Penny would do the same for me."

Ty tipped his head. "All the same, thank you."

Keira smiled. "You're welcome." Her gaze turned speculative, and she eyed him from head to toe. "So, you're investigating her uncle's death?"

"I am."

"And that warrants you traveling with her?"

Penny shot him a look over Keira's head, warning him to tread carefully.

"I thought it a good idea to be there to take possession of any physical evidence to maintain chain of custody. The prosecutors like that sort of thing."

Penny breathed a sigh of relief. He must have overheard their conversation. It would be much easier to convince Keira they were telling the truth if they both told the same story.

"That we do." Keira's eyes bounced between them. "But I'm guessing you found something else while you were there." A smile bloomed on her face as Penny's cheeks flamed.

Ty grinned. "You could say that, yes. Your friend is unlike any woman I've ever met before. I've enjoyed our time together."

Images of that kiss at the chapel flashed through Penny's brain as Ty looked her up and down. She resisted the urge to fan herself.

Keira's grin widened. "Okay then." She clapped her hands together. "So, who's hungry?"

Penny laughed at the abrupt change in subject. She could always count on Keira to keep things interesting. And to be hungry. The woman ate like a horse, but never packed any excess weight on her curvy frame. It probably had something to do with the fact Keira was never still. She was like the Energizer Bunny.

"Are you cooking?" Penny asked.

Keira looked at Penny like she had grown another head. "Like I'd let you near the stove." She turned to look at Ty. "When we were in high school, she wanted to surprise me for my birthday with a cake and my favorite food—mac and cheese. Both ended up as dismal failures and we went out for ice cream."

"Hey! I've gotten better since then," Penny protested. "Things are at least edible now."

Keira laughed. "But if I cook, it will taste good too." She looped an arm through Penny's. "Come on. Let's go see what I can scrounge up."

CHAPTER 28

P enny rolled over restlessly and stared out at the night beyond the window. Sleep was elusive tonight, the warm heat at her back that was Ty's long body, a stark reminder of why.

They were forced into the same bed because Keira overdid it on the wine—somewhat intentionally, Penny thought—and claimed the couch for the night.

Penny seemed to be the only one with a problem, though. She scowled and punched her pillow to fluff it up some more. After a brief bought of tossing and turning, Ty dropped off to sleep rather quickly, leaving Penny awake, aroused, and annoyed.

She flopped onto her back and sighed. This was stupid. Annoyed with herself, she closed her eyes and tried to will herself to sleep.

The sound of breaking glass made them pop open again. She sat bolt upright in bed.

Ty sprang up next to her.

Hmm. Maybe he *hadn't* been asleep. That thought made her feel slightly better about lying awake because of his presence next to her.

He glanced at her quickly before swinging out of bed to pad silently toward the window. He stood off to the side and peered out at the darkened lawn.

Penny shook off her distracted thoughts and followed him to the window. She took up a position on the opposite side where she could just make out their rental car. All the windows on it looked intact. So did those on Keira's car.

"All the car windows look okay," she whispered. "What was that?"

Ty shook his head. "I don't know. But all the tires on both cars are flat." He pushed away from the wall. "Get dressed. Grab the journal and the belt."

She squinted out the window again, and sure enough, both cars were resting on their rims. Alarmed, Penny scurried away to do as Ty asked. Something was happening, and she didn't want to get caught fighting in her pajamas.

Not caring that he was standing next to her, Penny ripped off her pajama bottoms and shimmied into a pair of jean shorts. Thankful she wore a sports bra under her pajama top, she quickly switched out the thin tank top for a t-shirt.

She threaded Hippolyta's belt through the loops on her shorts, then grabbed Theo's journal and stuffed into her backpack. Their passports, a change of clothes for each of them, and their wallets got stuffed inside as well.

When Penny looked up from her frantic packing, it was in time to see Ty had pulled on his jeans and t-shirt and was busy tying the laces on his boots. She thrust her feet into her tennis shoes and met him at the door.

"This is when I wish I had my gun," he muttered softly.

"My father had weapons." She looked up into his startled gaze. "There's a gun safe in the basement."

"Well. Then let's go get me armed, so we stand a chance at getting out of here." He cracked open the door and peered into the hallway. "Stay behind me," he said and stepped out into the hall.

Penny had no desire to argue with him. She hooked a finger through his back belt loop and followed in his wake.

They made it to the stairs when the smoke detector in the kitchen started shrieking. Penny's heart rate accelerated to a dangerous level.

Oh my God! They set a fire!

Hurrying now, they descended the stairs.

"Keira!" Penny shouted.

"I'm here!" Keira rushed up to meet them as they reached the bottom of the stairs. Smoke was filtering into the living room from the back of the house. They needed to get out, but they still needed to get to the weapons in the basement.

Ty made a beeline for the basement door.

"Where are you going? The front door is that way!" Keira motioned frantically toward the front of the house.

Penny shook her head, dread making her stomach want to heave. "It's a trap, Keira. We need to get my father's weapons from the basement if we're going to make it out of here."

Keira's mouth worked, but no words came out. If they weren't in so much trouble, Penny would have laughed. Keira was never at a loss for words.

Mindful that time was of the essence, she grabbed Keira's hand and pulled her along as she followed Ty downstairs.

Halfway down, Keira found her voice. "What do you mean, it's a trap? What's going on?"

"There's not really time to explain, but it all has to do with Theo's death. This fire is not an accident."

"Theo? Why would whoever killed him come after you? You didn't even know he existed a month ago."

"It's complicated." She really wanted to explain, but there was simply no time.

She turned to Ty. "The safe is over there." Penny pointed to the right-side corner opposite the stairs.

"I see it." He moved to the safe. "What's the combination?"

Penny stared at the lock in dismay. "Crap! I don't know," she whispered, tears welling in her eyes. She hadn't even thought about it being locked.

Ty's curse echoed her thoughts. "Do you know where it is?"

Penny shook her head. "It was probably with his stuff, but I packed everything away and put it in storage years ago. If he had it written down, it'd be at the storage facility in a box."

Ty cursed again. Penny beat back the tears of dismay and let her gaze roam the basement, searching for a weapon they could use to fight their way out. There were some loose boards propped against one wall and a few empty mason jars. Nothing that would defend them against a gun.

She looked up at Ty in despair. "What are we going to do?"

His eyes swung from her to the safe and back again. A hard glint of determination lit his eyes and Penny felt her own widen as she realized what he was thinking. She glanced at Keira, who looked as frantic as Penny felt and a whole lot more confused.

"It can't be helped. We need those guns," Ty told her, reading her thoughts.

Penny bit her lip. "We could go upstairs." It was the only way she could think of to keep their secret.

Ty shook his head. "We need to stay together."

Penny finally nodded reluctantly. So much for keeping Keira in the dark.

"Stand over there." Ty motioned them off to the side. "I don't know how this is going to go."

"What? How what's going to go?" Keira said, frowning at him.

Penny pulled a bewildered Keira to the side.

"What is he talking about, Penny?"

She didn't answer. Not that she had a chance to, though. As soon as they were out of the way, Ty braced one hand on the safe and grasped the handle. He took a deep breath, drawing himself into one tight coil. Penny could see the tension in every muscle of his body. Every ridge, every dip, was outlined in stark relief as he gathered his strength and prepared to unleash it.

Suddenly, he exhaled and pulled. The metal door groaned as it buckled in the middle.

Penny's mouth dropped open in disbelief. She hadn't actually thought he'd be able to do it. Ripping apart a wooden cabinet with his bare hands was one thing. Bending a solid metal, *locked* gun safe was something else entirely.

Ty readjusted his grip, curling his fingers over the edge near the lock, then inhaled again, gathering all that power. He exhaled once more and pulled. The door bent further and the lock popped free. The mangled door swung open. Ty grabbed a handgun and two full magazines off the shelf.

"Oh my God! How did you *do* that?" Keira cried.

"Genetics," Ty quipped. He handed a second handgun and ammo to Penny. "Keira, do you know how to use a gun?"

"I'm a Texan, of course I do, but—"

"Good." He thrust a loaded rifle into her hands. "Both of you stay behind me."

"Can someone please explain to me what the hell is going on?"

Penny looked back, already halfway up the stairs behind Ty. Keira stood poised at the bottom, rifle in one hand and the other fisted on her hip. She glared up at them.

Penny retreated down the steps and grabbed Keira's free hand. "Again, I promise I'll explain. Right now, though, we need to get the hell out of here." She looked down at her friend, trying to convey the seriousness of their situation. "Unless you want to become a crispy critter as this place burns down around us."

Keira shook her head, her curls bouncing riotously.

Penny took off up the stairs, pulling Keira behind her. Ty waited at the top, eyes roaming.

"The back door is fully engulfed. Our only way out is through the front."

Fear flared through her body, but Penny swiftly put a lid on it. It would not help them. If they had any chance of getting out of here alive, she needed to focus on strategy.

"So, what do we do?"

"How far do you think you can push that shifting thing?"

Penny took one look at the gleam lighting his eyes and felt her own widen. She was going to owe Keira a huge explanation when they got out of this.

She spun around and grabbed Keira's hand. "Keira. Don't freak out, okay? Ty and I have a plan, but you need to trust us."

"I trust you. But him?" Keira pointed at Ty. "I just watched him rip open a freaking gun safe with his bare hands. I'm having a little trouble putting my life in the hands of someone who can do that."

Oh, if she only knew.

"I understand, but he is one of the good guys, I swear. And Keira? The crazy stuff you can't believe isn't over yet."

Keira's eyes widened almost comically. "Oh, geez. Does he shoot lightning bolts out of his fingertips too?"

Penny couldn't stop the quick laugh that popped free. "That would actually come in rather handy right now." She looked up at Ty, curious. "You can't, can you?" Hercules was the son of Zeus, after all.

Ty held up a hand and aimed it at the wall, fierce concentration on his face. When nothing happened, he dropped his hand back to his side and shook his head. "Nope. Fresh out of lightning bolts. Zeus kept those for himself."

Keira looked down her nose at him, completely unamused. "Very funny."

Penny grasped Keira's shoulders and faced her square on. "The crazy stuff isn't about him this time. It's about me. Now, I'll explain the hows and the whys later, but right now I just need you to trust me and not freak out. Okay?"

Keira frowned, but nodded.

"This," Penny waggled her pistol, "is a precaution. If I do this right, we're going to walk right out of here with no one the wiser."

The frown wrinkling Keira's brow deepened. "How?"

"Like this." Penny stepped back and let the shift overtake her. Instantly, she was a spider at Ty's feet. Keira's shriek had her popping back to normal.

"Holy shit! How? Why?"

The living room window on the side of the house shattered before Penny could say a word. A flaming bottle flew through it and smashed onto the floor. The drapes caught fire in seconds as the bottle spilled its flammable contents and the flames spread.

"We need to do this now," Ty yelled over the roar of the flames that were quickly ascending the wall. "The backpack didn't shift with you. You need to get Keira out and get behind whoever's out front. Take a couple of them out so I can get out of here."

Penny looked at him through tearful eyes. "I don't want to leave you in here."

"You don't have a choice. One of us has to carry the backpack out. You're the only one who can shift any of us, and no one can walk out that door human, so long as all the bad guys are out there waiting. I'm trained for this stuff and can hold them off. She can't." He gestured at Keira. "Go."

Her heart warred with her mind as she considered his words. He was right, but it didn't change how she felt.

"Penny, go. Before none of us can get out."

He looked so handsome even with the sweat streaking down his face from the intense heat of the fire. A warrior come to life right in front of her. If they lived through this, she was done with the excuses why they shouldn't get involved.

She stood on her toes and pressed a kiss to his lips. "We'll hurry. Don't die on me."

Ty kissed her back. "Not a chance. Now go."

CHAPTER 29

"Y ou ready?"

Keira shook her head. "No. Yes. Aaagh!" She thrust her hands through her hair, making the already crazy curls crazier. "This is so nuts. I don't know what's going on, Penny, but I trust you. Let's do this."

Penny nodded and grabbed Keira's hand, preparing to shift them.

"Wait!" Keira cried. She turned wary eyes on Penny. "This won't hurt, will it? Not that I don't want you to still do it, I just want to be prepared."

"It doesn't hurt. It just tingles," Ty interjected.

Keira studied him briefly before she nodded. "Okay." She looked at Penny. "Do it."

Penny didn't give Keira a chance to change her mind. She let the shift happen, and they were quickly scurrying under the door and onto the porch.

As soon as they were through, Penny felt Keira climb onto her back like Penny told her to, so she wouldn't shift back. Penny fled across the porch to the bushes the best she could with Keira riding piggyback. The leafy plants rested against the porch railings in several places, making it was easy to get onto the leaves and inside the bush.

Once inside the foliage, she quickly shifted them to chipmunks so they could move faster while still going undetected.

They dropped out of the bush and made a quick pass around the perimeter of the house, pausing every few moments to renew the connection, so Keira didn't shift. Smoke billowed around them, making Penny thankful they were small and below most of the cloud flowing out of the broken windows. She tried hard not to let the pain of watching her childhood home burn override her concentration. If they were going to get out of here, she needed to remain focused. It would be terrible for them to be caught now.

Shoving her emotions down deep, Penny continued her circuit of the house. A gleaming, black SUV sat to one side of the drive opposite where Ty parked their rental. Keira's car sat behind the rental. She saw one man behind the SUV and another between their rental and Keira's vehicle. As she rounded the back of the house, she caught sight of a third man at the edge of the woods behind the house, watching the back door. All three held semi-automatic rifles in their hands.

Penny paused at the front corner of the house. They needed to get behind the gunmen.

She eyed the trees to the side of the house. The woods that surrounded the property were both a blessing and a curse right now. If she could get them to the trees undetected, they could use the thick foliage to get into position. But there could be men in the trees they couldn't see.

Keira poked her and pointed at the trees. Penny nodded, understanding. It was the best plan, even with the unknowns. They needed to hurry, though, which meant she needed to carry Keira more securely.

An idea took root and Penny sent a silent plea heavenward. *Please let this work.*

She motioned for Keira to climb onto her back. Concentrating hard, Penny tried to split the change and shifted just herself to a squirrel and left Keira as the smaller chipmunk.

Feeling herself grow, Penny knew that she at least was a squirrel now. She glanced back over her shoulder. Small paws circled her neck and tiny eyes in a little chipmunk face stared back at her.

It worked! Elated, Penny took off for the trees, hoping and praying the shifting shadows caused by the fire would keep the gunmen from seeing the bounding squirrel crossing the yard with a chipmunk clinging to its back like a monkey.

Once in the trees, Penny didn't stop. Fire now consumed the entire back of the house, and she could see the flames licking through the front windows. Urgency pounded through her veins. They needed to hurry, or Ty wouldn't make it out of the house.

She leaped up the closest tree and started jumping from limb to limb and tree to tree until she was behind the men near the vehicles. She scampered down and hid behind the wide trunk of an oak at the edge of the drive. Penny let the shift roll off, and they were human again.

"Oh my God," Keira breathed. "That was insane."

"We're not done yet," Penny whispered back. "I'm going to drop you off behind your car. Once I get on the other side of the bad guys' SUV, we're going to sneak up behind them and hit them over the head. Only shoot the guy if you have to. We don't want to bring the other one running out front."

Keira nodded and checked to make sure her pistol was ready to go. Before they had left the house, Ty had traded her for the rifle. "I didn't see anyone else in the trees. Did you?"

Penny shook her head. "No. I think these three are it." Thank God. She motioned to her back. "Climb on."

Once Keira was settled, Penny quickly shifted them and took off for the cars. She deposited Keira out of sight and raced across the drive to the other car. The man there was so focused on the house, he didn't notice the squirrel scurrying behind him. She hid beside the wheel and shifted back.

Cautiously, Penny peered around the SUV's back bumper to see if Keira was ready. The fire offered just enough light for her to see a thumbs up from her friend.

Sending a silent prayer through the night, Penny crept forward, pistol gripped tightly. Stomach churning, she brought the butt of the gun down on the man's head as hard as she could. The man crumpled to the ground like a ton of bricks. Penny resisted the urge to do a victory dance. She couldn't believe that had actually worked.

Noise from across the drive caught her attention. Penny looked over just in time to see the other man turn, and see Keira coming at him. He raised his gun, and the breath caught in Penny's throat.

Keira, gun already raised, fired two shots.

"Ty!" Penny yelled for him, all pretense of remaining quiet gone with the gunshots. She raced across the drive. "Keira! Are you all right?"

Shaking, Keira nodded. "I think so." Tears welled in her eyes and the gun fell from her hand. "Oh my God. I just killed a man."

Penny gathered her close. "You saved yourself."

CHAPTER 30

Ty barreled out the front door, rifle at the ready, as soon as he heard the gunshots and Penny's shout. He saw the women huddled between the cars, a figure sprawled at their feet. A quick glance across the drive revealed another lump on the ground at the back of the SUV. Not knowing if there were more hiding, he moved forward cautiously.

"There's a third coming from the back," Penny yelled.

He cleared the porch just as the third gunman Penny had warned him about rounded the front of the house.

"Drop it!" Ty leveled his rifle at the man.

The man didn't listen and swung his gun around to fire at Ty.

Ty pulled the trigger before he could get off a shot, the bullet connecting with the man's shoulder, rendering the joint useless. The gunman dropped the rifle with a scream, his right arm dangling at his side. Ty launched himself over the railing and grabbed him by the good arm. The man struggled despite his injury, trying to free himself.

Ty jerked him hard, making him cry out, and hauled him close. "Unless you want to get a bullet in the other shoulder, you will co-operate."

A half grin, half grimace creased the man's face. "You wouldn't."

There were times Ty enjoyed being six-foot-eight. Right now, he pressed his height advantage and loomed over the man. "I don't take kindly to someone trying to barbecue me and my friends. You're lucky I wanted you alive so I could question you, or right now you'd be down in hell or Tartarus or wherever it is you believe in. You keep giving me problems, and you might get more than a bullet to the arm. I'll use my bare hands to rip you to pieces." Ty jerked the man forward. "Now move."

More subdued, the man walked when Ty prodded. They headed across the yard to where Penny and Keira waited by the cars.

"Sit." Ty shoved the man to the ground. "Keira, give me your belt, so I can tie him up." The man might be wounded, but he still had one good arm.

Keira quickly did as he asked. Heedless of the man's wounded shoulder, he bound the mercenary's hands behind his back.

The gunman groaned. "Come on, man," he panted. "At least tie them in front."

"Shut up." Ty turned to Penny. "This one's dead, I see." He motioned to the gunman crumpled on the ground in a pool of blood. "What about that one?" He pointed across the drive.

"Out cold. I whacked him with my gun. Keira wasn't as lucky and had to shoot this one before he shot her."

Ty turned concerned eyes on the petite brunette. She looked a little pale, but not too freaked out. "You okay?"

"Oh, sure. I kill people every day. I'm just peachy." Her voice caught on the last word and tears welled in her eyes.

Ty squatted next to her and tried to reassure her. "Hey. It was him or you. He came here and brought this on himself. That's on him, not you. Okay?"

Keira sniffed and nodded. "I know. I'll be all right. It's just a bit of a shock."

Ty nodded, understanding completely. Killing was never easy. He'd done it more than he cared to admit as a SEAL. It was one reason he left the Navy. It had started to eat at his soul.

"We need to get out of here in case they have reinforcements coming." Ty looked at the three cars in the drive. Their rental and Keira's car were out. The gunmen made sure they weren't going anywhere. That left the SUV their attackers drove. Ty wasn't keen on taking it just because he didn't know what tracking devices were on it. But staying where they were wasn't an option. Taking the big, black SUV was their best bet until they could get somewhere safe and find a different vehicle, or he could disable the GPS.

He pulled the wounded gunman to his feet, getting a perverse satisfaction out of the groan the guy couldn't hold back as Ty hauled him up. He had no sympathy for the man and his buddies.

"We're going to borrow your ride, friend." He motioned for Penny and Keira to follow.

"Where are we going?" Penny asked as she buckled in beside him. Keira was ensconced in the back seat and both the remaining gunmen were trussed up like turkeys—complete with duct tape over their mouths from the roll they found in the car—in the way back.

Ty started the engine and swiftly turned around. "Some place we can regroup and figure out how they found us." Ty turned left out of the drive and started driving. He had no concrete place in mind at the moment. They just needed some distance between them and the house.

"We did go see Detective Carson. Maybe he told someone we were in town and they put two and two together and came looking for me at Mom and Dad's," Penny mused.

Ty tipped his head. "That's definitely possible."

Carson had certainly been disconcerted by their questions. If whoever was behind all this threatened his family again, Ty had little doubt Carson would have rolled on them. In his shoes, Ty would have done the same to protect his kids.

"Regardless, we need some place safe to go. We can't exactly waltz into a hotel with those two bound, gagged, and bleeding." Penny motioned toward the men in the back. "And the one you shot needs medical attention, or he's going to bleed to death."

"We could go to my parents' cabin," Keira suggested, leaning forward. "It's isolated and only a few people know they have it."

"No." Ty shook his head. "Your car was at the house. Police and fire are going to be all over that scene. Once they realize you're missing as well, they'll be looking for you. Family properties will be the first places they check."

Penny frowned. "So where do we go, then?"

The beginnings of a plan formed in Ty's head. It'd been years since he'd seen Leo Devereaux, but if the man still lived where Ty thought he did, they might have a place to go.

"I have a plan, but I need to make a call."

CHAPTER 31

"Did you get everything?" Penny took the bags from Keira so she could buckle her seatbelt.

"I think so." Keira settled into her seat, clicking the buckle into place. "Give me the phone and I'll get it activated."

Penny pulled the burner cell from the bag of supplies Keira picked up and handed it to her. She put the car in gear and headed back to where they dropped off Ty and the gunmen. Ty made them leave him and the two men—still trussed up like turkeys—at the edge of a rural road just outside of the next town while Penny and Keira went to get medical supplies and an untraceable cellphone. They decided it would be safest for Keira to go in and get what they needed while Penny waited in the car. With her curly hair twisted up on her head, Keira was the least remarkable of the three of them. Ty and Penny would both be remembered for their height. Keira looked like the girl next door. Thankfully, Ty thought to bring cash with them on their excursions around the world, so Keira was able to get what they needed without leaving much, if any, memory of her trip to the store.

Keira flipped the basic cellphone closed, finished activating it just as Penny pulled up to where they left Ty and their captives. Penny tapped twice on the horn in their prearranged signal that all was well.

Ty rose from the grass on her left. Penny and Keira hurried out of the vehicle. They rounded the back of the SUV as Ty pulled both men to their feet and hauled them up the embankment. Penny rushed to open the lift gate on the SUV so Ty could put the men inside. The one Penny hit over the head had long since regained consciousness and struggled against the tape binding his hands and feet. He glared at them as Ty propped the wounded gunman against the SUV's frame.

Ty ripped the tape off the wounded man's mouth. "I'm going to cut your hands free so we can bandage your shoulder. Don't try to run. We're in the middle of nowhere. There's no place for you to go, and you'll just end up pissing me off when I have to chase you down and bring you back. Understand?"

The man nodded weakly. Penny didn't like how pale and sweaty he was. The sooner they got him to a doctor, the better. Ty's plan better work, or they were going to be hauling a corpse around.

She helped Ty cut away the blood-soaked sleeve of the man's shirt. The wound still bled, but had thankfully slowed to an ooze. He uncapped a bottle of water and poured it over the wound. The man hissed as the water contacted his raw flesh.

"It's a through-and-through, so no need to go digging in there." A cold smile spread over Ty's face. "Lucky you."

The man grunted in reply.

"Now, the question is, do you want me to put a couple stitches in this or do you want to take your chances with the bleeding until we get to where we're going and can get to someone with numbing meds?" Ty held up the stitching kit that was part of the deluxe first aid kit Keira bought.

"Stitch it." The man's voice was tight with pain. "I've lost enough blood."

Penny helped Ty sterilize his hands while Keira got the kit ready.

"What's your name?" Penny asked, trying to distract the man.

"Alex."

"What about your partner?"

The man in question squirmed and glared again. Penny was sure he was cursing them loudly in his head. It was probably a good thing he was still muzzled.

"Seth."

"Who sent you after us?"

The man half laughed, half groaned as Ty put a stitch in. "Someone who's going to annihilate you. You and your band of merry friends don't stand a chance."

Fury, like she had never known, ripped through Penny. She was getting seriously tired of people wanting to kill her. "Really? Me and my 'band of merry friends' certainly kicked your ass." She looked up at Ty, who started on Alex's exit wound. "You sure there were no bullet fragments in there? Maybe we should rip out all those stitches and check."

Alex's eyes widened almost comically at the vehemence of her words.

Ty chuckled. "She's fierce, I know. But you're safe. Unlike you and your compatriots, we aren't heartless bastards who try to kill unsuspecting people." He stopped stitching for a moment and leaned in, menace sharpening the planes of his face. "But I will kill you if you push me. And you better talk. If you won't talk, you're no longer useful, and I don't need to be so careful the next time."

"You're a cop. You can't do that."

Penny sucked in a breath, both surprised and yet not by the fact these men knew who Ty was and what he did for a living.

Ty looked down at his belt. "I don't see a badge. Do you see a badge?" He grinned a mirthless smile. "You and I both know your employer doesn't want anyone to know about any of this. No one would believe it, anyway. Why should I play by the rules of polite society when we're operating outside their bounds?"

Alex's eyes bounced between her and Ty. Penny glared at the man. Genuine fear entered his eyes for the first time as Ty's words sank in. He was in between a rock and a hard place, and he now realized it. Penny got the feeling Alex and all his friends had underestimated how far Ty was willing to go. For that matter, she had a feeling they underestimated her as well.

"You want to talk now?" Penny asked as Ty resumed stitching.

Alex opened his mouth, but Seth kicked him before he could utter a word. Penny held her breath as Alex hesitated. Finally, he shook his head and clamped his lips together.

Disgusted, Penny whirled away. She busied herself making a bandage to go over the stitched wound. These men were lucky she was an inherently nice person with a strong moral compass. Otherwise, she'd be tempted to leave Alex's gunshot wound untended and open to infection.

Keira sidled close. "Penny?" she whispered. "What are we doing?"

Penny frowned, confused. "What do you mean?"

Keira opened her mouth, closed it, then tried again. "I mean, we've stolen an SUV—"

"That belonged to some seriously bad dudes."

"Right, but we're still in a stolen SUV. *With* the bad dudes who tried to kill us. We're in the middle of frickin' nowhere with no plan—"

"I have a plan," Ty interrupted.

Keira glared at him. "One beyond getting us to a safe place to regroup?"

Ty nodded. "Take out the head bad guy after us."

Keira's arms flew up over her head and she rolled her eyes. "That's not a plan!"

"It's the basis of a plan."

"But it's still not a plan!"

"Keira, I get that you're freaked, but now is not the time for us to discuss this," Ty said, casting a glance at their two captives.

Tension evident in every line of her body, Keira nodded after a moment.

"I promise, as soon as possible, we will explain," Penny said softly, grasping Keira's arm.

"This is big, isn't it?"

Penny nodded solemnly.

Keira bit her lip and whirled away. She pulled the hair-tie from her hair and ran a hand through her messy curls.

"All right. That should do it." Ty set the stitching paraphernalia down and held out his hand to Penny for the bandages. She handed it over and watched as he slapped the pads over both wound sites, none too gently. Alex moaned.

"You want to wrap this while I hold it, Penny?"

Together, they made quick work of bandaging the gunman's shoulder. Once done, Ty rebound the man, but this time strapped his arms to his sides with the duct tape so he wouldn't rip out the stitches. Ty slapped another piece of tape over his mouth and sat him back in the cargo area of the car next to his buddy.

"What's next?" Penny asked as Ty slammed the back gate shut.

Ty turned to Keira. "Did you get the burner phone I asked for?"

She nodded. "It's up front."

"Good. Now I make a phone call and hope to hell Leo hasn't moved."

They made their way back to the front of the car. Keira pulled open the passenger door and grabbed the phone off the console, then handed it to Ty.

Ty thanked his lucky stars the military taught him to memorize information. He pulled Leo's phone number from the dregs of his memory and keyed it into the burner as he held his breath. He hadn't actually talked to Leo in nearly a year. They emailed every once in a while, though, and he hadn't mentioned moving.

A low growl rumbled through Ty's ear as the line connected. "'Lo?"

"Leo, it's Ty Farris," he said, recognizing the man's voice.

A beat of silence passed. "What the fuck, Farris? Do you know what time it is, man?"

"Yeah, I do. I'm sorry to wake you, but it's important. Do you still live in the back of beyond?"

More silence passed and Ty could practically hear Leo's mind try to shake off sleep and catch up to the conversation. "Yeah. Why?"

"It's a little hard to explain over the phone, and honestly, I don't have time, but my friends and I need a place to lay low for a few days. Do you mind some visitors?"

This time, the comeback was much quicker. "Lay low? Everything all right?" Before Ty could respond, Leo spoke again. "You know what, never mind. I don't care. Of course you can come here."

Ty breathed a sigh of relief and looked over at Penny, giving her a quick nod. "Thanks, Leo. I appreciate it."

"No problem. When should I expect you? I'm assuming you're driving if you want to fly under the radar. So what? Late tomorrow?"

"Actually, I'm in Texas, so we should be there by late morning."

There was a pause. "What the hell are you doing in Texas?"

"I'll explain everything when we get there. There are a couple things I need, though, before we arrive. I have some—not friends—with me and they need a secure place to stay."

Leo's low laugh rumbled over the line. "Man, this is going to be some kind of story you're going to tell. I've got just the place to stash your *not friends*, so they stay put."

It was Ty's turn to laugh. "Awesome. We also need someone with some medical knowledge who knows how to keep a secret. One of our not friends is injured pretty badly. I've patched him up, but he's probably going to need some antibiotics and fluids."

"Okay. I'll see what I can do."

"Thanks, man. I appreciate it. We'll see you soon."

"Anytime."

Ty disconnected the call and smiled at the women. "How's Louisiana sound?"

CHAPTER 32

Penny stared at the massive cabin that seemed to appear out of the trees as they passed into the clearing around the house. The single story, sprawling structure was painted a deep red and sat on stilts in the middle of the clearing. A porch extended the length of the front of the house and rocking chairs sat motionless and inviting, waiting for someone to sit and relax. Towering cypress, oak, and ash trees surrounded the property. Spanish moss created a curtain that hid the house and its outbuildings from view beyond the clearing. It was quite the idyllic setting, if a bit isolated. But right now, isolated was exactly what they needed.

Ty pulled up next to a burgundy extended-cab pickup. As he put the SUV in park, a tall blond man walked out of the house, followed by a behemoth of a dog. The screen door slapped closed behind them. Ty shut off the car and stepped out. Penny and Keira followed. By the time the women reached them, Ty and Leo were shaking hands and exchanging a man hug. The dog wagged its tail, happily circling the pair.

"So these are the friends you need to lay low with?" Leo asked, looking them over.

Penny couldn't help but notice his eyes lingered on Keira just a little longer than they did on her. Keira had that effect on men. Her youthful, open face, wide eyes, and curvy frame were like catnip to the male half of the species.

While he was distracted, Penny took a moment to study him. He was about her height, maybe a couple of inches taller, and muscular, but not overly so. His hair was dark blonde and shaggy, but not unkempt, and his dark eyes held a keen intelligence. The air surrounding him said simple country boy, but Penny had a feeling this man was anything but.

Ty quickly introduced them all before motioning to the car. "Our *not friends* are secured in the back of the SUV. I'd like to get them settled. They're probably in pretty desperate need of a bathroom and some food by now. We tried to let them out to relieve the call of nature about halfway here, and the uninjured one decided to be an idiot and try to run. I hope whatever place you have in mind for them can be battened down like Fort Knox. He is one determined SOB. Not real bright, but determined."

Leo grinned and hooked his thumb toward the house. "I cleared out a closet and turned the doorknob around. I added a couple of locks too, both deadbolt and slide locks. It's got a chem toilet in it now and a stash of water and snacks."

"Sounds perfect."

"I've also got a medic friend on standby to come out and take a look at the one guy. I just need to give him a ring."

"Good." Ty started toward the back of the SUV. Leo followed, as did the dog. The large animal bounded over to the women, eager for attention. Keira shrieked and backed away as the dog sniffed her.

"Clyde, sit." Leo barked.

The dog dropped to his haunches and stared up at Keira. He let out a soft whine and his tail swished in the dirt.

"Sorry about that, *chère*," Leo apologized. "He forgets he can be scary. He really is harmless, though."

Keira nodded shakily. "It's okay. I'm just not much of a dog fan."

With good reason, Penny thought as she moved closer to her friend. Keira was attacked as a child by one of her grandfather's Dobermans. Thankfully, Penny was with her and had run for help. Keira's dad came right away and called off the animal before he could do serious, permanent damage, but the experience left Keira wary of large dogs.

Leo called the dog to his side and motioned for Ty to open the lift gate. He let out a low whistle when he saw the two men bound in the back. "Mercenaries?"

Ty gave a short nod. "I think so. They lit Penny's house on fire with us in it and then waited outside so they could pick us off as we tried to escape the fire."

Leo's gaze snapped to Ty. That relaxed air of his was gone in an instant, morphing into something edgier. "How did you get away?"

Ty reached in and grabbed Seth. "*That* is a question for after we get these two squared away." He hauled the man out, who immediately started to struggle. Ty shook him hard. "Dude. Did you learn nothing from the last time? If you want to be able to do more than get your pants unzipped to take a piss, you had best knock it off."

Seth glared at him but relented.

"You're right. He's not very bright," Leo said with a grin.

"Nope." Ty stepped back so Leo could help Alex from the car, then followed his friend into the house. Penny and Keira fell into step behind them.

Leo led them down a long hallway to a door about halfway down that led into a bedroom. Inside, Penny noted the boarded-up window and the utter lack of *everything* in the room. Only the bed and dresser remained. She was glad Leo had prepared for the possibility the men might escape the closet. She glanced back at the door and saw the new locks there as well. They'd hear them breaking out before they actually escaped.

Ty ushered their prisoners into the room's walk-in closet. From her vantage point, she could see that Leo had set up a small cot along the back wall and stocked the built-in shelves with water, snacks, and some MREs.

Ty helped Alex sit and made quick work of ridding him of the tape binding his arms. "We'll get someone here to look at you and get you some pain meds. Try to rest in the meantime." Alex nodded and leaned back against the wall, eyes dropping closed.

Turning, Ty eyed their more fractious captive. "You try anything and, so help me, I will make you look like a duct tape mummy. Got it?"

The man nodded.

Ty peeled the tape off his mouth and went to work on his hands while Leo stood in the doorway, blocking it.

Finally free, Seth eyed them belligerently, but made no move to get out of the closet.

"Don't try to escape. You won't get far," Leo said. "Even if you get past us, you're in the middle of the swamp." He grinned wickedly. "And the gators are hungry sons-a-bitches."

Ty slid past, and Leo closed the door with a laugh.

"Call your medic friend," Ty said once Leo turned to face him after locking all the locks on the door. "We get the one checked out and we'll fill you—and Keira—in on what's going on." He spared a glance at the woman who stood with Penny.

Glancing over, Penny laid a hand on Keira's shoulder. Her friend still looked a little shell-shocked, even after all these hours. She hoped she could handle their revelations.

The foursome filed out of the room and down the hall. Leo told them to have a seat, then left to make a phone call.

Penny's adrenaline fled now that they were safe. She sank into the soft couch and closed her eyes. The next thing she knew, there was a knock on the door. Jolting awake, she turned to see Leo let in a man carrying a small duffel bag. He spared her and Keira a quick look before following Leo and Ty down the hall.

Her stomach grumbled, reminding her it had been a long time since they ate anything substantial. She got up and went to the kitchen, searching for something quick and found sandwich fixings. By the time the trio returned, she had plates ready for everyone.

Leo let his friend out, then followed Ty to the dining room.

"I hope you don't mind," Penny said, carrying plates into the room. "I was hungry and needed something to occupy myself."

He waved a hand. "Not at all." He held out a chair for Keira, then sat down.

Penny passed out the plates and took a seat.

"Okay, fill me in." Leo lifted his sandwich and took a bite.

Ty held up a finger, devouring his food. Penny didn't know where to even start—Keira wasn't the only one still shell-shocked—so she let him take the lead. After several large bites, his sandwich was gone, and he dove into the story. The more he talked, the quieter Keira grew and the larger Leo's eyes became.

Penny glanced at Keira, fully expecting to see a similar expression to Leo's on her face. She looked surprised all right, but there was also something else there. It looked like fear, but it was more than that.

"Keira? Are you okay? I know this is a lot to take in." Penny placed her hand over Keira's arm.

Keira swallowed hard and tears welled in her eyes.

Penny sat up straighter in alarm. "Keira?" This was not at all like her friend. The Keira Penny knew was the type to take a problem by the throat and wrestle it into submission. She should have been throwing out suggestions about how they could eliminate the threat so they could get back to their lives. Not fighting a breakdown.

"I'm sorry, Penny."

"Sorry for what?" Penny frowned.

"This is all my fault."

Both men sat forward, looks of intense interest on their faces, while Penny did a double take. What the hell was she talking about? "How is any of this your fault?"

Keira sniffed and swiped at the tears streaming down her face. "Because I know who's after you."

CHAPTER 33

P enny opened and closed her mouth several times. She knew she looked like a fish gasping for air, but she couldn't formulate any words.

"What do you mean, you know who's after us?" Ty finally asked, echoing Penny's thoughts.

Keira turned to him. "The name you mentioned—Artemenko—I know it."

"How?" Ty's voice had taken on an edge Penny was sure had criminals spilling all their secrets. It promised violent retribution for anything less than the complete truth.

"It's my family name," Keira said softly, her gaze dropping.

Confusion furrowed Penny's brow. "Your family name is Artherton."

Keira nodded and looked up. "It is now. But it didn't used to be. My grandfather changed it before I was born and convinced my dad and uncle to do it as well. I wouldn't even know about it except I found the documents in a trunk in my grandfather's attic when I was looking for stuff for costumes for that Halloween party we went to our senior year of high school."

Penny sat back, stunned. How did she not already know this? "Why didn't you ever tell me your family changed its name?" She was genuinely curious. Had Keira's grandfather, Victor, asked Keira not to say anything? Or had Keira decided it wasn't worth telling anyone? Somehow, Penny didn't think it was the latter. Changing the family name would be something Keira found interesting and noteworthy.

Keira shrugged. "It didn't seem all that important—interesting, but not important. And when I asked my dad about it, he said it was a cultural thing and asked me not to tell anyone. He said they did it to help them fit in better, and that he didn't want any of my friends to see me differently since we were recent immigrants. You remember what it was like for anyone with a 'foreign' sounding name at our school. Dad said he had faced similar problems at work. Shortly after they changed the name, he took a position at a different law firm, and, well, you know the rest."

That she did. Dominic Artherton was one of the premiere corporate attorneys in Austin.

Ty steepled his fingers and rested his chin on them. "I still fail to see how this is your fault." He eyed her speculatively. "Unless you've been in on this the whole time."

"No!" Keira shouted. "No. I would never do anything to hurt Penny." She turned and grasped Penny's hands. "You have to believe me, Pen. I had no idea my family had anything to do with your troubles until you mentioned the old family name."

Penny gulped, not sure what to think. Her heart screamed Keira was innocent, but her head said it was certainly possible she'd known all along. Her eyes slid to Ty, imploring him for help. He simply raised an eyebrow as if to tell her she had to decide on her own if what Keira said was true.

"Explain how you think it's your fault," Ty demanded, saving her from answering.

Keira closed her eyes briefly, gathering herself. She locked her eyes on Penny, regret stamped all over her features. "That night you arrived in Austin at your parents'—when Dad called?"

Penny's eyes widened, understanding dawning.

"I had a big case at work that day, and he was calling to see how it went. He heard the door bang shut and asked me where I was. I told him you were home for a visit and that you brought a friend."

Penny felt the bottom drop out of her stomach. That explained how they knew to attack the house. She couldn't believe that people she'd trusted nearly her entire life wanted her dead. She had spent almost as much time in Keira's home—with Dominic and Keira's mother, Sara—as she had at her own.

"Shit," Ty muttered. "They've been tracking us since we got back to the U.S." He pushed away from the table to pace to the window. He stared out at the yard and the trees beyond before spinning back around. "Do they know where we are now? Did you call anyone when you went to get medical supplies and that burner phone?"

Keira shook her head emphatically, setting her curls to bouncing. "No. I was afraid to use my cell for fear that whoever was working with the guys we captured would think to track it. I knew you both turned off your phones, and that you disabled the GPS in the SUV. I didn't want to be the one to lead them to us." Her voice broke on the last word, and she buried her head in her hands, more tears leaking around her fingers.

Ty walked back to the table and sat in his chair, scooting it closer to Keira. "I need you to tell me everything you can about your family. What they do for a living. Where they frequent. Which ones want power. Who's capable of murder."

Keira's head sprang up at that. "No one's capable of that! They're all good people. Kind. And they all know Penny and love her."

"At least one of them doesn't," Leo spoke up. "Or you wouldn't have had to turn into a spider to escape a house fire set on the orders of a member of your family." Leo looked at Ty. "That begs another question: did they know she was in the house?" He tipped his head toward Keira.

A strangled sound passed through Keira's lips.

Penny acted instinctively and wrapped the smaller woman in a tight embrace. "No," she told Leo. "I refuse to believe her family knew she was in the house and set it on fire, anyway. They might want me dead for what I have, but Keira was totally innocent in all of this until yesterday." She gestured down the hallway. "They sent their lackeys to do their dirty work. I bet they didn't even know what Keira looked like beforehand."

Ty stood abruptly. "Let's ask them." He motioned for them all to follow.

Penny rose, still holding Keira. As hard as this had been for Penny to deal with, she could only imagine how Keira felt. Her entire life had just been tipped on its head and spun around even more violently than Penny's.

She clung tight to her shaky friend and followed Ty and Leo down the hallway.

Reaching the bedroom, Ty drew his weapon as he approached the closet door. A glance behind him showed that Leo also had his gun drawn. Penny wanted no part of the potentially explosive situation, so she and Keira hovered near the bed.

CHAPTER 34

Ty took the set of keys Leo held out. While Ty unlocked the deadbolts, Leo took up residence on the other side of the door and grasped the doorknob.

Leo gave a quick nod, signaling he was ready. Ty pocketed the keys and slid the last slide lock free. With a quick turn of the knob, Leo pulled the door open while Ty swept into the doorway, weapon at the ready.

Seth, having heard the door unlock, stood ready to attack, but backed off when he saw the guns trained on him. Alex sat on the cot looking weary.

Ty eyed Seth as he motioned Keira forward. The man might seem to have learned his lesson, but Ty still didn't trust him. He lowered his weapon to pull Keira into the doorway. Leo stood guard just inside the closet.

"Do either of you know who this woman is?"

Two sets of perplexed eyes met Ty's question.

"Should we?" Seth asked.

Ty hummed a non-answer and let Keira retreat to Penny's side. He eyed both men speculatively, trying to discern if they were lying. Seth still watched them, the set to his jaw belligerent, but Alex seemed curious now. Intelligence shone from of the man's eyes. Ty had a feeling there was more to this mercenary than they initially believed. He just hoped he didn't have the black soul so many men for hire seemed to possess.

Ty made a split-second decision. "Alex, come with us." While he didn't trust the man completely, he had a feeling he could use that intelligence he saw to their advantage. Ty didn't think this was a man who had any strong allegiance to the Arthertons. No. This man was a hired gun who went where the money was. So did his partner. The difference between them, Ty hoped, was Alex knew when to cut his losses and jump ship. Seth didn't. Ty was betting on Alex seeing reason and helping them defeat his employers. With the situation they were in, Ty would take any help he could get.

Seth's eyebrows slammed down in a frown, and he took a step toward Ty.

"Uh-uh-uh." Ty waggled his pistol at the man. He so wanted this jackass to make a move. Unlike his partner, Seth was a thorn in their side, and Ty couldn't wait to be rid of him. He didn't know how that would happen yet, but it would. "You can go sit over there." He pointed at the cot. "Alex has been cooperative and gets some freedom."

Alex pushed himself off the cot and slowly shuffled toward the door without even a glance at his partner.

Yeah, Alex was definitely the smarter of the two. There didn't seem to be any love lost between the men, either. That would definitely work in their favor.

With a last long look at Seth, Ty shut the door after Alex and locked it.

"Why are you letting me out?"

"Because we need answers, and I think you have some." Ty took the man by his good arm and led him back to the kitchen.

"I already told you I'm not telling you anything. You shot me. Why the hell would I help you now?" Alex grumbled as Ty led him down the hall.

"Yeah, well, we have some new information, and we need you to fill in some blanks. And you tried to kill us first, so I think we're even. Have a seat." Ty pushed him down into one of the kitchen chairs. He pulled a chair in front of the gunman and turned it around to straddle it. Leo pulled one up behind the gunman until he was practically breathing down his neck.

"Tell us what you know," Ty demanded.

Alex just sat there, stone-faced.

"You should talk," Leo urged, tone menacing. "I'm not as nice as him and I don't like it when people try to hurt my friends." He practically breathed the words into the gunman's ear.

Alex clamped his mouth shut and looked at a point over Ty's shoulder.

Frustration ripped through Ty. They needed to know the scope of the Artherton family involvement. The sooner the better. Ty had a feeling something was headed their way, and he wanted to be ready for it. They didn't have time for this crap.

"Seriously? This is how you interrogate someone?" Penny stepped up next to Ty and glared at him. "How are you ever effective in your job?" She shook her head and went to the fridge, where she pulled out the sandwich fixings they just put away. He frowned as she quickly slapped a sandwich together and held it out to Alex.

"Go on," Penny urged when he hesitated to take it. Alex finally grabbed the sandwich and took a huge bite. Penny made a shooing motion at Ty. He arched an eyebrow at her, but stood. He didn't know what she was doing, but he could tell she had a plan of some sort. He could see it in her eyes. He stepped back and let her have a go at the man. She certainly couldn't do any worse than he and Leo.

She took his seat. Ty moved behind her to rest his hands on her shoulders. She eyed Leo, silently telling him to move. With a glance at Ty, who nodded, Leo stood and moved over near the counter next to Keira.

Alex watched her warily over his sandwich. "You think feeding me and calling off the dogs is going to make me talk?"

Penny shook her head and smiled. "No. But I'm hoping kindness might. I feel like you're not used to it. That you're more used to violence and money doing the talking. And, while you don't always like it, it's the way of the world for you."

Alex shifted uncomfortably in his chair. Penny's strategy was already working. Ty could see the indecision creeping into the mercenary's eyes.

Penny sighed. "Look. We don't want to hurt you. We just want answers. I don't think you particularly care whether we die or not. This job is just a paycheck to you. So, why don't you give up what you know? We're not letting you go, so you're never going to see any of the money they promised you. Knowing how ruthless they've been in their pursuit of me, even if you were to escape *and* kill us, I doubt they'd let you live to collect." She held up a hand as he started to protest. "And just so you know, we know who sent you now."

Alex's eyebrows shot up at that. He looked around the room at all of them. "You do?"

Penny nodded.

"Then why am I out here?"

"Because you can fill in the details."

Alex took another bite of his sandwich and chewed thoughtfully. *That a girl, baby. You've got him.*

Ty had been right about the man's intelligence. He was weighing his options. Ty would bet dollars to donuts Alex was about to roll on his employer. He needed to put Penny in an interrogation room with all his suspects. She was a natural at making people relax and willing to spill all their secrets.

"Who do you think it is?" Alex finally asked.

Penny pointed at Keira. "Her family."

Eyes wider than Ty thought possible, Alex stared googly eyed at Keira. He gulped audibly. "Who are you?"

"Keira Artherton."

Alex closed his eyes and muttered a curse. "You're Dominic's daughter."

Keira nodded. "Is my father involved?"

"You really don't know what any of this is about?"

She shook her head. "I didn't until Penny and Ty told me. And you didn't answer my question. Is my father involved?"

Eyes closing again, Alex nodded.

Keira's knees buckled. Leo reached out and caught her, wrapping an arm around her waist to hold her up.

Penny swallowed hard, tears threatening to spill over. Ty was impressed as she pulled herself together in an instant, putting a firm lid on her emotions and turning back to Alex. "Did Dominic know Keira was at my house last night when he ordered you to burn it down with us inside?"

"Dominic didn't issue the order. And no, I don't think any of the Arthertons knew she was there. Dominic only mentioned Keira once. She called during a meeting. When he hung up, he smiled and said it was his daughter, Keira, then apologized for the interruption. Said he always answered when she called. His affection for her was clear. If he knew she was there, we would have been told to get her out before burning the house down."

"Who issued the order if it wasn't Dominic?" Ty asked.

Alex's gaze swung to Keira. "Your grandfather, Victor," Alex answered after a beat. "Dominic just went along with it."

Ty winced as a wail ripped free from Keira. Leo pulled her closer and held tight.

"Talk," Ty growled. "Who all is involved besides Dominic and Victor?"

Alex raised his face to the ceiling, cursing. "This is all such a cluster now," he muttered. He dropped his gaze back to them. "I think Greg was involved on the periphery. He was at the meeting where we discussed the—issue—but wasn't directly involved. There were a few others there. Victor's other son, Max, and both of Max's sons, Nick and Luke. Max was knee deep in it, but his sons didn't seem to be directly involved, just like Greg."

Penny sucked in a breath while Keira—tears streaming down her face—sagged against Leo, too stunned to support herself.

"Who's Greg?" Ty asked her. His relationship to the others was the only one not clear.

"Keira's brother."

Jesus. This just kept getting worse.

"Do they have any way of tracking us here? Anything we don't know about? I already disabled the GPS. And we left your phone and Seth's in Texas." Ty highly doubted there was a way someone could find them, but something about the sudden change in Alex's demeanor at the question was shouting otherwise. A bad feeling settled in Ty's gut.

Alex muttered another curse. "The SUV has a special tracking system. It's got a remote activation to it. Unless you removed it and smashed it, it can be turned on again. There's a hidden battery inside."

Expletives flew around the room.

"Jesus," Leo muttered. "What is this family? The mob?"

Keira stiffened and shoved out of his arms. "We are not the mob!"

"Really, sweetheart? Because it kinda sounds like it to me."

Ty thought Keira was going to slap him. She didn't, but she didn't let him off the hook either. As best she could, at a foot shorter than Leo, she got in his face, waving her finger at him. "My family is involved in legitimate businesses. I am a prosecutor for the city of Austin. I think I would have noticed or heard rumblings about my family being mob-like."

Leo leaned down until they were nose to nose. "Maybe so, but something's definitely not right. Normal people don't put specialized GPS devices in their cars."

"Can we get back to the subject at hand, please?" Ty patted the air with his hands, trying to calm the atmosphere. The last thing they needed was to fight amongst themselves. They were going to need every last person to stop the invasion he was suddenly sure was coming.

Leo and Keira turned their attention back to the table, albeit a little reluctantly. They could fight later. Right now, they needed to plan. And fast.

"Alex, how long do you think we have until someone shows up here?"

Indecision lit the man's eyes, and he hesitated.

Ty bit back a growl. He leaned down, trying to impress on the man the seriousness of their situation. "I get it. You want to complete your contract. But I'm telling you, they will not let you live. You've become a liability. Not only did you fail, but you know too much. And what you don't know, they'll think you do know. If you help us, I will do everything I can to get you out of this alive. You won't get paid, but you won't be dead either."

Alex frowned as he considered Ty's offer. "Why do you want to help me? Why trust me after what we did?"

Ty went for broke. They needed information, and they were short on time. "Because I can see you aren't a heartless bastard, even though you try to be. You don't have any compunction about killing for money, but you draw the line somewhere. Now that you've gotten to know us a little, I'm betting you'd have a hard time killing us. We aren't just a face to you anymore. I also think that while what you do is despicable, you have some standards. What her family wants to do—and I'm sorry, Keira—is literal world domination and they don't give a flying fig who they stomp on to achieve it."

"Whoa, whoa, whoa. Back up," Alex said, raising his good hand. "What the hell are you talking about? World domination? All they said was she had something that belonged to them and they wanted it back." He pointed at Penny.

"I possess an ancient artifact the Arthertons want. It does not belong to them. It belongs to my family and always has. My family hid it centuries ago to keep it out of their hands. They've been looking for it ever since."

Alex looked perplexed. "All this over some ancient piece of crap?"

"There's a bit more to it than that," Penny said, exasperated. "What's important is that we keep it *out* of their hands. It will change the course of history if we don't."

"How?"

"I can't tell you that. You just have to trust me. Trust us."

Alex searched her face, and Ty held his breath. He was banking that all that cunning intelligence Alex exhibited would sway him to their side.

"You'll let me go after all of this if I help you? Just bam, I'm free?"

"Yes," Ty and Penny chorused.

Alex searched both their faces for deceit. Ty knew he wouldn't find any. It cut against the grain to let a guy like this go, but if it meant saving them all—and keeping the world from tyranny—he could shove those feelings aside and strike a deal.

"What about Seth?"

"What about him?" Ty asked. "He's been less than cooperative. As far as I'm concerned, the Arthertons can have him. If they can get to him. He's going to stay locked in that closet for now."

Alex nodded. "Fair enough. The guy was a tool, anyway. All right, I'm in."

A collective sigh went around the room. "Great. Now tell us how long you think we have."

Alex rubbed his jaw. "They probably activated the tracker this morning when we didn't report in. We were supposed to call in at seven and let them know the job was done."

"Why not right away?" Leo asked.

"Victor likes his sleep, but he didn't want anyone to know before him. He's a bit of a control freak, I've noticed."

Keira let out an inelegant snort, and all eyes swung toward her. "I agree with that. Granddad likes being the head of the family. He's never mean about it, though. And he's a creature of habit. He does things a certain way every day."

"How were they planning to get the artifact? You don't know what it is, and my house would not only be in ruins, but a crime scene. You all weren't exactly subtle in setting that fire."

Alex frowned. "Their plan was to buy your assets after your death, since you don't have any family. I still don't understand why they decided to burn the house, though. I figured anything they were looking for would just burn. And that fire was all Seth. I wanted to make it look more like an accident. A leaky gas line or something. He thought it would be better to try to smoke you out, then shoot you. To make absolutely certain you were dead. Victor put him in charge, so I didn't have a choice but to go along."

"Why him and not you?" Ty asked.

Alex's mouth quirked up ruefully. "I'm not an ass-kisser like Seth. I just wanted to do the job and get paid." He looked at Penny. "So, what is it they're after, anyway? They never said."

"And I'm not either." She might trust this man to help them plan a defense and even a counter-attack, but she was not going to trust him with her secrets.

Ty waved a hand, dismissing the thread of conversation. "Forget what they're after. They're coming and that's all that's important. So, they're already on their way, is what you're saying, right?"

Alex nodded.

"Great," Ty muttered. "Would they drive or wait for us to stop and then fly to us?"

"Probably drive. It might take longer, but it's less hassle and they're better able to change direction if we do."

Ty looked at his watch. "It's one now. It took us eight hours to get here, and that was in the middle of the night. We stopped for an hour to bandage you up, so they're probably only about four hours behind us."

"Which means we don't have long," Leo commented.

"Are they likely to hit us tonight?"

Alex shook his head. "No. Maybe if they'd gotten here this morning, but it'll be late afternoon. They'll want time to recon and plan an attack." He looked at Leo. "You're an unknown and they don't like unknowns."

"So, tomorrow night?"

"Possibly. It depends on how easily they think they can get to us here. If they need reinforcements or more firepower, then it'll be two days from now." Alex looked at Leo with a thoughtful frown. "Do you have any defenses in place here?"

Leo scoffed, while Ty just grinned and shook his head.

"Do I have any defenses? That is a stupid question. I may live in the middle of the swamp, but I spent too many years covering my ass to stop just because I was stateside again."

"What *do* you have, anyway?" Ty asked.

"I've set up some perimeter alarms, so we'll know when anyone's coming. I've got cameras throughout the woods too, so we can watch their progress. I used some Cajun ingenuity as well." A wicked grin split Leo's face. "There are a few traps out there."

"Aren't you concerned about wildlife tripping one of your traps?" Keira asked, her voice still a little testy. She obviously hadn't forgiven Leo yet for the mob comment.

Leo shook his head. "We don't get much large wildlife out this way except boar and gators. It's too swampy. I rigged all the trip lines high enough only a human can trigger one." He held up a hand. "And before you ask, no, I'm not concerned about someone stumbling into one. No one goes for a stroll through my woods unless they're with me. For one, I'm too far off the beaten path. And two, why would you want to? It's a frickin' swamp."

"Okay, so we let the traps pick some of them off and then watch the progress of the others until they reach the house," Penny stated. "What do we do once they get here?"

"First, we fortify those defenses in the swamp, so fewer of them get through to the house. We'll have to be careful and work quickly, since they'll likely be out scouting soon. Second, we need to set some traps at the house. Lure them in where we want them and not let them just come at us willy-nilly." Ty ticked the points off on his fingers.

Leo grinned. "I think I know how to do that."

Ty gave a quick nod. "Good. I know you have an arsenal here, so we need to get it ready."

"Keira and I can handle that," Penny said. Keira nodded in agreement.

"What do you want me to do?" Alex asked.

"For now, just fill in where you're needed. But when the action starts, I'm going to need you to help us predict what these guys will do. You'll be familiar with many of the men who come, yes?"

Alex nodded.

"You're going to be our ace in the hole." Ty paused and bent down to make his point clear, his countenance suddenly deadly. "Do not screw us over or I will end you."

Again, Alex nodded. "I won't. You were right. I might be a heartless bastard most of the time and kill without compunction, but I'm not an idiot. There are things going on here I don't understand. I want no part of it anymore. I signed up for a simple contract hit, not this—this cluster it's become. I will help you so I can live through this, then I'm gone."

"Good." Ty looked at each person in the room, eyes intense. He felt optimistic for the first time. Having Alex on their side gave them an advantage the Arthertons wouldn't be expecting. It was time to end this once and for all, and it would end in *their* favor. "Let's get busy."

CHAPTER 35

"Are you doing okay?" Penny asked Keira several hours later. They were seated at the table again, this time cleaning weapons and inventorying ammo and grenades. Leo had an impressive amount of firepower, for which she was thankful. They were going to need it.

Keira shrugged and ran the cotton swab through the barrel of a Beretta pistol, her expression pinched. "Honestly? Not really. I know it'll probably be the goon squad that comes after us and not the men in my family, but it still hurts to think my dad and my grandfather sent them here."

"Maybe you should leave," Penny suggested. "There's no guarantee your dad or your granddad won't be out there waiting. In fact, I would bet at least one of them will be in the area. With the way this is set up to go down, if they were to somehow win this battle, someone needs to sweep in after it's over to get the belt before the police get it. If it's confiscated by the authorities, it could be years before they're able to get their hands on it. If at all. I heard Ty as Leo about his brother, Gabe, so I know he has family his property would pass to. Your granddad would not leave to chance who gets the belt."

Keira sighed. "I know. But I don't want to leave you in the lurch. You're going to need all the bodies you can get to fight back. I know Ty and Leo can hold their own, but they're only two men. Our converted mercenary is only half a man right now with that hole in his shoulder. That leaves you. Against probably half a dozen or more men from what Alex said." She set the swab down and started stuffing bullets into the gun's magazine. "No. I'm staying. Even if it means I have to face my family. They can't get away with what they've tried to do. What they did to your family."

Penny blinked furiously, trying to keep the tears at bay. Keira's words meant a lot. It couldn't be easy for her to come to grips with the fact her family murdered Penny's in their quest for power. Keira's entire world had flipped upside down overnight, and rather than leaving the situation behind, she wanted to stay and make it right. It wasn't her fight, but Penny was grateful for her help.

She gathered Keira into a hug and squeezed tight, trying to convey her gratitude. "You're the best. I hope you know that."

Keira smiled and patted Penny's hand. "I know."

Her simple reply made Penny laugh. She pulled back and dragged a box of bullets closer. "All right. Let's get this finished so we can go help the guys set up outside."

After a thorough briefing on what defenses Leo had in place and where they all were, Ty, Leo, and Alex went outside to fortify the traps and to set new ones designed to cut off access to all sides of the house except the back. They'd debated leaving the front open because blocking the drive would be difficult, but ultimately decided on the back. Its lack of a porch left it wide open all the way to the tree line, which made it easier for them to pick off the bad guys as they tried to reach the house.

In theory, it was a sound plan, but without more manpower, Penny wasn't sure it would work. They were still going to have to spare someone to watch the front. Alex said there were at least eight other mercenaries waiting in the wings, and they could hire more once they got here if they thought they needed them. When Penny asked how that would be possible, all three men had looked at her like the naïve woman she was and explained it was very easy to hire people who would kill for money if you knew where to look. Alex promised her the men he worked with would know where to look. Penny sat back at that point and let them plan without further questions from her. It might be her problem that brought them all into this mess, but they obviously knew what they were doing, so she stayed out of their way.

Ty and Leo figured they likely wouldn't face more than twelve men and prepped accordingly. They seemed to think any more than that would hamper the enemy's ability to coordinate in a fluid situation.

Even with the odds stacked against them, Penny still wished Keira would leave. She hated the thought that her friend might have to face down her father or grandfather, or even her brother. That she might very likely have to watch one of them die. It just seemed like a cruel twist of fate that Keira's family was involved in this.

Footsteps sounded on the porch steps, distracting Penny from her thoughts. She looked up in time to see Ty pull open the screen door. Sweat dotted his forehead and glistened on his forearms. His damp t-shirt clung to his chest, outlining every muscle.

Penny quickly looked back down. She swallowed hard, trying to moisten her suddenly dry mouth. He set her on fire without even trying. She cleared her throat. "Everything set?"

"Almost. We still need to work on blocking the driveway, but we got the traps fortified and placed a few extra in some strategic locations.

Leo's out rigging a few surprises for our friends, with Alex's help." He walked over to the table to survey their handiwork.

"You trust that guy enough to let him do that?" Keira set down the magazine she loaded.

Ty sat in the chair next to Penny and began twirling a strand of her ponytail between his fingers. Tingles spread outward from her scalp. Heat pooled low in her belly, the spread outward. Why did he have to be so utterly masculine?

"He's actually proven to be fairly good at all this booby trap stuff, and made some great suggestions while we were checking things out. I think he really does want to help."

Keira scoffed. "He's a mercenary. He ought to be good at booby traps."

"Not necessarily. Most of them are good at following a subject unseen and covering their tracks, but they tend not to set too many booby traps. Traps to lure in their mark, yes, but they don't normally string them up from a tree with a snare or set a trip line to drop a large branch on their head."

Penny made a face at the visual Ty created. She was under no illusion this fight wouldn't be bloody. It didn't mean she wanted to imagine it ahead of time.

It served as a reminder, though, why she needed to continue to resist the hold Ty had over her. Being distracted could get them hurt or killed. But she was starting to wonder if resisting their attraction wasn't just as distracting.

She chanced a glance at him. He stared down at her, his bright blue eyes smoldering as if he could tell what she was thinking.

She cleared her throat and did her best to pretend the mere sight of him didn't affect her. Penny had a feeling she failed. "So, what now?"

"Now, we wait."

CHAPTER 36

Small sticks and dried leaves crunched under Penny's feet as she walked into the woods, looking for Ty and Leo. After Ty checked in with them earlier, he went back out to help Leo and send Alex in to rest. That was a couple hours ago, though, and it was hot today. Penny knew he didn't take any water with him, so she decided to bring them some while Keira finished loading the last of the weapons.

"Ty? Leo?"

She heard Leo shout an okay in the distance and followed his voice. Passing through a heavy stand of trees, she stopped short, unable to do more than stare at the sight before her. Leo stood on the ground, shirtless, looking up at the tree. It wasn't the sight of Leo's naked torso that gave her pause, though. It was Ty's. He was thirty feet off the ground, standing on a branch while he leaned against the trunk to keep his balance. His bare chest gleamed gold in the sunlight filtering through the canopy overhead. Muscles rippled as he wound a rope around the branch above him. He knotted it, then jumped off, using the rope to lower himself down.

The strangled moan that got stuck in her throat must have been louder than she thought, because they both turned toward her, the hard, cold look of a soldier falling over their faces. In an instant, Leo had a knife in his hand, ready to throw it.

Penny held up her hands. "It's just me!"

Both men straightened, their shoulders relaxing. Leo flipped the knife over his fingers and slid the blade back into the sheath attached to his belt.

She blew out a breath, her heart beating overtime, both from their reaction and from seeing Ty shirtless.

"What are you doing out here? It's dangerous to walk through the woods," Ty said, walking closer.

"I was careful. It took me fifteen minutes to walk this far because I didn't take a step before looking all around." She was not about to get strung up in a tree because she was dumb enough to walk into one of Leo's traps. "Here." She held out a water bottle. "I brought you guys some water."

Ty took the bottle and turned, tossing it to Leo before taking the other one from her and twisting off the cap. All the blood in Penny's head rushed south to flood her core as he upended the bottle and gulped down the clear liquid. His Adam's apple bobbed, the thick muscles in his neck working as he swallowed.

She forced her eyes to look away, knowing if she didn't, she'd never be able to make her feet move and walk back to the house. There was already very little blood left in her brain to keep her body functioning.

The crinkle of the plastic bottle drew her attention back to him. He wiped the back of his hand over his mouth.

"Thanks. It's hot."

Her head moved in a semblance of a nod. "You're welcome." Her eyes landed on his chest, right in front of her. Fingers itching to touch him and see if he was soft and supple or smooth and hard, she looked away again and balled her fists. "So, what are you doing with that tree?" She pointed to the one he just jumped out of.

He glanced back. "Setting a snare."

She took in the length of rope trailing the ground and frowned. "With that long of a rope?"

"No. It just needs to be that long so I can get down." He spun around and walked back to the tree. Tossing her the water bottle, he picked up the rope. "I'll pull it down and we'll tie it off."

Her frown deepened. "How?"

He grinned. "Like this." He looked at Leo. "You ready?"

Leo nodded, gulping down the rest of his water. He screwed the cap back onto the bottle, then shoved it into his pocket. "Go for it."

Ty wrapped the rope around his right arm and pulled. Penny's mouth dropped open as the tree bent. He wove the rope around his other arm and repeated the process, bringing it lower. Hand over hand, he pulled the tree down until she was sure it would snap. Leo moved around behind him to wrap the rope around a stake. Ty stood there with his heels dug into the dirt, holding the tree in position like it weighed no more than a heavy box.

"Okay, you can let go." Leo picked up a net, then wove the end of the rope through the loops on it before arranging it over the ground. Ty helped him scoop leaves and dirt over it to disguise it.

"And there you have it. One snare," Ty said.

Leo chuckled. "Easiest snare I've ever set. It helps having a human winch."

She tilted her head to look up at Ty. "It's good to know you've embraced your strength."

He lifted an arm and flexed. His biceps bulged, making Penny all tingly again.

"Now that I know it's there, it just feels natural." He shrugged. "It's still weird, mentally, but using the strength doesn't feel that way."

She understood what he meant. "I get that. Using my shape shifting abilities is as easy as breathing, but wrapping my head around being able to do it is another thing. It's not the first thing I think of using when a situation calls for it."

"Like at the house fire, right?"

She nodded.

Leo walked toward them, carrying his tools and shirt. "That was the last one. I'm going to head back to the house."

Ty nodded. "We'll see you there."

Penny watched him go, lamenting the loss of their buffer. She kept her eyes on his retreating form longer than necessary, knowing if she looked at Ty, she wouldn't be able to keep her hands to herself. There was no one else around to help keep her desire in check.

"You know, it's too bad you weren't here sooner. You could have helped me get up into those trees. I had to climb every time to get the rope up there."

She chanced a look at him. He flashed her a smile, then bent over to pick up his shirt.

Don't put it on!

Penny shoved her hormonal inner voice back into its box. He needed to put the shirt on and preserve her sanity.

He didn't, though, stuffing one corner into his back pocket instead. She tried not to stare at his butt and failed miserably. Cursing herself, she turned away and wandered closer to the snare, pretending to look at its simple construction.

"Hey, are you okay?"

Penny jumped as his deep voice rumbled from just a few feet behind her. She spun around and looked up, nodding. "I'm fine. Why?"

He shrugged, those steely muscles moving gracefully under his silken skin. "You seem a little tense."

"We're running from contract killers. I have a reason to be."

"Yeah, but not right now. We're safe for the moment."

A breeze kicked up, tousling her hair. A strand got caught on her mouth, and Ty took a step toward her, then reached up to clear it away. His fingertip brushed her lips and all coherent thought fled from her mind. Her body took over, and she swayed closer.

His eyes darkened and the hand brushing her hair back slid around her neck. He speared his long fingers into her hair, cupping the back of her head.

Penny's hands rose on their own to rest against his muscled chest. Silky softness over steel met her touch. He sucked in a shaky breath and shuffled closer.

"Why do you tie me up in knots the way you do?" His voice was low, just loud enough to carry over the wind.

"For the same reason you do it to me."

His head dipped. "And why is that? Fate?"

"I don't know, and right now, I don't care. I just want you to kiss me."

"This is a bad idea." His words contradicted his actions. He leaned down. "We don't need the distraction."

"No, we don't." Like a magnet to metal, she rose up on her toes, bringing her mouth to within millimeters of his. He groaned and closed the distance. Penny's heart stopped as he pressed his lips to hers, only to start up again like a jackhammer. She knew what to expect after the spectacular kiss they shared in Greece, but it didn't matter. Her body reacted like it was the first time. She slid her hands up to circle his shoulders and hung on for dear life.

His hands roved over her body, heightening her arousal and making her wish there were fewer clothes between them. Her breasts ached to feel his bare chest pressed against them.

But the wilderness, feet from a trap meant for people who wanted to kill them, was no place for stripping, so she left her shirt alone and did what she could to satiate her need fully clothed. She nipped at his lips, soothing the sting with her tongue, enjoying the feel of his chest rumble beneath her hands and against her breasts as he moaned. When he moved away from her mouth, she tipped her head to give him unfettered access to her neck, loving the feel of the stubble on dusting his jaw against her sensitive flesh.

He palmed her butt, rocking her hips into his. Penny rubbed against the hard ridge beneath the fly of his jeans, lifting one leg to lock around his thigh. When she raked her nails over his back, he growled and broke away.

"We need to stop. I don't want to, but the last thing we need is to have Leo come back for us and find us rolling around on the forest floor buck naked."

Penny bit her lip at the thought of Ty in all his glory, but she nodded, knowing he was right. She let her leg slide down his and took a step back. "I guess we should head back to the house." She ran a hand through her hair to disguise the shakiness in her limbs. She felt like she could fly back—without shifting. "Could you do me a favor, though, and put your shirt on?"

A wicked look entered his eyes, and one corner of his mouth lifted. He tugged his t-shirt from his pocket.

Penny blushed and rolled her eyes. "Don't even act like you don't know how you look."

He grinned and pulled the shirt over his head. "I just like that you noticed."

"I'd have to be dead not to. Even then, I'd probably stare down at you from heaven."

He laughed. "Well, that feeling is mutual."

Penny's eyes widened.

"Don't look so shocked. You're beautiful, Penny."

She bit her lip and glanced away. "I know I'm not horrible, but beautiful?" She just didn't see it. She was too tall. Too plain.

He turned her to face him, holding her face in his hands. "I don't know why you don't see what I see, but I will never let you forget that you're gorgeous." He leaned down to press a quick kiss to her lips.

Penny's heart flip-flopped. Tendrils of some intense emotion snaked through her, taking root in her chest, glowing bright. Her cheeks flushed and glanced away. "Thank you."

He took her hand. "You're welcome. Let's head back. It's getting late, and I'm starving."

She smiled. "Keira was going to make some pasta primavera thing from the stuff she found in Leo's garden once she finished loading the last few weapons. She's probably cooking now."

"Awesome." He tugged her forward. "Let's go."

She laughed as she hurried to keep up with his long stride. "Even if she's finished by the time we get there, they won't eat it all."

"You don't know the way Leo eats. I've seen him demolish a giant plate of food before the rest of us even got halfway done." He paused, a thoughtful frown pulling down his brow. "You think we could fly back? It would be faster."

Penny laughed. "No. You can walk. I already told you I never wanted to carry you like that again. You're heavy!"

He grinned. "Make me a mouse. You can pretend I'm your prey." The predatory gleam in his eyes sent a delicious shiver up her spine. "I think I might like it if you had your way with me."

Penny's blush returned full force. She smacked his arm to cover how flustered he made her. "Well, if I fly you, any ardor I feel right now will be lost to the tense fear that I'll drop you."

His mouth turned down. "We don't want that." He sighed. "I guess we're walking."

She laughed again. "You'll live." She tugged on his hand. "Come on." He flashed her a smile, then followed her out of the woods.

CHAPTER 37

Ty leaned against the doorjamb of Penny's bedroom, drinking in the sight of her silhouetted by the moonlight streaming through the window. She stared through the glass, dressed in one of his t-shirts he didn't know she took from his backpack. The thin material ghosted over her curves, hinting at what was below. His hands itched to slide under the shirt and discover what was beneath.

He was still amazed at how quickly she'd become important to him. It had only been a week, and he already couldn't imagine life without her. He hadn't been looking for someone to share his life with, but it seemed he found her, nonetheless. They just needed to set their world right before they dove headfirst into a relationship.

He shook off his lustful, distracting thoughts. Seducing her wasn't the reason he stopped by her room at this hour. He simply wanted to say goodnight before turning in for a few hours; he had to be up for his turn on watch duty at three o'clock. Leo was up now, monitoring things. Ty's shift ran from three until dawn. He and Leo decided they didn't trust Alex *that* much to let him take a turn on guard duty and sent the man to bed an hour ago. Leo added a couple of additional slide locks to the bedroom door so Alex could sleep on the bed and not fight Seth for the cot in the closet.

Penny sighed and rested her forehead against the cool glass of the windowpane. Ty couldn't take the brooding and slightly sad look on her face anymore and moved into the room. He walked up behind her until he could circle her waist with his arms, unable to resist touching her. He let his chin rest on the top of her head. She fit so perfectly in his arms. He could curl around her and surround her until she felt like a part of him. He'd never had that with any other woman.

"You okay?"

She tilted her head to look up at him. "Yeah. I was just thinking about Keira. I feel so bad for her. Everything she's ever known has been yanked out from under her. I mean, it's one thing to learn your identity has been a lie, like I did, but quite another to learn your entire family is in the business of murdering people so they can take over the world." She sighed again. "I know she's putting on a brave face, but she's bleeding so badly inside. I see it every time she thinks no one is looking."

Ty squeezed Penny's waist tighter and brought his head down until his cheek rested against hers. He hated that she was hurting for her friend. He hated that both of them had lost so much in this quest. It didn't seem fair.

"I'm sorry. I wish we had a magic wand to fix all this."

She sighed. "Me too." She wrapped her hand around his arm and leaned against him. They stared out the window together for several minutes before Penny broke the silence.

"Will you stay with me?"

His entire body clenched at her words.

She spun in his arms and looped her arms around his neck.

Ty hesitated. "Penny..." He really wanted to, but he knew if he did, there would be more than sleep happening. They'd both agreed this was a distraction they didn't need.

She threaded her fingers through his hair. Tingles raced across his scalp and down the back of his neck, weakening his resolve.

"I know it's not wise. I've grappled with this decision all evening, and realized fighting the attraction has become almost as big of a distraction as being together would be. And after nearly dying, then watching the house burn, all the while knowing you were in it—I don't want to wait anymore. I want us to grab any happiness we can now. There may be no tomorrow, and I don't want any regrets."

Her words speared him, crashing through the wall he'd built around his feelings concerning her. He had boxed them up and walled them off until there was a better time to deal with them. With one conversation, she smashed down the wall and broke the box wide open. Every emotion she made him feel rushed to fill his chest.

Ty shifted and ran one hand up her back until it rested at her nape, under her hair. The silky black curtain fell through his fingers and over his arm, cool against his heated skin. He angled her head and held it, mouth hovering just above hers. Her warm breath fanned over his face, stoking the fire building inside him.

"Kiss me, Ty," Penny whispered, her eyes locked on his lips.

Ty didn't disappoint her. He lowered his mouth the last inch and sealed his lips over hers. Passion flared immediately, the heady feeling making his blood burn.

He walked them backward until they reached the bed. Turning when the backs of his legs hit the mattress, Ty broke the kiss to deposit Penny on the bed. He took two long steps to the door and threw it closed, flipping the lock. He spun around, one hand already on the neck of his shirt to pull it off, when the sight before him froze him in his tracks.

"Penny? What's going on with your eyes?" He peered closer at her. "They're—they're burning. They look like golden flames." It was the eeriest thing he'd ever seen, but strangely beautiful.

She sat up on her knees, staring at him just as intently, shock coloring her face. "Yeah? Well, yours are dancing with blue fire."

He moved forward and climbed onto the bed, kneeling in front of her. He touched her face with just his fingertips, transfixed by the sight of her eyes. Even in all the times he watched her shift, he never saw her eyes do this.

"What's going on?"

She shook her head slightly. "I don't know."

He could feel the power swirling between them. This was something more than simple attraction. Exhilarating, yet terrifying, because this level of power was frightening. Even when he had tapped into his strength to open the safe or pulled those trees down, he hadn't felt this kind of power. It was raw and unfettered.

And it wasn't just his power, but hers as well. It flowed off of her in waves, reaching out to him to pull him in. It almost felt sentient in nature. He could feel it calling to him, wanting to mingle with his own power.

"None of Theo's papers talked about anything like this." She smiled ruefully. "Although, I don't think Theo ever felt this level of attraction to someone with divine blood before, either."

"We're not going to spontaneously combust and burn the house down if we continue, are we?" He wasn't sure he could stop himself from making love to her, even if they did. His desire for her was mingling with the pull of their powers and quickly ratcheting up his arousal. He had a feeling he was going to combust no matter what.

She scooted closer and wrapped her arms around his shoulders. "No. But honestly, I don't care if we do." Then her mouth was on his and Ty stopped thinking. He let instinct take over and tucked Penny into his chest. His hands spanned her back, roaming the long expanse up to her neck and down to the curve of her hips, over and over. She whimpered and tried to wiggle closer, toppling them onto their sides on the mattress.

Ty's hands slid under the hemline of her t-shirt to find bare skin. Her tiny gasp of pleasure spiked his pulse and had him gathering the material in his fingers to pull it up and over her head. As the shirt landed on the floor next to the bed, he pulled back to look down on her near naked form. A golden light dusted her olive skin. It shone like a beacon, calling him home.

Helpless to resist, Ty reached out to trace her curves, only to see a blue glow on his own skin. His eyes snapped to hers. The flames were still there, dancing for him.

"This is nuts," he whispered reverently.

Penny placed her hand on his arm and lightly traced the muscles in his forearm. The light gliding over their bodies flowed over them both to blend.

"I can feel it." She watched the colors mix. "It's like coming home. It recognizes you." Astonishment filled her voice.

Ty's control snapped as the very feelings she talked about washed over him. He lowered himself back over her. "Let's let it get reacquainted, then, shall we?"

Penny grinned and put her arms around his neck. "Let's."

His mouth crashed down on hers. The light erupted around them, flowing along their skin. It was like she touched him everywhere at once, threatening to overwhelm him as his need surged.

Their passion built until Ty thought they really would combust. He sat up long enough to shuck the rest of his clothes and her panties before falling back to the bed, their limbs twining. His mouth moved over her silky skin, tasting every inch.

Her skin was warm beneath his mouth and fingers. Ty set about fanning the heat building between them. He trailed kisses along her jaw and down her neck. His hands skated along her sides, over her hips and back again. Her body was magnificent. Long and lithe. Strong and lean, but curvy in all the right places. She fit against him like she was made to be there.

Considering the reaction their bodies were having to each other and the weird eye thing, maybe she was. He could almost touch the thread of power connecting them. He wondered what it would look like—what it would feel like—once he was actually inside her. His erection pulsed at the thought, and he ground against her belly, trying to assuage some of the need. He'd had good sex before, but never anything like this. Kissing Penny, knowing where this was headed, was an adrenaline rush on steroids. He could feel the blood of his demigod ancestor pulsing through his veins. It was a heady feeling. Power and a sense of rightness thrummed along his nerve endings, toppling him into a sea of sensation.

Head dipping low, Ty's mouth closed over the tip of her breast. He sucked it between his teeth and rolled the nipple with his tongue. Penny gasped and clutched at his hair, holding him in place. He switched his attention to the other breast, palming the one his mouth just left. With her hips rocking against his, Ty lifted her legs to wrap them around his waist. She locked her ankles behind his back, the move putting her hot, wet core right against his throbbing erection. Ty fought for control as the sensation nearly sent him spiraling over the edge.

CHAPTER 38

Penny almost wept in relief as Ty probed at her entrance. She wanted him inside her. Now.

"Please, please tell me you're on the pill," he muttered, voice strained.

Penny opened her eyes to stare into the flames lighting his eyes. "I'm not, but we're safe."

He stroked through her wet folds once and poised the tip of his shaft at her opening. "You're sure?"

She gave a jerky nod and tried to push up to take him inside her. The steel bands of his arms wouldn't let her. She whimpered, her need for him driving her closer to the edge of ecstasy. "Yes. I track it. We're safe." She wiggled some more. "Please, Ty. I need you. Now."

On a groan, Ty pushed inside her, pulling a shout of pleasure from her. She wiggled in his arms when he stayed still.

"I need a second," he ground out between clenched teeth. The muscles in his neck strained tight. Penny nipped at the tendons at the base of his throat and wiggled again. He felt delicious inside of her. He filled her so completely, and she was desperate for him to move. She tried her best to move her hips, but his hands gripped them tightly, holding her virtually immobile on the bed. All she could manage was a small wiggle.

"Shit, I'm not going to last, Pen."

Sensations bombarded her as he pulled back slightly and slammed into her again. "I'm not, either, so you're good. Just don't stop. And don't be gentle." She thrust her hips up as he drove into her again.

"Yes, ma'am."

His thrusts increased their tempo, and Penny felt her release build quickly. Within a few strokes, Penny broke. Waves of white-hot pleasure crashed over her, and his name flew from her lips. Ty soon followed her over the edge, her name leaving him on a hoarse groan.

Mingled with the intense pleasure, power surged through Penny's veins, more intense than what she felt from the belt or even when she shifted. She opened her eyes to look at Ty and was taken aback at what she saw. The light flowed along their skin, skimming just above their flesh. The two colors seemed to dance as they wove together, faster than before, excited. They twined into a tight bond until both colors swirled together over both their bodies, fading from one to the other. It was both beautiful yet terrifying, because she had no idea what it meant.

Ty inhaled sharply as power flowed over him. "I can really feel your abilities now. I didn't know you had all that inside you."

"Same here. I know I've seen it in action, but your strength is amazing." Penny dropped her legs from around his waist and relaxed into the mattress. Ty rolled to the side, pulling her with him. She let her hand rest on his chest, one leg draped over his, and watched the colors tangle and shift. Over several minutes, the swirls calmed until they settled into a stationary glow over their skin. The light faded before it seemed to just melt into them.

Penny looked down at her now glow-free arms, then back up at Ty. His eyes were normal again. "I can still feel you. It's like a beacon pointing straight at you. Can you feel me?"

Ty concentrated a moment, then nodded. "I can. It's like we're linked now."

Penny nodded fiercely. "Exactly. I wonder if the feeling will fade."

Ty shrugged. He wondered the same. "I guess we'll find out." He reached over to shut off the bedside lamp she'd left on. "But it won't be right now." He yanked the covers over them and pulled her close.

"We didn't set the house on fire," Penny stated with a sleepy chuckle.

He chuckled. "No. Just each other." He hugged her tight, and Penny quickly fell into a deep, restful sleep.

CHAPTER 39

Ty woke Penny in the dead of night when it was time for him to get up for his shift. He knew he should let her sleep, but he couldn't leave without one more taste of her.

"I have to go," he murmured softly against her lips.

She growled at him before locking her arms tight and pulling him in for a searing kiss.

Crap. He was going to be late. With one touch, she destroyed his defenses and sent him straight to full arousal.

This time, when the glow erupted between them, Ty wasn't surprised. In fact, he barely paid it any attention. It was as natural to him already as the desire building between them. It simply was a part of them.

They went slower this time. Their need less frantic, they took the time to explore each other, learning the other's body. He learned she loved it when he brushed his rough jaw on her neck and shoulder as he kissed her neck. She learned he lost it when she raked her nails over his head.

Ty filled his hands with Penny's curves, their lushness spilling over his hands, and pushed inside her once again. He kept the pace slow, driving them both mad with desire. She clung to him like an extension to his body. Ty pulled strength from way down deep to keep the steady pace. The struggle to keep from speeding up only seemed to intensify the sensations surging through them. When they finally spiraled up and out of control, it was ten times more powerful than before. She touched his soul and set it alight. Feelings he'd only scarcely acknowledged flooded him with warmth.

Unsettled by the strength and depth of his feelings, Ty buried his face in Penny's hair so she wouldn't see the emotions sure to be on full display across his face.

CHAPTER 40

Penny stroked Ty's back as she willed her heart and breathing back under control. Her body hummed after the intensity of their lovemaking. She didn't think it could get better after the last time, but it did. The connection she felt the first time was still there, but this time it was so much deeper. It brought out the depth of her feelings. Love pulsed through her veins, followed close behind by the shock from that realization.

She supposed it shouldn't be such a surprise. He was an amazing man. After a bit of a hiccup at the beginning, he'd taken her story as truth and done everything he could to help her. What really surprised her was how fast she fell. Again, she shouldn't be. It was only natural to have heightened emotions when in such a tense and life-threatening situation, but she still never imagined she would fall in love so fast.

It was terrifying and wonderful all at the same time.

Ty shifted, removing his weight from her body. He pushed up on his hands above her and looked down. Penny's breath caught at the intense look on his face. She had a feeling he was realizing the same things she just did.

He traced her cheek with one finger. "I really do need to go now. Leo will wonder where I am."

Penny ran her hands up and down his biceps and nodded. "I know. I can't wait until this is over. I want to see where this—where we—go without the threat of death hanging over our heads."

Ty stared at her intently for several moments before leaning down to press a kiss to her forehead. Penny shut her eyes against the tears that threatened at the tender gesture. He pulled back to look at her again. "I want that too, Penny. I'm going to do everything I can to make that a reality."

"I know." She wrapped her arms around his neck and pulled him down to her, pressing a soft, lingering kiss on his lips, willing him to feel how she felt. He returned her tender kiss with one of his own.

Ty groaned as he pulled back. "Now I really don't want to leave."

Penny snickered. She tugged on his hair and gave him a quick, hard kiss before pushing him up and away. "Go. Before Leo comes looking for you."

Grumbling, Ty climbed off the bed and gathered his clothes. Penny sat up and watched with unabashed interest as he dressed. The man was magnificent, and she wasn't about to miss the show.

Ty looked up and caught her watching. Fire leaped to life in his eyes. "Don't look at me like that, Pen." He paused with his pants half-zipped.

Penny bit her lip and let her eyes roam over his muscled chest and abs. "Like what?" she asked innocently.

He glared down at her. "Penny."

She grinned devilishly and relented. "Fine. I'll behave."

Ty growled and stalked toward her. "Why don't I believe you?" He kissed her hard and backed away before she could grab onto him. He picked his t-shirt up off the floor and tugged it over his head.

Penny pouted at the loss of the view.

He grinned at her before he fastened his pants and grabbed his boots. "Get some sleep, sugar. I'll be back in the morning."

She nodded and watched him walk out the door.

Alone with her thoughts, Penny fell back on the bed. The reality of where he was going and why brought home just what they were attempting to do. They were trying to stop a gang of mercenaries from killing them with some backcountry Cajun traps, the abilities of two demigod grandchildren, and Leo's arsenal. It seemed nearly impossible. If they were going to win, they needed to outwit and outsmart their opponents.

They had to find a way, though. She meant what she said to Ty—she wanted to see where they could go. She wanted a life with him, and she wanted to figure out how to navigate the world with their abilities. Together.

Penny just prayed they got that chance. This needed to end.

She pulled Ty's pillow down to her chest and hugged it, inhaling his lingering scent and doing her best to push the tumultuous thoughts from her mind so she could sleep.

It was easier said than done.

CHAPTER 41

Penny woke to the smell of fresh coffee, frying bacon, and sunlight streaming through the window. Yawning widely, she pushed off the covers and padded over to her backpack to grab her last change of clothes. Eager to see Ty and to find out if the night was uneventful, she quickly dressed. In the bathroom across the hall, she brushed her hair and teeth, then made her way to the kitchen.

Leo was standing at the stove tending the bacon, while Keira sat at the table, glaring daggers at his back. Penny arched an eyebrow. Apparently, they were still at each other's throats. She smiled inwardly. One of these days, that chemistry was going to backfire on them and they would end up going at each other in a completely different way. Considering all that Keira learned in the last twenty-four hours, Penny decided not to enlighten her friend about that fact. Instead, she grabbed a mug from the cabinet and poured herself a cup of coffee, nodding a good morning at Leo as she did so.

"Where's Ty?"

"Outside." Leo lifted strips of the splattering bacon from the skillet and laid them on a plate covered in paper towels.

Penny took a seat at the table and greeted Keira, but Ty's shout for Leo from the porch had her rising again. They hurried to the door.

"There's a car coming up the drive." Ty stood at the bottom of the porch steps, eyes glued to the trees where the driveway disappeared from view. They could all hear the growl of an engine and the crunch of gravel under tires as a vehicle wound its way up from the road.

Leo stepped forward, and the men strode down the drive to intercept the vehicle. Penny, heart pounding, retrieved the rifle from inside the door while Keira grabbed another from the hall closet. The two women stood guard on the porch, ready to defend the men and themselves if necessary.

This didn't feel like an attack, but it could be a distraction so the real one could begin. She scanned the trees around the front of the house, worried about what they couldn't see from around the back.

Before she could further contemplate taking a peek behind the house, a truck crawled up the drive and stopped just past the tree line. A man got out, completely relaxed, until he saw the guns in Ty and Leo's hands. Penny could barely make out what was said. Something about a package. Leo reached out and took a padded envelope from the man.

Message delivered, the man climbed back into his truck and quickly left. Ty and Leo shared a look, Leo turning the package over in his hand before they both holstered their guns and jogged back to the porch.

"That was weird." Penny propped her rifle against the house.

Keira nodded and did the same. "I agree. What's that?"

Leo held it out to her. "He said someone paid him to bring it out here. It's for you."

Keira reared back like she'd been slapped. "For me? From whom?"

Leo shrugged. "Guy didn't say. Just that he was supposed to give it to Keira Artherton." He waved it at her. "Open it."

After a moment's hesitation, Keira took the envelope and ripped it open. She pulled out a basic cell phone and a folded sheet of paper. Penny took the phone so Keira could read the note.

"It's from my dad. He wants me to call him."

"So do it," Leo said.

Keira glared at him. "What if I don't want to talk to him?"

Leo shrugged again. "He obviously has something to say to you. Maybe he just wants to convince you to come home so you don't get hurt. Maybe he wants you to negotiate with us for the belt. Who knows? He's got something to say and whatever it is, could give us a clue about what's coming. Call him."

Keira continued to glare at him, and for a moment, Penny thought she might refuse just to spite him. Leo had gotten under Keira's skin from the very beginning, and she was now opposed to everything he said. But it wasn't long before his words sank in, and Keira wavered.

"Just see what he wants," Penny encouraged softly. "You can always hang up on him and shut the phone off if you don't like what he has to say."

Keira nodded finally and turned on the cell. "At least I don't have to worry about leading them to us now. They apparently already know where we are," she muttered as she punched in her father's cell phone number.

Penny scanned the trees again, thinking the same thing.

"Put it on speaker," Ty said as Keira went to hold the phone to her ear.

Keira nodded and punched the button just as the call connected.

"Keira?"

"Hi, Dad."

"Are you all right?"

A deep frown marred Keira's face as she stared at the phone. "That depends on your definition of all right. Physically, I'm fine. Mentally and emotionally, I'm not so sure. It's a bit of blow to learn your family has *murdered people* for their own gain." Anger clouded her accusatory tone. Penny thought it was a good thing—for Dominic Artherton—that he wasn't standing in front of his daughter at the moment. Keira was beyond angry at her father.

Dominic's hearty sigh came through the line loud and clear. "So, you've figured it all out. I'm so sorry you had to learn about all of this the way you did. We were hoping we wouldn't have to involve you, but it seems it was out of our control. I knew encouraging you to befriend that girl would come back to haunt us all. I'm sorry I ever agreed to do it." Regret dripped from his words.

It was Penny's turn to frown. She shared a confused look with Keira.

"What do you mean?"

"When your grandfather found Penny again, he thought we could gain more information if you befriended her. He was practically giddy when you came home from school and mentioned you made friends with her. He told me to encourage and foster your friendship. I was wary and wanted to discourage it, but he insisted, and I caved. I'm sorry. If I hadn't, you might not have been in danger the other night."

"I'm not," Keira retorted hotly. "Penny's worth a thousand of you all, and apparently the only family I have now."

"Keira, no. While I admit I've made some mistakes, you have to know I love you. If you come home, we can explain this more, and you'll see that what we've done is all for the greater good. Think of how much suffering could be eliminated if there was one ruling party. We could unite resources from all over the world to help those who truly need it."

Keira scoffed. "Is that the line of bull crap Granddad's been feeding you, or did you come up with that on your own? I know him. He just wants control. He might make an effort to help others, but for him, this is truly all about control. I've seen how he runs the family. How he railroaded you and Greg into becoming lawyers. Greg wanted to be a doctor, did you know that? But he gave in to you and Granddad with your pointed words and expectations of him to be an attorney.

"And don't even bother trying to tell me that a majority of your clients aren't somehow associated with Granddad. I'm betting he's sent you most of them over the years, *and* I'm guessing you've granted them all favors and made sure there were loopholes allowing them to take advantage of the system. I've dealt with a few of them in court when their plans backfire. *And* don't think I don't remember how disappointed he was when I chose to pursue criminal law and join the prosecutor's office instead of going into contract and real estate law like the rest of you. This is not about altruism. This is about greed, pure and simple."

Dominic's silence was answer enough.

Penny spared a glance at Ty and Leo. Both men looked shocked at her outburst.

"Wow," Leo mouthed. A new admiration sparked in his eyes for Keira. He finally seemed to be shaking free of the assumptions he made about her.

"Keira, regardless of what you may think, you still need to come home. Your grandfather needs you. He was hoping to do all of this without you, but it seems you're vital in our quest." His voice took on a hard note. "You can either come home voluntarily, or, after we kill all of your friends, you will be forced to return and then be put under lock and key until you cooperate. It's your choice."

Shock crossed Keira's face. It quickly turned to anger, and she moved to disconnect the call. Penny's hand on hers stopped her.

"Ask why," she breathed. "Why are *you* vital?" She jabbed a finger at Keira.

Keira nodded and turned her attention back to the phone. "Why does he want me? He's been disappointed in me for years now. And it's not like I could represent him in court even if I wanted to—which I don't. We're family."

"It's not about that." Dominic hesitated. "Look, I'd really rather not discuss this over the phone. Besides, it's easier to just show you than to explain it."

"Explain what?" Keira demanded.

Dominic sighed again. "You always were stubborn," he muttered. "Your birthright," he said, louder. "It became yours when your Aunt Lana died. Your grandfather thought it best to withhold the knowledge until necessary."

"My birthright? What birthright? Aunt Lana had nothing of value except her house to leave to anyone and Granddad sold that."

Understanding struck Penny upside the head. She slapped her hands over her mouth to hold in a squawk. Keira gave her a sharp look. Penny just flapped her hand.

Holy crap. This couldn't be.

Could it?

If she was right, this could be a game changer.

Keira shot her another bewildered look before turning her attention back to her dad. "Look, I'm not coming home. And I don't intend to come quietly either. You just said I was stubborn. You have no idea. What you all have done is just wrong, and I refuse to be a part of it. You can capture me and lock me away for the rest of my life, but I will never help you. I love you, Dad, but I can't be a part of this."

This time when she went to hang up, no one stopped her. She quickly turned off the phone, then looked at Penny.

"What? What are you all freaked out about?"

Penny took a deep breath. "What if... what if you're like me? And Ty? What if you have some special ability we don't know about, but your grandfather does, and he wants to exploit it?"

Keira's eyes widened, and both Ty and Leo sucked in a breath.

"No. No, that's simply not possible." Keira held up her hands and backed away. "I'm just boring old me. Nothing special about me except my ability to put the bad guys in jail."

"No, that makes sense," Ty remarked, regaining his composure. "Why else would they *need* you? They might *want* you, so you'll be safe, but your dad said they actually *need* you. There's something about you, specifically, that's special. I mean, what else could your birthright be that's so important?"

"I don't know, but it's not that." Keira stomped her foot and put her hands on her hips. She would look like a petulant two-year-old if the situation weren't so dire.

"We need to call Jack. Have him do some research on Iphigenia," Penny said. The sooner they knew more about her, the sooner they could figure out just why Keira was so important.

Ty nodded and started for the house. "I'll get him on the line."

They all traipsed back inside, Keira sputtering about how it wasn't necessary. They all ignored her. Leo went back to finishing breakfast while Ty booted up the laptop and got Jack on the secure video chat.

"Hi, Dad."

"Son. It's good to hear from you. I know you called and said you were safe, but I hadn't heard anything since. I was getting worried. How are things?"

"Interesting." Ty filled him in on the events of the last thirty-six hours.

"Every time we think we've figured this out, it grows another head. Maybe there's something to that hydra thing after all," Jack muttered. "Metaphorically, of course."

"Right. But listen, we need some more information. What do you know about Iphigenia? Other than what you told us before. Does she have any divine history?"

Jack frowned. "Divine? Well, yes, actually she does. There's one myth that states after Artemis saved her, she later turned Iphigenia into the goddess Hecate and sat her on her court of ladies-in-waiting. Why?"

"Because we think Keira might have some divine ability like Penny and I do, passed down from her divine ancestor."

"I do not!" Keira put her face in front of the camera. "Hi. I'm Keira. I'm not special. I'm an attorney. Tell them they're wrong," she pleaded.

Jack sat back and stared at them thoughtfully through the video feed. "I can't. It's certainly possible you have some latent ability if Ty and Penny are any indication. Although, since Hecate's divinity was given to her by Artemis, and she wasn't born of it like Hercules or Thetis, I can't be sure. Have you tried to access any abilities?"

Keira shook her head fiercely. "No. Because. I. Don't. Have. Any."

"Keira, I know this is hard to fathom, but we didn't think we could do the things we can either until we tried," Penny said, her tone soothing. "Maybe we should look into this more."

"I don't even know what to try," Keira said, hands flying. "I don't know the first thing about Iphigenia or Hecate or whatever her name was."

Leo thrust a plate of bacon and eggs in front of Keira. "Here. Eat and calm down. Listen to what Jack has to say and maybe you'll get some answers."

Penny bit her lip to keep from laughing at the look of pure hatred Keira shot at Leo. Keira grabbed the plate from him, though, and stuffed a piece of bacon in her mouth. Penny caught Leo's smirk as he turned back to the stove.

"Hecate was the goddess of witchcraft and necromancy. She had a strong knowledge of potions and magic. In modern times, she's heavily associated with Wicca."

Keira gulped down her bacon and stared wide-eyed at Jack. "So, I'm a witch?" she whispered, appalled.

Jack tipped his head slightly. "It's certainly possible."

"Do you feel witchy?" Penny asked, mouth quirking.

Keira whacked her on the arm. "It's not funny!"

Penny rubbed her bicep and smiled fully. "Would you relax? I'm just trying to lighten the moment. So you might be able to do magic. Cool. I can turn myself and others into any animal I want, and Ty can bend trees and rip apart metal with his bare hands. It's all good. So, let's just simmer down and take it one step at a time. Okay?"

Keira took a deep breath and collected herself. After a moment, she nodded, much more settled. "You're right. I'm sorry. I'm just completely freaked out by all of this. None of this is supposed to be real, much less happening to me." She looked at Jack on the screen. "So what do I do? What should I try?"

"Do you remember any stories you heard as a child? Anyone with any special ability?"

Keira started to shake her head, then stopped. "Wait." She looked at Penny. "My aunt. Lana. I remember she used to have all these books with herbs and what-not in them. I would look through them sometimes, but I didn't really understand any of it. I was only maybe six or seven. She died not long after that."

"Do you remember any of it?" Ty asked.

Keira thought hard for a moment before shaking her head. "No. Just vague images of old books and pictures of plants. I couldn't even tell you what plants they were."

They all frowned.

"What if we hold a seance?"

As a group, they spun to look at Leo, who, until now, quietly listened to the exchange.

"Huh?" Keira finally said.

Leo shrugged. "He said Hecate's the goddess of necromancy. That means she can communicate with the dead. What if we try to communicate with the dead? Maybe you can get a hold of this aunt of yours and ask her for help."

There was a brief pause before Jack spoke again. "That's actually a great idea. If she's going to have an ability, necromancy might very well be it."

They all turned back to Jack and stared at him.

Penny was the first to recover. "Okay. So, what do we need to do if we want to do that?"

Jack steered them toward some books they could get online that would help them. Leo grabbed his tablet and started pulling them up.

"It looks like I have everything we need here if I improvise a bit," Leo said after quickly flipping through a couple of them.

"Good. Do it soon. You need to know what you're up against and what it is they want from Keira."

Ty thanked his dad and cut the connection. He sat back and looked at them all. "So, I guess we're holding a seance, then."

CHAPTER 42

"How many walk-in closets does this house have?" Keira asked an hour later as they crammed themselves and their supplies into Leo's bedroom closet.

After their conversation with Jack, Ty and Penny took Alex some breakfast and checked on Seth while Leo and Keira scrounged up what they would need to conduct a seance. Now they were gathered to perform it.

Leo set the small pot he grabbed from the kitchen atop the chafing dish he dug out of his camping supplies. They put a couple of cinnamon sticks in it, along with some sandalwood essential oil and distilled water. He lit the dish to heat the mixture while Keira drew a pentagram on the hardwood floor with chalk. She placed candles—sourced from emergency supplies—at the points and lit them. She surveyed the set up and nodded.

"Okay. I think we're ready. Everyone pick a side and sit." She motioned to the circle. Ty sat with his back to the back wall of the closet. Penny sat on his right, Leo on his left. Keira took up residence by the door.

"Join hands, please," Keira requested.

Keira took a shaky breath. Penny bit back a smile as she saw Leo squeeze Keira's hand in encouragement. For all the animosity between the two, they seemed to care about one another. His reassurance seemed to work, too, for she squared her shoulders and a determined glint entered her dark eyes. Penny was glad to see it. Once Keira set her mind to something, she rarely failed. Penny was counting on that now.

"Bear with me on this. I'm not quite sure what I'm doing, so I'm going to wing it and hope for the best." Keira took a deep breath and began her chant, calling forth the spirits.

The longer she chanted, the more Penny felt the power build and the more melodic Keira's voice became. Penny could feel the trance Keira weaved as she spoke. Maybe there really was something to her having hidden abilities, after all.

Suddenly, the atmosphere in the room changed. A darkness settled over them, thick and fluid, making Penny's heartbeat quicken. She clutched Ty's hand harder. The steam coming off of the pot on the chafing dish began to swirl and form shapes.

Keira stopped chanting and stared at the steam.

"I call forth Lana Artherton." Keira's voice was sound and resolute. It brooked no argument.

The steam swirled angrily.

Keira called for Lana again.

This time, after a brief angry twirl, the steam settled, and a voice spoke out of nowhere. "Who calls me?"

They all jumped at the sound.

"Holy shit, it worked," Leo murmured.

Penny shushed him and focused on the steam and Keira.

"I do, Aunt Lana." Keira stared into the steam.

All Penny saw were swirls and vague shapes. She had a feeling Keira saw much, much more.

"Keira?"

"Yes."

"I see you've discovered who you are."

"Sort of. Who am I, Aunt Lana? How is this possible?"

"One woman from every generation of our family can do what you can do. In my generation, it was me. You are the one for yours," the voice intoned.

Could she be any more vague, Penny wondered?

"I don't understand, Aunt Lana. What is it I can do? Talk to the dead, obviously. Is it more than that?" Keira pleaded with the spirit.

"It's so much more, child. So much more. You have magic in your veins. You just have to tap into it."

"How do I do that?"

"Focus within. You'll find it."

The steam began to swirl again. "I have to go now. Focus within, Keira."

Keira stared at it for several moments before dropping Penny's and Leo's hands. "She's gone."

Penny stared at Keira in awe. "That was amazing."

"It was weird." Keira rose, agitated, and left the closet.

Ty and Leo blew out the candles and snuffed out the chafing dish while Penny followed Keira. She stood at the window, staring out at the yard beyond. Penny decided to offer silent support and wrapped her arms around Keira in a hug, resting her cheek on top of the smaller woman's head. After a moment, Keira wrapped her arms around Penny's waist. She heaved a giant sigh and Penny hugged her tight, trying to comfort her friend.

"This is so bizarre," Keira said softly, breaking the silence.

Penny let out a snort. "Tell me something new."

Keira gave a brief laugh. "I know. I'm being a flake. It's just so hard to take all of this in. I'm trying. Really."

Penny nodded. "I know. I wish we had more time for you to come to grips with it all, but we don't." She took a deep breath and pulled back a bit so she could look down at Keira. "Did what Lana said make sense? Do you know what to do now?"

Keira dropped her arms and hugged herself. "Crazily enough, I think so. When we were in the middle of that... I felt... something. It's hard to explain. It was like there was something inside of me that woke up during the seance. I can still feel it. I don't really know what it is, but it's there, shouting at me that it's awake."

Again, Penny nodded. "I know what you mean. It's like an invisible tool you always carry with you. Always ready to be pulled out and used. Its weight is reassuring. You know it's there for you to use whenever you need it."

Keira's eyes widened. "Yes, exactly." Her face fell as she frowned. "But I'm not sure if I can control it if I access it. It's so big, it's scary."

"You'll never know if you don't try. You want to go practice?" If Keira had any hope of getting a handle on what she could do, she needed to examine it closer. That meant bringing it out to play.

Keira took a deep breath, then nodded. "Let's do it."

CHAPTER 43

"All right," Penny said a short time later. "Let's see what you can do without a spell book. Mostly since we don't have one." She grinned at Keira, who smiled back. They were out in the yard, well away from the house, just to be safe.

"How do I do this, Pen?"

"Look inward, like your aunt said to do. Focus on that new thing you can feel. Let it take shape, then reach out and touch it with your mind. I'm hoping it will tell you what it can do. Ty and I had the advantage of already knowing what we could do, so it was just a matter of tapping into our abilities. Just be careful when you decide to use it, though, since we don't know what it is. Think small."

Keira nodded. She shook out her arms and took a deep breath, closing her eyes. "Okay. Find the thing and talk to it." She inhaled once more and went quiet.

Penny watched as Keira turned her focus inward, looking for what had awakened. She was a little apprehensive about what Keira would uncover. Magic and witchcraft were powerful tools. Uncontrolled, they could cause a lot of damage. Penny was grateful Keira was on their side. She could understand why Victor wanted Keira now.

After several minutes, Keira opened her eyes. Excitement shone in their brown depths. "I think I found it." She walked over to the woodpile near the shed. "I'm going to try something. Stand back."

Penny stepped back until she stood several feet behind Keira. She had no clue what Keira intended to do.

Hands out in front of her, Keira stood, focused on the woodpile. Suddenly, several of the logs shot up off the pile to wobble unsteadily in the air. Slowly, they lowered until they rested in a teepee formation on the ground in front of Keira.

"I did it!" Keira lowered her hands and turned with a squeal.

Penny was stunned. Holy crap! Keira could move things with her mind.

"I'll say. So, you can move things with your mind. That's—that's more than I was expecting." To say she was disconcerted was an understatement. It hadn't really hit her how big of a deal it could be for Keira to have Hecate's abilities until now.

Keira's smile faded at the look on Penny's face. "What were you expecting?"

Penny gave her a sheepish smile. "To be honest, I'm not really sure. Maybe an illusion of some sort?"

Keira regarded her with a thoughtful look. "Let's try that, too." She focused inward and within moments, Penny was staring at her friend, who suddenly had a pink cowboy hat on her head.

A saucy grin bloomed on Keira's face. "What do you think? Is it me?"

Penny couldn't help but laugh. As freaky as Keira's abilities were, it was nice to see her personality come back out to play.

Stepping closer, Penny peered at the hat on Keira's head. It certainly looked real. "Can I touch it?"

Keira shrugged. "Try it."

Penny reached out and poked at it with one finger. It held, but seemed to blink.

"Whoa. Gotta hold it a little harder if it's going to hold up to physical manipulation." A frown marred Keira's face as she concentrated. "Try it again."

Penny poked it again. This time, it stayed solid and didn't waver.

"Try to take it."

"Are you sure?" Penny frowned. Sweat dotted Keira's face. "I don't want you to overtax yourself."

Keira nodded. "Yes. I'm okay. If it gets to be too much, I'll just let the illusion go."

Penny hesitated another moment before reaching out. "All right. If you're sure?"

"Yep. Do it."

Taking an illusionary hat off her best friend's head ranked right up there as one of the weirdest things she had ever done, Penny decided as she took the hat. Again, it stayed solid and seemed as real as it would if it actually was.

"This is insane." Penny turned the hat over in her hands. It was perfect. It looked just like a straw cowboy hat. There were no gaps, no areas where the weave was blurred. The color was uniform over the entire thing. It even had teal feathers hanging off of the white leather string. Keira had some serious mojo.

Penny put the hat back on Keira's head just as Ty and Leo walked around the side of the house toward them.

"Where on earth did you find that monstrosity?" Leo asked as they came to a stop next to them.

Keira grinned at Penny. There was a purely devilish glint in Keira's eyes. Penny just shook her head. Leo was about to get schooled.

"Well, it came from the same place as your pants," Keira told him, still grinning.

Leo frowned. "My pants? I'm wearing jea—" His words cut off as he looked down and saw not the jeans he put on that morning, but tight, pink and purple-striped slacks. They hugged his legs and hips, leaving absolutely nothing to the imagination.

"What the hell!" Leo turned a full circle, trying to look at the full extent of his clothes.

Penny and Ty erupted into laughter. The look on Leo's face was priceless.

"What happened to my jeans?" He surveyed his pants again before looking back up to spear Keira with a glare. "Keira, give them back."

She just laughed. "Oh, I don't know, Leo. I kinda like the look. Shows off all your manly bits." She bit her lip as she stared gleefully at his lower half.

That sent Ty into even bigger peals of laughter. Tears streamed down his face, and he leaned against the woodpile. Penny covered her mouth in an attempt to stifle her own laughter.

Leo suddenly grinned. "If you wanted to see all my manly bits, all you had to do was ask, *chère*."

It was Keira's turn to glare at Leo. "You can keep your bits to yourself."

Penny thought for sure Keira would give him back his jeans. To her amazement, though, Keira's grin reappeared and Leo's tight, tight pants turned into parachute pants. Shiny, bright, neon orange parachute pants.

A satisfied smile stole over Keira's face. "There. No more bits in sight. I do like the color. How about you?"

Leo looked down and just shook his head, muttering under his breath. "I look like a fuckin' genie."

Keira's eyes lit up once more, but fortunately for Leo, Ty moved away from the woodpile, distracting her before she could make him look any more ridiculous.

Wiping the tears from his face, Ty struggled to get his laughter under control. "Keira, that was awesome. Thank you. I will never let him live this down."

"Screw you, Farris," Leo growled. "Can I have my jeans back now, please?"

Keira ignored him and readjusted her hat.

"How did you do that?" Ty asked.

Keira shrugged. "I tried."

She certainly did, Penny thought, mirth still rolling through her. "Show them what else you can do."

"Oh, Jesus. There's more?" Leo complained. "Don't maim me, woman."

The devilish gleam reentered Keira's eyes. One of these days, Penny mused, Leo would learn to stop antagonizing her.

Arms crossed, Penny waited to see what Keira would do to show the men her telekinetic ability.

She didn't have to wait long.

Leo jumped and yelped. He turned around to see a thin stick floating in mid-air right at the level of his backside.

Keira ticked her finger, and the stick came at him again. Leo scurried back. Keira poked him with the stick and laughed.

Leo just stopped and glared.

With one last laugh, Keira relented. She dropped the stick and crossed her arms, an eyebrow arching in his direction, daring him to comment.

Leo glared, but kept his mouth shut, which was probably wise. The poor man still had on his parachute pants. Penny hated to think what she would do to him if he sassed her again. She was also amazed at how long and easily Keira could hold the illusion. She still had her hat, too. It was almost like once she did it that first time and figured it out, it became as natural as breathing.

"Is there anything else you want to demonstrate?" Leo asked, rubbing his backside.

Keira smiled and shook her head. "No. I'm good."

"Cool. How about giving me back my jeans?"

She waved a hand. "Later."

Ty barked another laugh before he schooled his features and controlled himself. "So, how does this work?" He circled Leo, looking at the orange monstrosity covering Leo's lower half. Ty rubbed the material between his fingers. "They certainly feel real."

"They are so long as I can hold the illusion. I'm not exactly sure where it comes from, but it's some kind of energy that's all around us. I can feel it and manipulate it to do what I want. I didn't actually pick up the stick. I used the energy to surround it. By manipulating that energy, I could then control the stick. The pants are similar. I told the energy what I wanted, and it did it."

Leo looked down at his pants with newfound respect. "So, you literally made these out of thin air?"

"Well, *I* didn't. The energy did. I just told it what I wanted and helped it find its shape."

"Could you make anything, then?" Ty asked.

Keira tapped her chin thoughtfully. "No. I think there are limits to what I can control. I'm not quite sure what that is, but I can feel a limit to the ability."

That would make sense, Penny thought. Keira was human. The source of her power rested with her divine ancestor, Hecate. Only a fraction of that would be passed down. Just like Penny's own ability and Ty's strength. Both Thetis and Hercules could likely do a lot more than either of them could ever dream of.

"I guess the question now is, how do we use this to help us fight?" Penny said. "What do you think, Keira?"

Keira shrugged again. "I'm not a strategist, so I'm not sure." She looked at Ty and Leo. "What do you two think?"

They looked at each other, silently communicating. Penny could tell they were both running battle strategies in their heads, trying to figure out where Keira's abilities would be most beneficial. Penny wondered the same thing, but like Keira, she was no strategist. She was suddenly very thankful for Ty and Leo's military expertise.

"Do you think you could put up and maintain a net or a barrier around the sides of the property we were already trying to booby trap?" Ty asked.

"I can try."

"Do it. Let's see what you can do."

Focus turned inward again, Keira stared off into space as she concentrated. Penny felt the hairs on the back of her neck rise as the air fairly crackled with energy. She looked around warily, half expecting to see lightning come streaking down out of the sky.

The pink cowboy hat blinked in and out of focus, as did Leo's pants as Keira drew on all of her power to put the barrier in place. Sweat popped out on her brow and her breathing quickened.

Penny didn't like this. Keira seemed to be taxing herself to the max. Even if she could erect the barrier, Penny doubted she could defend it once attacked.

When blood dripped from Keira's nose, Penny intervened.

"Keira, stop!" She grabbed onto Keira's biceps. When she sagged, Penny tightened her grip, so she didn't crash to the ground.

Leo swooped in and wrapped his arms around her before she could completely collapse. "Whoa there, *chère*. I've got you."

Keira shook her head and pushed against Leo's chest, trying to stand on her own. "I'm okay. I think we found the limit to my ability, though."

Leo held on, refusing to let go just yet. "Yet you still held on to the illusion of my pants until the very end."

Keira glanced down at his now denim-clad legs and smiled. "My bad. Here, let me fix it."

The parachute pants came back, this time neon green.

Leo laughed. "Yeah. You're going to be just fine." He loosened his grip on her, holding her arm until he was sure she was steady on her feet.

Penny stepped forward. Keira needed a break. Hell, so did Penny after that. "Come on, Keira. Let's go clean up your nose."

With a frown, Keira raised a hand to her face. "My nose? What's wrong with my nose?" She touched it, her fingers coming away bloody.

Eyes wide, she stared at it. "Holy crap." She looked up at Penny. "I see why you stopped me now."

Penny nodded, shoving back the fear she'd felt. She never wanted to see her friend like that again. "Don't ever push it that far again. You scared the crap out of me."

"I think I scared myself." She took a deep breath and brushed her hair back from her face. "I think I can make small barriers here and there, but a large one surrounding the house will be impossible."

Ty laid a hand on her shoulder. "We'll take whatever you can give. I'm sorry I asked you to do that."

Keira waved him off. "Don't be. Now I know what I can and can't do." She patted his hand and took a step toward the house. "I'm going to go in and clean up and get some water."

Penny watched Keira let go of all the energy. Her body relaxed, and Leo's pants transformed back into jeans.

She followed the smaller woman back to the house, her thoughts jumbled. Victor was going to be doubly aggressive now that Keira was on their side and not his. He knew what she could do—had known all along—and would respond accordingly now that Keira knew too.

Outrage at the man for keeping such a secret from her friend surged through Penny. She understood why her own family left her in the dark. She didn't particularly like it, but she understood it. It had kept her safe and undiscovered all these years. If Theo was still alive, Penny was sure she would still be in the dark about her heritage.

Not telling Keira also kept her safe, but it wasn't done out of love. Victor's intent had been malicious. She had a feeling he knew Keira would refuse to help him on his quest. Keeping her in the dark hadn't been about keeping her safe—it had been about making sure she didn't use her powers against him.

Penny hoped Victor showed up to this fight. She looked forward to seeing his face as Keira strung him up and kicked his ass.

CHAPTER 44

Ty set down the tools he was using to rig yet another trap. They were hoping to discourage anyone from taking certain routes to the house. Building an actual barricade all around the property would take too long and would give Victor's forces too many places to hide in the already dense swamp. Simple snare traps and large branches rigged to drop from the trees were much simpler, but still effective, and now scattered the forest and swampland surrounding the house.

All except for one area just off to the west. It had its own natural trap in the form of the "meanest, orneriest, gator to ever walk the Louisiana swamp," according to Leo. He said if any of Victor's men dared to step through that part of the swamp, the gator would make sure they never did again.

Ty wasn't about to argue. No one knew these swamps and forests better than Leo. He ran a survival guide business and a camping outfitter in this area. He practically lived in the trees and swamps. If he said there was a mean, territorial gator lurking off that way that would chew up a man and spit him out, there was a mean, territorial gator off that way that would chew up a man and spit him out.

A crunching noise behind him made him whirl, his hand going to the pistol tucked into the small of his back.

"It's just me," Penny said, emerging from the trees.

Ty let out a breath. This attack needed to happen. He was so on edge, waiting for men with guns to jump out at him from around every corner. He left the SEALs to avoid ambush situations just like this. Although, if someone was going to ambush him, he preferred it to happen in the desert. Fewer places for the bad guys to hide.

Penny walked up to him and right into his arms. She threaded her fingers into his hair and leaned close. Ty settled his hands at her waist. She raised her face for a kiss, and Ty was happy to oblige. Only the fact they were too exposed out here allowed Ty to keep a reign on his control. She was potent.

He pulled back and smiled down at her. "As nice as that was, I know you didn't come out here for just a kiss."

Penny smiled back. "No. I wanted to talk to you without anyone overhearing."

Her expression was so serious it immediately set him on alert. "What? What's wrong?"

"Nothing," Penny hastened to assure him. She sighed and took his hand in hers, tugging him to a fallen tree.

"Okay, something's bothering you." He took her face between his hands after they sat and forced her to look at him. "Tell me."

She wrapped her hands around his wrists and leaned forward until her forehead rested against his. "It's not really *bothering* me, it's just something I need to get off my chest. I'm just going to come out and say it."

She pulled back enough so she could look him in the eye.

"I love you."

All the air left Ty's lungs in a rush. Emotion clogged his throat and his heart thundered in his chest. Before he could speak, she rushed on.

"I know it's soon and we haven't known each other long, but all this—" she gestured around them, "has made me realize that life is short and nothing is guaranteed beyond the now. All day you—*us*—has been on my mind. Last night was amazing. Life-changing. I can still feel you. It's how I found you. I just focused on you and let it lead me here. I don't think I'll never *not* know how to find you for the rest of our lives."

Ty agreed. He could still feel her, too. He'd been aware of her all day long, even when he couldn't see her and didn't know where she was. Instinctively, he'd known he could find her without having to ask where she went. Their connection was beyond the emotional and physical. Something spiritual now tied them together.

"Listen to me," he said, still cupping her face. "It is not too soon for you to say that because I feel it, too. I love you, Penelope Dimas. You have come into my life and flipped it upside down and inside out. I cannot imagine living without you, and I don't plan to. Whatever happens here, I will forever be by your side."

He kissed her then, trying to convey the depth of his feelings.

And they were deep. He could scarcely comprehend them himself. She was a part of his soul now. He couldn't remember how he felt without her presence glowing inside him.

Ty pulled her closer as she kissed him back just as passionately. He let the kiss linger for several moments before he groaned and pulled back. "What I wouldn't give to be back in the house, so I could strip you naked right now."

Penny chuckled. "I know. We wouldn't have any privacy, though. Keira's rummaging around looking for stuff so she can try her hand at some warding spells, and she corralled Leo and Alex into helping her."

Ty smiled at the image. Whether Leo knew it or not, he was a goner. Keira had him wrapped around her little finger. "She's really taken to this whole divine powers thing. I'm surprised. She seemed pretty freaked out in the beginning."

Penny nodded and snuggled into Ty's chest. "She's pretty resilient. And determined. She's never not accomplished something she's put her mind to. I think she just decided fighting the inevitable was stupid and proceeded to embrace the crazy like the rest of us."

Ty chuckled. "Crazy is about right. I wonder if our lives will ever be normal or if there will always be some greedy, evil, otherworldly element on the back burner."

"God, I hope not. I just want to finish my accounting degree and run Theo's business. I will gladly leave fighting the bad guys to you."

"I just want normal bad guys again."

Penny laughed and looked up. "I love you."

Ty's heart swelled at the words. He would never get tired of hearing that.

"I love you too."

As he lowered his mouth to hers for one more kiss, he realized that regardless of all the crazy, he wouldn't change a thing.

It led him to her.

CHAPTER 45

Penny woke from a dead sleep, instantly on full alert. Her heart hammered as she stared around the dark room, listening intently. Something had pulled her from sleep.

The eerie silence made her pulse thunder in her ears. She slid out of bed and quickly dressed. Something didn't feel right. She decided to see if she could find Ty, who was on guard duty.

Before she could make it to the door, it creaked open. Penny looked behind her, realizing she left the pistol on the bedside table. Deciding there were other ways to fight, Penny shifted into a mouse and scurried into the corner.

"Penny?"

Her breath whooshed out in relief. She quickly shifted back. "Ty?"

He opened the door fully and stepped in. "Good, you're awake. They're here."

He was so calm, it took Penny a moment to comprehend what he said. Once she did, any relief she felt quickly evaporated. Her heart picked up its tempo again as adrenaline rushed into her veins. "Seriously?"

Ty nodded and handed her a set of keys. "Go wake up Keira and Alex. You can let Seth know, but leave him in the closet. I'm going to wake Leo."

"Leo's awake," Leo said from the doorway.

Penny jumped a foot. She hadn't heard the man approach. "Holy crap!" She put her hand over her now triple-timing heart.

Unaffected by Leo's sudden appearance, Ty continued like they were never interrupted. "I'm going outside with Leo to set the last traps and barriers. You, Keira, and Alex keep the house secure for now."

He swooped down and placed a hard, potent kiss on her lips.

"And put your comms in."

Penny nodded, her hand coming to rest on his cheek.

Ty covered it with his own. "I love you. Stay safe, Pen."

She nodded. "I love you, too. Be careful."

With a nod, he and Leo swept out the door as quickly as they came in, leaving Penny alone with her adrenaline. She sucked in a deep breath, trying to get herself in check so she could think clearly.

Okay. First, she needed shoes.

A quick glance around the room revealed her tennis shoes peeking out from underneath the rocking chair. Penny hurried over and thrust her feet into them. Next, she put on the belt, then grabbed the pistol off the nightstand. Keys in hand, Penny rushed out of the bedroom.

Just as she reached Keira's door, it flew open and Keira emerged, hair wild, but wide awake and dressed.

"Leo woke me." Keira's voice was still rough with sleep.

Penny fished a hairband out of her pocket and handed it over so Keira could tame her wild locks.

"It's really happening now, isn't it?" Keira gathered her riot of curls together and wrapped the band around them.

Penny nodded. She tamed her own hair into a messy bun. "Yep. Ty and Leo just went outside. I'm going to go get Alex."

"I'll go get all the weapons out and ready."

Keira sprinted past while Penny hurried down the hall to the bed-room turned jail. She quickly slid open the locks and unlocked the deadbolt on the door.

"Alex."

The man sat up as she stepped into the doorway. The sheet fell to reveal the stark white bandage on his shoulder. Penny caught his wince in the moonlight streaming through the window.

"Penny? What's going on?"

"The bad guys are here. Get dressed and meet me by the back wall of the great room."

He nodded and swung his legs off the bed.

"Let Seth know what's coming." She didn't wait for him to reply, simply spun on her heel and hurried to the back of the house to help Keira.

"Grab the other one," Keira yelled as Penny came flying around the corner to the great room. They had piled the guns and ammunition into two laundry baskets, making them easy to transport. Keira pulled one across the floor to the window. Penny grabbed the other from where it sat out of the way by the wall.

"Do you see anything?" Penny asked as she settled in next to Keira. She grabbed a rifle from the basket and checked it.

"Not yet."

They both stared out the window, looking for movement. They had luck on their side tonight. The moon was full and there wasn't a cloud in the sky, which meant they could see all the way to the trees fairly easily.

Alex hurried up to them. "Anything?"

Penny shook her head. She picked up the infrared scope from the table behind them and scanned the trees. A few small animals hid in the scrub and up in the trees, but no humans were visible. Whoever was out there was still deep in the swamp.

Keira picked up the comm units from the table and passed them out. Penny was thankful Leo was who he was. His business and military connections gave him access to many, many useful things, like the comm units.

Making quick work of donning the device, Penny pressed the button on the mic wrapped around her neck. "Ty? Do you copy?"

"Copy," his whispered voice came back in her ear.

"We're set up," she told him. "I scanned the back with the scope. No signs of intruders."

The comm clicked as Ty replied. "They tripped an alarm at the edge of the property. Looks like they came in by boat. Leo and I are finishing the driveway barricade. We'll be back to the house in five."

Penny acknowledged him and sat back to wait. She could only hope the traps took out most of the men. The fewer they had to face, the better.

CHAPTER 46

Ty and Leo returned to the house in record time. The driveway barricade took little to finish. It was just a matter of laying the spikes they'd fashioned from the frame of an old airboat into the trench they pre-dug in the drive and filling it in with dirt. To keep anyone from walking through, they dragged a bunch of brambles onto the drive and piled them high. Obstacles, snares, and tree limbs rigged to fall littered the tree line all around the house.

"Start flipping through the camera feeds. I'll hook up the laptop so we can both monitor their whereabouts," Ty said to Leo.

They worked swiftly to get things set up. Ty didn't know how quickly their attackers would get through the woods, and he wanted to be ready. They needed to get an accurate count of the intruders and their positions before they breached the tree line.

He plugged the laptop into Leo's main computer and got it set up. Black and white infrared images popped to life on his screen.

"You take the east and south. I've got the west and north," Leo said.

Ty grabbed the feeds from the system and split the frames on his screen. Leo's set up was amazing. The man had some serious technical know-how in addition to his survivalist skills.

Alex came around to peer over their shoulders. He grabbed a pen and a pad of paper and started tallying bodies as they walked past the surveillance cameras. Every time Ty thought they found them all, another one would cross in front of a camera. The odds were not looking good. In five minutes' time, they counted ten men. There were likely one or two others they hadn't seen yet. He prayed their traps worked and picked a few off, and that they had enough firepower to hold off this many men. All of them were carrying semi-automatic rifles and had at least one pistol strapped to their bodies. Several of them carried heavy packs, hiding heaven only knew what.

Victor, it seemed, decided not to underestimate them this time. Ty had a feeling that had more to do with the fact he knew his grand-daughter was against him, and what she was capable of. He knew he would need to split her focus if his men had any chance of breaking through and getting to Penny.

Ty did his best to compartmentalize his feelings. He was livid Victor Artherton thought he had the right to come after Penny and not only to take the belt from her, but to eliminate her in the process. He was having a hard time holding back the rage. His feelings for Penny were definitely clouding his judgement. But he knew if he wanted to be effective in this fight, he needed to push all those feelings aside and look at the situation from a strictly military point of view. This was an operation like any other. It just had a different setting than he was used to. The wilds of Louisiana differed vastly from the deserts of Afghanistan.

Over the next ten minutes, Ty's eyes bounced from one viewing pane to another on his screen. He watched the snares take two and another one get tagged by a branch as he tripped one of the limbs they had rigged to fall. A man on Leo's screens got hit by a limb as well.

Ty definitely liked these odds more. The two hanging tangled in netting wouldn't be a problem unless one of their buddies climbed a tree and cut them down. The other two could come around and rejoin the fight, but they would at least be out cold until a few more of their friends were hopefully out of the picture.

"Those traps worked great," Alex murmured. "I'm glad I'm on this side and not out there."

Ty concurred. He would almost always rather be on the defensive; to have the stronghold and dare others to breach it.

"They're coming through the trees now!" Penny's urgent cry pulled Ty's attention away from the monitors. He hurried over to the window and took the scope from her.

"Over there." She pointed to the right. "And there."

Ty counted three coming to rest behind the first line of trees to the east and north. "There are still six out there, at least." He would bet at least two of them were trying to circle around and come through from the front of the house.

"Alex, take the other scope and go check the front."

The mercenary quickly did as he was told. Ty still didn't completely trust the man, but he'd shown he was willing to work, and to fight, over the last day and a half. He hoped that stayed true once the bullets started flying.

Suddenly, a scream pierced the air from the west, followed by a wild burst of gunfire. They all swung that way to look.

"What do you see, Leo?"

Leo quickly scanned through the monitors. "Nothing."

"Then what the hell was that?" Keira asked.

Ty looked over at his friend to see him grinning.

"Clancy."

"Who?"

"The gator," Leo explained.

Keira's eyes widened. "You were serious about that?"

"I never kid about gators," Leo deadpanned.

Ty bit back his smile as Keira rolled her eyes and turned back to the window. Those two were going to kill each other or end up falling in love. Knowing Leo like he did, Ty was betting on the latter.

Shaking off the distracting thoughts, Ty turned back to the window and scanned the tree line again. One more man had emerged, bringing the total to four. The location of the other two worried him. They were probably trying to breach the front. He just prayed there were only two. But he didn't think so. This had the hallmark of being led by former military. The men were too evenly spaced, outfitted too well. There were definite amateurs in their ranks—they would have caught fewer in their booby traps if they were all former military—but whoever led them knew what he was doing.

"Alex," Ty activated his mic. "Who do you think is leading these guys?"

A moment of silence met Ty's question.

"Probably a guy named Travis Eversole. He was Marine recon. Would still be if he hadn't got caught killing civilians. He told me he didn't understand why his commander was so angry. They were all terrorists to Travis, and he didn't care to differentiate."

Shit—a psychopath. A psychopath with black ops training. Just what they needed.

"Wonderful. Do you see anyone yet?"

"Not yet, no."

Ty held back a growl. He wanted locations on the remaining men. He pressed his mic again. "Keep looking. Report as soon as you see anything."

"Copy."

"What are they waiting for?" Penny crouched at the bottom of the windows, peering out at the trees. "They're all just standing there."

Ty held up the scope and looked again. All four men still hovered behind the trees. It hit him suddenly what their plan was. He sat back on his heels and looked around at the others. "They're waiting on the rest of the men to get around front, then they're going to come at us from every side." It's exactly what he would do in a situation like this—it's exactly what he'd done on numerous SEAL missions.

"That's why we set so many traps, though, right? To stop them from doing that?" Penny said.

"We set them to *try* to do that. They were always more likely to just make it more difficult, though."

"So we're still going to get attacked from all sides, even with all the prep work we did?"

Ty grinned, quickly switching gears. "Not if we attack first."

"Hell, yeah." Leo pushed away from the monitors and grabbed a rifle. "Let's take these assholes down."

Brain firmly in operations mode, Ty grabbed a rifle and double-checked it. Years of tactical training kicked in, and he started issuing orders. "Penny, Keira, one of you go up front and help Alex keep watch."

"I'll go." Keira grabbed the scope and scurried off.

"Penny, watch the monitors and see if you can spot the rest of the men trying to go around to the front. We need eyes on all of them, so none of them slip in unnoticed."

"Got it."

Ty turned to Leo. "You ready for this?"

Leo grinned. "You know it."

Both men quickly traded out the standard scopes on their rifles for night vision ones. Again, Ty was thankful for Leo's array of equipment. Thankful and impressed. He hadn't expected to find such good equipment outside of the military or SWAT. Leo had it all, and then some. It was the survivalist in him coming out, Leo told him earlier.

Whatever it was, it was coming in handy.

Ty aimed the rifle through the open window and peered through the scope. "You take the left."

"Copy."

Ty wanted to laugh as he sighted his targets. None of the mercenaries hid very well. For as stealthily as they approached and the equipment they sported, they were terribly undertrained. It had to chafe on a guy like Eversole to work with such amateurs.

He had a feeling Victor hired these men for their willingness to kill and hadn't bothered to check their skill sets.

They were going to pay for that now.

"We'll probably only get one good shot each, so we need to make them count," Leo said.

"Agreed. We'll shoot on three." Ty took aim. "Ready?"

"Ready."

Ty touched the trigger. "One... two... three."

Both men squeezed the trigger. Ty watched his man fall. Shouts erupted from the remaining men even as Ty swung his rifle toward the other one on his side of the yard. The man ducked behind the tree before Ty could get off a shot.

"Come on, you bastard. Peek," Ty murmured.

"I've got movement out front." Alex's voice came through the comm. "From the east. Can't see anyone yet, but I can hear them. You guys hit someone? Because they are all kinds of agitated if the shouts are anything to go by."

"Two," Ty replied. "Keep an eye out."

"Copy."

"I got one!" Penny cried.

"Where?" Ty asked. He still looked through his rifle scope, keeping the gun trained on the second man, just waiting for him to poke his head around the tree.

"To the west. Must be one the alligator missed. He keeps looking behind him like he's expecting something to jump out and attack."

"Good ol' Clancy." Leo chuckled.

Ty smirked. Who'd have thought the big, bad ex-SEAL would have a soft spot for an alligator?

Leo's rifle barked, swiftly followed by a curse. "Damn. I missed. The asshole moved."

The man in Ty's crosshairs was smarter and continued to stay tucked away. Ty got a glimpse of shoulder every so often, but nothing of substance.

"We've got a problem!" Keira came running up, heading straight for the stash of weapons. She pulled two rifles off the stack.

That pulled Ty away from the scope. "What?" Dread punched him in the gut at the look of fear and disbelief on Keira's face.

"Two men just emerged from the east. One of them has a grenade launcher."

He exchanged a look with Leo. This was not good.

Leo stood. "I'll go with her and send Alex to you. We'll stop him."

Ty nodded. He caught Penny's wide-eyed, frightened gaze and tried to send her a reassuring smile before turning back to sight the targets behind the house. His own gut churned. Leo needed to stop the guy with the grenade launcher. If the attackers took out the house, they would all be sitting ducks out in the open. The only other structures that offered any protection were the shed and detached garage, but there were yards of open grass to cross before they could get to either.

Rifle raised again, Ty sighted his targets out back. Leo's man was still in the same place, but Ty's had disappeared.

Curses Ty thought he left behind with his SEAL days slipped free.

He tapped his mic. "We've got one MIA."

"Copy," Leo answered.

"Pen, check just north and east of the house and see if you can pick him up."

He heard her fingers clack on the keyboard as she pulled up the right screens. Ty continued to scan the trees.

Alex moved up to the window Leo had occupied, carrying a rifle.

"There's one at about eleven o'clock," Ty said, not bothering with a greeting. "Watch him."

"Yep."

A rifle cracked from the front of the house.

"He nicked one," Keira reported. "There's no good angle on the guy with the grenade launcher. He's holed up behind that massive oak to the right of the driveway."

Ty knew which one she meant. The tree was three hundred years old if it was a day. It towered above the yard like a proud sentinel. Right now, though, it was more like a giant shield.

"Get down!" Leo's shout echoed through the house.

Ty launched himself at Penny and pulled her from the chair. He rolled them beneath the table and covered her with his body.

A boom sounded from outside, accompanied by a bright flash.

Ty pressed his mic. "Did he miss?"

"Keira steered the grenade away. It hit in the yard." Awe tinged his voice.

Ty couldn't blame him. He was impressed, too. Turning Leo's jeans into some monstrosity was a far cry from grabbing a high-speed projectile in the air and pushing it away. The woman had one hell of a learning curve.

"She did what?" Alex asked. He pushed up from the floor to kneel at the window again, a confused look on his face. "How did she steer it away?" He glared at them now. "What the fuck haven't you told me?"

Ty exchanged a look with Penny, but before either of them could reply, a flash of light from the trees caught their attention.

Eyes wide, Ty dove at Penny again.

"Incoming!"

CHAPTER 47

Penny coughed and pushed against the splintered wood lying across her back. Pain split her head. She pressed a hand to her forehead, where it was the worst. Blood smeared her hand.

Ignoring the wound for now, Penny looked around, trying to get her bearings. "Ty?"

A groan answered her from beneath the rubble and the pile shifted. Penny grabbed a board and tossed it away. "Ty!"

The pile shifted again as he pushed up to his knees. Boards and debris fell away. He shoved at what was left until he could get to his feet beside her.

"Oh my God! Are you okay?" She ran her hands over his head and down his chest, looking for injuries. There had been so much stuff on top of him. He had to have at least some broken ribs.

He grabbed her frantically searching hands. "I'm fine. I'm fine, sugar." He frowned down at her. "Are you all right? You're bleeding."

Penny touched her head again. It still ached like mad, but the bleeding had already slowed to a trickle. "I'm okay."

He kissed her quick before stepping back. "Good. Where's Alex?"

Penny's eyes widened. Oh, God! He had been right in front of the window.

She spun around to see a giant hole where the window and part of the wall used to be. More pieces of debris littered the floor, and a foot stuck out from beneath the rubble.

They rushed over and started pulling at the debris. Ty quickly uncovered his head. His quiet curse made Penny stop short.

"Is he..."

Ty touched Alex's neck, then nodded.

Tears welled in Penny's eyes. Alex was by no means a friend, but he wasn't an absolutely terrible person either. He'd been trying to do the right thing in the end.

Ty stood. "Come on. We need to find Leo and Keira and regroup. We're sitting ducks by this hole, and I think the house is on fire."

Penny sniffed and did indeed smell smoke.

Leo's voice suddenly sounded in their comms. "Are you guys all right?"

Ty was quick to reassure him. "Penny and I are fine. Alex is dead. We're coming to you."

"Copy."

Following Ty's lead, Penny picked up a rifle, pistol, and as much ammo as she could stuff into her pockets, then headed for the front of the house. She wished they could take the baskets with them, but hauling them out of the house would just slow them down.

Keira ran at them and grabbed Penny in a fierce hug. "I was so worried. I wish I could have stopped that one too."

So did Penny, but it took them all by surprise.

Ty handed boxes of ammo to Leo.

"We need to get out of here." Leo took the boxes and started stuffing them into every pocket he had.

"Yep. The house is smoldering." Ty put a hand on Leo's shoulder. "I'm sorry I brought this to you. I never dreamed they'd try to blow us up."

"Hey, no worries, man. We're brothers. I'd have volunteered if you hadn't asked. The house can be replaced. You and your woman can't." He gestured at Penny.

Ty gave a quick nod of thanks while Penny felt the tears well again, thankful once more for Leo, and not just for his arsenal this time. The man was a gem. He had offered them a chance to take a stand instead of continuing to run, and lost nearly everything in the process.

Penny swiped her eyes and crouched down behind the men. Ty trained his rifle on the trees, looking through the scope.

"Where's the one with the grenade launcher?" he asked, glancing at Leo.

Leo grinned and didn't say a word.

"Okay, then." Ty's head bobbed. He put his eye back to the scope. "I see two. And there are two more lurking somewhere." He pulled back to look at the group. "We can't rule out the ones who got beaned by the tree limbs, either."

"Which leaves seven." Penny's eyebrow quirked. "That's better than the twelve originally. I'm still impressed at how you guys nailed that number." She was happier than ever to have the two former SEALs on her side. She'd likely be dead or still on the run without them.

"So, what's our plan?" Keira asked.

Ty surveyed the area beyond the house. Penny could see the gears working in his mind as he planned. She could tell by the crease between his eyebrows that the unknowns in the situation bothered him. He didn't like not having all the information, and the missing men were a glaring hole.

"We're going to head for the garage. It's the closest place to offer any cover. Once we're there, Penny, you and I are going to shift and go scout the locations of our missing friends."

Eyes wide, Penny nodded. It was a sound plan.

She was still terrified.

Guns and battle were not her thing, but if it meant staying alive and keeping the others alive, she would do whatever was necessary.

Ty took her hand and squeezed it, somehow knowing she needed the reassurance. Penny clung tight.

"Leo, you stay with Keira and keep her safe. Keira, if you get a chance to drop something on someone or string someone up by his ankles, do it."

They both nodded.

Another blast shook the house as a second grenade flew through the hole created by the first one. It landed near the counter that separated the kitchen from the living area, sending debris flying. Flames erupted immediately, reaching the ceiling as the gas lines from the stove caught fire.

"Let's get the hell out of here," Leo growled.

Penny concurred. It was time to move on.

Hands shaking, Penny took two steps toward the door, following Ty, when she remembered Seth.

She grabbed Ty's arm. "Wait. What about Seth? We can't just leave him in here to die."

Ty closed his eyes, muttering an oath. "I'll go get him. Leo, get the women to safety."

Penny immediately protested. "We need to stick together."

"She's right, Ty," Leo agreed. "We *all* stand a better chance of reaching the garage if we leave at the same time. If you come out with Seth alone, you're going to be an easy target."

Penny didn't give him a chance to argue. She turned and ran down the hall. Footsteps sounded behind her as the others followed.

Ty caught up to her as she reached the closet door. "This independent streak of yours is problematic."

Penny grinned at him. "You love it. Now open the door, frogman."

Ty quirked a half-smile at her and did as he was told. Seth stood in the middle of the closet floor, eyeing them warily.

"Come on." Ty motioned the man out. "The house is on fire."

Seth's eyes widened. He hurried out of his makeshift cell.

Leo had his pistol out and trained on the man. "Let's get one thing straight. We still don't trust you. You try to run away, I will shoot you. You try to hurt any of us, I will shoot you. You so much as breathe the wrong way, I—"

"Will shoot me. Yeah, I get it." Seth waved his hand, cutting off Leo. "Let's just go. I've no desire to burn to death."

Penny's eyebrows slammed down into a frown. Was this guy for real? "You don't want to burn to death? Seriously?"

Keira raised her rifle. "Can I just shoot him?"

Ty glowered at their prisoner. "I'm tempted to let her. You're lucky we're not murderers like you." He grabbed Seth's arm and pulled him into the hall. "And that we have little time before we *all* burn to death. Come on. Before I change my mind."

Smoke now filled the hallway, thick and disorienting. Ty led the way, one hand clutching the back of Seth's shirt and the other trailing along the wall to keep his bearings.

By the time they reached the end of the hallway, Penny's heart hammered in her chest. An inferno ripped through the back of the house. The entire kitchen and back wall of the house were ablaze. Flames leaped up the walls, consuming everything they could reach.

Thankfully, the fire hadn't spread to the front of the house yet, but it wouldn't be long.

"Form a chain," Ty yelled over the sound of the fire and the shrieking smoke alarms. Penny hooked her hand in the back of Ty's jeans. She felt Keira's hand clutch the hem of her shirt.

Heart in her throat, Penny fell in step behind Ty as he moved forward toward the door. She hoped they didn't miss it. It was impossible to see through the thick, choking smoke.

"Oomph!" Penny landed hard against Ty's back as he crashed into a piece of furniture, coming to an abrupt halt.

"Sorry. I can't see a damn thing." Ty coughed and moved around the chair he fell over.

Suddenly, the smoke cleared, revealing a path to the door. It was like a perfect tunnel. Penny straightened and looked over her shoulder. Keira grinned back at her.

All right, then.

Now able to see, the group took off and fled through the house. Cautious of bad guys lurking and ready to take them all out, Ty slowly opened the door. He pushed Seth ahead of him.

Knowing he was the most likely to get shot, Seth struggled. Leo's pistol against his back calmed him. "Either you go, or I shoot you, and you won't have to worry about your friends out there."

Seth glared at Leo, but turned and walked out. The others followed when no bullets flew. They formed a circle, walking back to back, rifles and handguns at the ready.

Penny watched the trees with a wary gaze. Shadows flickered in the firelight, making her jump. The house fire brought back memories of their harried escape from the other night, ramping up her adrenaline to the nth degree. The garage seemed miles away.

The crack of gunfire joined the roar of the flames from the house. Penny ducked and yelped as a bullet winged over her head, imbedding itself in the house.

"Move!" Ty yelled. He picked up the pace, and they all but flew across the space between the house and the garage. More shots pinged off of the metal building. Penny heard Ty grunt as he busted through the side door and they stumbled inside.

Bent double, Penny struggled to catch her breath. "Can we stop running out of burning buildings, please?"

Keira bent over next to her and nodded, raising a finger. "I second that."

"Shit."

Leo's curse made Penny straighten. She turned to see what brought on the outburst and nearly collapsed at the sight.

Blood poured down Ty's arm to drip off his fingers onto the floor.

"Oh my God, you've been shot!" Penny rushed to him and peeled his t-shirt away from his bicep.

"I'm fine. It's a through-and-through." He tried to pull away, intent on getting to the door.

Penny grabbed on with both hands and glared at him before turning her attention back to his arm. "You are not fine. You're dripping blood everywhere."

Ty glanced at the wound. "Just wrap it. It'll be fine. I've had worse."

Leo took off his t-shirt, then ripped off the bottom. He thrust the long strip of cloth in front of her face, saving Ty from another tongue-lashing. Penny bit her tongue and took the fabric, realizing now was not the time to get into it.

She guessed she should be grateful the injury wasn't worse or that more of them weren't shot. That had been entirely too close, though. Seeing the blood and bullet hole brought home the deadliness of the situation. Until now, none of them had been injured. Seeing it unnerved her.

It also brought home the depth of her feelings for Ty. She knew she loved him, but now she knew she couldn't live without him.

"There. That should keep you until we can do more about it." Penny tied the final knot in the fabric around the wound.

Ty lifted his arm to check out her handiwork and nodded at what he saw. "All right. Let's do this. I'm tired of being shot at and nearly burned to a crispy critter. Let's go stop these assholes."

Penny took a deep breath before placing her hand in his. Nerves made her shake, but resolution flowed through her. They—she—could do this. Ty quirked an eyebrow at her, silently asking if she was ready. She nodded and squeezed his hand.

Ty looked at Leo, then at Seth. Penny belatedly realized he was trying to keep their secret. Again, she was glad for his military training. If left up to her, she would forget about everything except the current situation.

The moment Leo distracted Seth, Penny shifted them into rats, and they fled the garage. She hoped they just looked like a couple of scared animals fleeing the loud humans who just invaded their territory.

Penny let Ty lead the way, hanging onto his tail with her teeth. It was unconventional, but it worked and kept them moving.

Soon, they were behind the first man. Ty pulled his tail free and shifted back to human. Penny let the change roll over herself and squatted beside him.

He put a finger to his lips and motioned for her to stay put. Penny nodded. Ty crept forward, not making a sound.

The mercenary never knew what hit him. Ty put in him a sleeper hold, and he was out in moments.

Working quickly, Ty pulled the strap off the man's rifle and secured his hands before finding a handkerchief amongst the mercenary's things and stuffing it into the man's mouth. He liberated him of his weapons and ammo before returning to Penny's side.

She just stared at him in awe.

"What?"

"That was amazing. I think from start to finish, you were only over there a minute."

Ty shrugged. "I've had some practice."

She could imagine. She also realized he could have done a whole lot more to that man and hadn't. Penny had no idea what they were going to do with these men when this was all over, dead or alive.

Worrying about that now would just distract her, so she shoved the thoughts away and focused on keeping up with Ty, who was now moving through the forest, looking for another mercenary.

They found one lurking near the oak tree. The body of the man Leo shot earlier was sprawled only feet away.

Penny turned her head and fought the urge to gag. Leo was an excellent shot. He hit the man square in the head. The damage wasn't something Penny was likely to forget seeing anytime soon.

The other mercenary had picked up the grenade launcher and was preparing to fire it at the garage. Ty grabbed him, but because of the weapon, couldn't put him in a sleeper hold like the last man, and they ended up grappling. Penny held her breath as she watched them fight. This man wasn't like the others. She had a feeling this was Eversole. He was cockier than the others and a better fighter.

He slipped free of Ty's hold and they squared off.

"You must be the cop Victor told us about. You might be huge, but you're no match for me. I'm going to kick your ass, and then I'm going to gut you and watch you bleed. After that I'm going to find your lady friend and do the same to her."

Ty's nostrils flared. "Good luck with that. Did Victor also tell you I was a SEAL?"

Penny smiled as a slight hesitation hitched the mercenary's shoulders before he squared them again. The cocky grin grew.

"Even better. I'll get bragging rights about how I killed the big, bad SEAL."

Ty scoffed. "Whatever, dude. Quit talking. Or are you too chicken to attack me?"

The grin slipped off Eversole's face. He took a step toward Ty, feigning a punch only to swing out with the other arm. Ty saw it coming and blocked it, throwing a punch of his own. His fist connected with Eversole's jaw, and the man's head snapped to the side. He stumbled back a couple feet before regrouping.

"Not so cocky now, huh?" Ty grinned and waved the man forward. "Come on, you bastard."

Eversole charged, and Ty lifted a booted foot in the blink of an eye. It connected with Eversole's jaw, and he dropped like a sack of potatoes, out cold.

"Wow. That was incredibly easy." Ty stared down at the now unconscious man, shaking his head.

Penny stood from her hiding spot. He turned and offered her a smile. Her heart skipped a beat, as it always did when he smiled at her.

"I really wanted more of a fight." He nudged the man onto his stomach with his boot. "Oh well. The end result is the same, I guess."

Penny laughed softly and walked toward him. "It really isn't much of a contest when your opponent is human and you have the strength of Hercules running through your veins."

Ty smiled sardonically as he trussed up Eversole, just like his comrade. "It would have been nice to at least have a challenge. This guy was all bluster and no skill."

He stood and handed her the weapons he liberated from Eversole. "I wonder if the others will keep fighting now that we've incapacitated their leader?"

Penny opened her mouth to respond but never got any words out. The sound of a vehicle coming up the driveway had her snapping her mouth shut and clutching the pistol Ty handed her.

He urged her back further into the trees and crouched beside her.

"Leo, I took out two, but we've got a car coming up the drive now," Ty whispered into his mic.

"Copy."

From their vantage point, Penny and Ty could see a black SUV, like the one they took from her house in Texas, come to a halt just short of the barricade Ty and Leo erected across the driveway. Four men climbed out of the vehicle, fully automatic rifles in their hands.

"Oh, shit," Ty muttered.

Penny's stomach lurched and her heart lodged in her throat. This was not good.

The four men clambered around the obstacles blocking the drive and lined up on the other side, weapons pointed at the garage.

"Oh my God," Penny breathed. "Eversole must have radioed our position before you took him out. They're going to shoot up the garage."

Ty pushed his mic button. "Leo, get down!" he whispered urgently.

The words were barely out of his mouth before the four men opened fire and strafed the garage.

Penny watched in horror as bullets ripped through the metal siding on the garage, leaving hundreds of holes in their wake. The barrage continued for several long seconds. When their magazines ran dry, each man swiftly replaced it and started firing again.

By the time they ran out of bullets completely, tears streamed down Penny's face. She buried it in Ty's chest and bit her lip until she tasted blood, trying to hold back the sobs.

Through her tears and her own shakes, Penny felt Ty's body vibrate with rage. She had a feeling he was about to go full Hercules.

She was okay with that.

She was going to get him over there so he could.

Tears drying up as determination took their place, Penny looked Ty in the eye, silently conveying her plan.

As soon as he nodded his understanding, they were back in rat form and scurrying through the forest. They slipped easily through the brambles and emerged directly behind the men, who now had pistols in their hands as they prepared to advance on the garage.

Penny released Ty and let the change roll over them. He launched himself at the two on the left, while Penny shifted herself into a mountain lion and leaped at the two on the right.

She made good use of the cat's body and let loose a fierce yowl as she dove forward. Both men swung around just as she reached them. She caught the one nearest to her in the chest. Claws sinking deep, she curled her paws and flung the man sideways while she rolled in the opposite direction. She let her claws rake through his flesh as he flew away. The man went down with an agonized scream, which quickly gave way to gurgles as his lungs filled with blood.

Penny felt no remorse. No one messed with her family. Not anymore.

She swung around and stalked toward the second man. His hand shook as he aimed his pistol at her. Penny shifted to the rat and bound forward. When she reached him, she shifted back to the cat and swiped the gun from his hand. He screamed in terror and backed away, eyes wide. Penny stalked forward. He turned and ran. She lunged after him. He wasn't going anywhere.

Her claws caught him in the back, and she pushed him to the ground, landing swiftly on top of him. One swipe of her massive paw across his head knocked him unconscious.

Penny spun around, intending to help Ty, only to see one man sprawled at his feet while he flung the other through the air. The man hit the oak tree thirty feet away with a sickening thud, landing on the ground in a heap.

She ran forward anyway, knowing there were still others hiding in the woods. As soon as she reached Ty, she turned them small again and made a beeline for the garage. They had to check and see if the others were still alive. She prayed they were still alive.

In seconds, they were scurrying through the door of the garage. Penny let them shift back.

"Keira? Leo?" Penny looked around, frantic.

"Penny."

Heart in her throat, Penny whirled around at the sound of Leo's voice. He kneeled in the corner behind the door, cradling a very weak-looking Keira across his knees.

Penny and Ty rushed over.

"Oh my God! Is she okay? Was she shot?" Penny asked, landing beside them. Keira's face was almost pure white in the moonlight coming through the window. Blood flowed out of her nose in a steady stream. She looked terrible.

Leo shook his head. Tears shimmered in his eyes. "No." His voice cracked. He swallowed and tried again. "No, she wasn't shot. She stopped the bullets from hitting us."

Penny's eyes widened.

"All of them?" Ty asked, incredulous.

Leo nodded. "When you told us to get down and the first rounds ripped through the building, we dropped to the floor. A couple flew right over our heads. One hit Seth." Leo tipped his head to something just beyond them. Penny and Ty turned to see Seth sprawled on the garage floor, lying in a pool of blood, unmoving. It looked like a bullet had caught him in the chest.

"The next thing I knew," Leo continued, "there was some kind of energy shield over us and the bullets were just bouncing off." He looked down at the woman in his arms, admiration and respect shining from his eyes. "She saved our lives."

Wow. Penny was flabbergasted and at a loss for words. Keira had put her own life on the line to save them.

"Keira." Penny touched her friend's face. "Keira, wake up."

She moaned and shifted.

"Keira," Leo tried. "Hey, I need new pants. You need to wake up and make me wear something ridiculous."

Penny smiled at his cajoling. If anything would bring Keira around, it would be Leo's teasing.

Keira's eyelashes fluttered and a small smile ghosted over her lips. She inhaled deeply and opened her eyes briefly.

"That's it, *chère*. Wake up."

She moaned again. "Mm. You... you don't need new pants. Those show off your manly bits just fine. But a jaunty beret might be nice." Her voice was weak and shaky, but she was awake. Penny sent up a prayer of thanks and blinked furiously against the tears welling in her eyes.

Leo barked out a laugh before hugging her to his chest. "I'll wear whatever you want me to, *chère*. Anytime." He pressed a kiss to her curls and rocked her.

The sound of clapping coming from the doorway made them all swing around.

"Very, very impressive. It's too bad it was all for naught."

Rage, worse than what she just felt, flooded Penny's body.

She knew that voice.

CHAPTER 48

"Granddad?" Voice weary and weak, Keira struggled to sit up in Leo's hold.

Victor spared her a dismissive glance before turning to Penny. He had a rifle slung over his shoulder, which he swiftly brought up to aim at her chest.

"Ah, finally. You know, your uncle did an excellent job at dropping off the map with you after your parents died."

"You mean after you *murdered them*?" Penny's hands clenched into fists at her side. What she wouldn't give for Ty's strength right now. She so badly wanted to deck this man. She wanted to *throttle* him and all his minions for killing her family.

Victor waved a hand. "Semantics. The point, my dear, is that while he buried his identity and yours under layers and layers of deceit and shell companies, we still found you. And now I intend to take back the power denied to us, with or without our enchantress." He looked at Keira, who now stood next to Leo, his arm wrapped tightly around her, holding her up.

"The belt is not yours to command. It was given to *my* ancestor, not yours," Penny retorted angrily.

He wagged a finger and tsked at her. "Ah, but that's where you're wrong. Ares gave *Hippolyta* the belt, not Penthesilea. Penthesilea only got it because Hippolyta died. Upon her death, it could have gone to anyone," he reasoned. "Why not my family?"

"Because it was never intended for you. Ares entrusted it to the Amazons. Not some human family out for a power grab."

Victor shrugged. "Well, regardless, I intend to take it from you and rule mankind." Victor's voice rose as he spoke. It reverberated through the night. "I dare anyone to challenge us."

A sense of foreboding hit Penny square in the chest. Something bad—very, very bad—was coming.

She didn't have to wait long to find out what.

A loud roar began to move through the trees, audible from in the garage. It sounded like a freight train moving in. As Victor turned to look, Ty took advantage of the distraction and rushed the man. They tumbled through the doorway into the yard.

Penny, Leo, and Keira followed them out.

Ty had Victor on his back, one hand clutching Victor's wrist, holding the rifle immobile. The other was wrapped around Victor's neck.

"This ends tonight," Ty growled.

Victor struggled against Ty's hold, trying to break free, but he was no match for Ty's superior strength.

Before Ty could do more, the wind swirled, kicking up leaves and dirt. Branches swayed overhead and bent toward the ground. The flames from the house fire licked skyward, melding into the swirling wind and debris.

Ty looked up, but kept Victor pinned to the ground. "Pen? What's happening? Is this Keira again?"

Penny shook her head, watching the wind coalesce into a twisting column of swirling debris. Keira stood next to her, looking only marginally better than death warmed over. Leo still held her up. She looked as surprised as the rest of them at the swirling column.

"No. She's still spent from stopping the bullets. I don't know what this is, but it isn't her, and it doesn't feel good."

The wind spiraled until a single, narrow column of dust and debris swirled on the ground, extending up past the treetops. Ty yanked the rifle free of Victor's hand and released him. They both scrambled to their feet.

Air howled and whistled around them as the column of air and debris spun faster, the circulation becoming tighter.

"Where's this coming from? There isn't a cloud in the sky," Ty yelled over the wind.

"Can't you feel it?" she yelled back. "It's not natural. There's a power crackling through it." She showed him her arm. All the hair stood on end, and goosebumps covered her skin.

Penny focused on the power emanating from the cloud. It was an awesome and terrifying power. It felt bigger than anything she had ever experienced and a hundred times more deadly. It put her power and the power in the belt to shame.

The swirling cloud seemed to reach a fevered pitch, bowing all the trees toward it before it collapsed violently to the ground, coalescing into one singular point.

Penny stared in disbelief as a man rose from the settling dust. The light from the house fire made it easy to make out his imposing figure. He was at once one of the most handsome, yet terrifying men she'd ever seen. Every bit as tall as Ty, if not taller, his wavy black hair fluttered in the leftover breeze. Otherworldly, dark eyes seemed to suck in all the light while simultaneously shining bright from his chiseled face. A dark beard dusted his jaw, giving him a rakish look. Tight black pants encased his muscular legs and a long leather duster worn over a snug, black shirt outlined his impossibly broad shoulders and chest. Tall, lace-up, black leather boots sheathed his feet. In one hand, he held an iron staff as tall as he was. All-in-all, he was frighteningly beautiful.

He faced Victor and grinned a bone-chilling smile. "I'll take that challenge."

Penny had to hand it to Victor. After an audible gulp, he stepped forward and put on a brave face for the stranger. She was happy to stay pressed against the garage wall.

"And who are you?" Victor asked.

The man's grin widened and, if possible, he looked even more dangerous.

"Hades."

Oh my God.

Penny thought her eyes would fall out of her head. This was not happening.

The god of the underworld was real and still alive.

And he wanted to challenge Victor in his quest for world domination? This was *not* good.

"Holy shit." Ty came to stand next to her. "This just keeps getting better and better. How do we stop the lord of the dead?"

"I have no idea." Her words came out in a terrified whisper.

"Penelope." Hades spun her way and Penny jerked at the sound of her name falling from the god's lips. "Or should I call you Penthesilea?" He quirked one dark brow and gave her a devilish grin. "Come here, little minx."

Ty's hand clamped down on her wrist, holding her in place as she moved to go to Hades. "No," he whispered fiercely.

Penny speared him with a look, imploring him to understand. As much as she wanted to stay where she was, she feared what would happen if she didn't go to Hades more than she feared what would happen if she did. "I have to. One doesn't say no to the god of the underworld."

Hades took a step toward them. "Bring your friend, since he seems reluctant to have you in my presence." He laughed, his voice low and rumbly. "Not that I blame him."

Ty squeezed her wrist one last time before releasing it. Penny grabbed his hand, willing some of his strength to her, and gulped as they stepped forward.

Oh, lord have mercy, this was scary. Penny's heart triple-timed as they stepped closer. Hades could kill them both with a crook of his finger. Belt around her waist or not, she didn't think it would stop him from squashing them like a bug.

They stopped when they were at the edge of the circle created by the god's entrance.

"I was very pleased to hear Victor issue his challenge. It meant I could get involved. You see, I've been following your little fight here. Watching." Hades paced his circle, speaking to them all. "Waiting. I don't care for humans the way my brother, Zeus, seems to, but I do find that you hold a purpose in our universe." He shrugged nonchalantly. "And you keep me in business."

He pointed at her waist. "That belt of yours has the potential to change not only this world, but the nice, orderly world of the gods as well. I can't let that happen."

"How?" Penny asked.

Hades frowned and halted his pacing, clearly not expecting her to question him. "How do I intend to stop it, or how can the belt change my world?"

"Either. Both." Penny wanted to know both, but each answer, particularly how he intended to stop them, scared the crap out of her.

"Hecate isn't happy being an underling goddess." Hades looked back over his shoulder at Victor. "I'm sure you know all about this. *You* were never intended to have the power. It was all supposed to go to her."

Confusion lit Victor's face.

Hades smiled a truly devilish smile and barked out a delighted laugh. "Oh, this is grand. You didn't know." He spun around and stalked over to Victor. "She's been using you—*all* of you—since the very beginning. She planned all of this and has been biding her time. I don't think Artemis knew just how cunning and manipulative Iphigenia was when she saved her and turned her into a goddess." He shrugged. "Or maybe she did. She's never been particularly fond of me. It'd be just like her to give me a good kick in the ass like this.

"Anyway, she intends for you to win the belt, and then have you bring her to the mortal realm, so she can amass an army and invade the underworld," Hades stated, matter-of-fact.

Victor drew himself to his full height. "Well, we just won't summon her here." He smiled. "Problem solved."

Hades shook his head. "No. You're forgetting she's had the last several thousand years to plan this. She's likely got contingencies for her contingencies. If she doesn't get you and your family to do it, she will find someone else. Or she will trick one of you into summoning her. That cannot be allowed to happen."

Penny straightened as the meaning of what Hades wasn't saying hit her. "Dear God," she whispered. "He's going to take it."

"Over our dead bodies," Ty muttered.

Penny looked at him with wide, scared eyes. "Exactly."

Ty's own eyes widened. "We can't let him win any more than we can Victor."

She felt sick to her stomach. "I know. I'd say we run, but I don't know that he wouldn't be able to track us. I don't know how all this godly stuff works," she whispered frantically. Penny's mind whirled with possibilities. She couldn't see a way out of this, but they had to try.

"You're quite right, Penelope. On all counts." Hades broke into their quiet conversation.

Penny and Ty both jerked at the intrusion.

"There is nowhere for you to run that I would not find you. And I do intend to take the belt. By any means necessary."

Penny bristled.

Hades held out a hand, stemming her objections. "But I don't intend to use it. It has become too dangerous to stay in the mortal world any longer. It needs to be returned to my realm to maintain order."

"But it didn't come from *your* realm. It came from Olympus," Penny retorted.

Hades rolled his eyes. "Come now. Don't be so nitpicky. You know perfectly well I mean the *immortal* realm."

"No, I don't," Penny dared to argue. "I don't know anything about you other than what I've read, and hardly any of that was flattering. And it certainly didn't fill me with hope that we could trust you not to use the belt for your own gain."

Hades laughed. "You do have quite the wicked tongue." He swirled a finger at her. "That's the Amazon in you coming out. I bet you're spirited in *all areas.*" His mocking tone left no question as to his meaning. Neither did his eyes as he raked them up and down her tall frame.

Ty growled and took a step forward.

Hades's eyes lit with amusement and he stepped forward to meet Ty's challenge. "Yes, yes, grandson of Hercules. Do try to take me on. I haven't had a good fight in centuries."

Ty frowned. "You know who I am, too?"

"I told you, I've been watching." Hades stepped closer until he was practically nose to nose with Ty.

Penny couldn't help but stare at the sight. Both men were enormous, their genetic connection clear. They were like two giants amid mere men. The tension between them was so thick it felt tangible.

"You take me on in a fair fight, and I guarantee I'll wipe the floor with your godly ass." Ty didn't back down to Hades's slightly superior size and overwhelming power.

A corner of Hades's mouth quirked. "Ah, yes. Possibly. But I never fight fair. Comes with being the lord of the underworld."

He backed up a step and gestured to include all those watching. Penny was astonished to see that the rest of Victor's men had come out of the trees to see what was happening.

"Tyreece was correct. This ends tonight. That belt will no longer be a pawn in your scheme. I hope you all have said your prayers because you will be going to your chosen afterlife tonight."

Gasps and cries of alarm rent the air. Black shapes emerged from the trees behind Victor's men. The cries of alarm turned into screams of terror. Rustles in the trees and splashes in the swamp belied Victor's men trying to run away.

Hades laughed evilly. "Yes. Do run. It's more fun for my friends."

More screams echoed through the trees as those who escaped death earlier were caught by the black shapes roaming through the woods.

Penny moved closer to Ty and clutched his arm. He was stiff with tension, his muscles coiled and ready to spring at a moment's notice.

"What's out there?" Victor demanded. "What have you done?" His face held a sickly pallor, even though his cheeks were flushed bright red with anger.

Hades laughed again. "I just brought some demon friends along to the party."

"Yep. This *really* just keeps getting better and better," Ty muttered.

The black shapes emerged from the trees. They were men, but not men, huge and cloaked in black, with eyes that looked like the pits of hell. Penny shuddered at the sense of darkness and evil now filling the yard.

Several of the demons carried bodies, some of them two or three, which they unceremoniously dumped at Hades's feet. Penny realized they brought not only the ones they just killed, but all the ones that died earlier, before Hades arrived.

"Very nice, boys."

He turned to Victor. "Now it's your turn," he said and reached out with his staff.

"No!" Victor's shout seemed to freeze in mid-air as Hades touched his staff to Victor's chest without warning. Penny watched in horror as an internal fire glowed bright from Victor's heart and spread outward.

Keira's scream made Penny turn.

Faster than she'd ever seen her move, Keira ran past them and right at Hades. Raw energy blasted from her hands and knocked Hades across the yard all the way to the trees. He slammed against the trunk of one and fell to the ground. Keira kept moving until she landed at her grandfather's side.

"No! Granddad!" She caught him as he fell. Fire still burned in his chest, tendrils now snaking out to fan down his arms and up his neck.

Penny ran to her, Ty on her heels. Leo beat them both there.

The old man reached out and touched Keira's cheek. His breath hitched raggedly as the fire progressed throughout his body. "I'm sorry... my dear. I... never meant... for... things to end... this way. We... we were just following... our destiny."

"Well, it's not my destiny, and I don't intend to die. I don't want to rule the world," Keira told him, her voice wobbling.

He smiled faintly. "No. You never did." His hand fell away from her face. "Tell your father... and the others... that I love them." With that, his eyes rolled up and he went limp. The fire burned brighter and burst down his torso, making his entire body glow bright. They all scrambled away as his back suddenly arched. His eyes snapped open, his mouth wide in a silent scream. Flames erupted from his eyes and mouth. The fire glowed brighter, flames shooting higher and erupting down his body until he completely blackened and crumbled to embers.

"No!" Keira wailed. Huge wracking sobs tore from her chest. Leo reached out to enfold her in his arms, murmuring softly. After a moment, though, she shoved him away suddenly and stood.

"No. I don't need to be coddled right now." She sniffed and wiped the tears from her face, determination seeping into her expression.

Penny's sense of foreboding returned. She rose and touched Keira's arm. "Keira. Whatever you're planning—don't do it."

"It wasn't your family he just killed." She pointed at the pile of bodies several feet away.

Penny's eyes shifted to the pile. They widened as she got a look at some of the faces, seeing Keira's brother and her cousins along with all the other men Victor hired.

Dread settled low in her belly. Oh, this was *bad*.

Keira always had a bit of a temper. Penny feared what she would do now that she had magical abilities on her side, as well as righteous anger.

Penny stepped in Keira's path. "He might not have killed my family, but my family is gone, too. Victor killed them."

Keira frowned fiercely. "Are you telling me it's okay my grandfather is dead? That my brother and cousins are dead?" Her voice rose several octaves. "All because they killed *your* family?"

"No." Penny hastily shook her head. That came out all wrong. She took a deep breath and tried again. "No. I just meant we have all lost someone in this fight. It's not worth it to continue it. And that's frickin' *Hades*." She pointed to where the god was just now getting up off the ground. "You can't win against him, Keira."

"She's right, Keira." Leo came up behind her and slid his hands over her shoulders. "It would be suicide."

Keira sagged into Leo, her face crumpling again. His arms wound around her and he pulled her into his chest. "I'm so sorry, *chère*."

Sardonic laughter drew their attention to Hades. "Very nicely done, witch. It's been a long time since someone has taken me by surprise and knocked me on my ass." He strode toward them, his long legs devouring the ground. He stopped only a few feet away. "Seeing as I just killed your grandfather, I'll let you live. This time."

Keira laughed darkly and broke away from Leo. "Do you think I care? Bring it, you immortal bully!" Energy crackled over her head as she prepared to blast him again.

Penny stepped between Keira and Hades and held up her hands. "Let's not get carried away."

Hades straightened, some of the fight leaving him. "You're right. While it might be easier for me to get the belt if I just kill you all, I don't really want to. Contrary to what all your stories tell you, I'm not a completely ruthless bastard."

Penny straightened at that and lowered her arms. He didn't want them dead, too?

"What do you mean? Why don't you want us dead? You had no qualms killing Victor and his henchmen."

"Because you and I fight on the same side. All we want is the safety of the world. To maintain the status quo. Your family has never used the belt for evil gain and has protected it well all these years."

"Then why not let her keep it?" Ty asked. "Why take it away now? You've smashed the Artherton's rebellion. You know Keira won't be a problem, and I doubt you'll get much grief from whoever's left now that you've killed the entire family and she's on our side."

Hades was shaking his head before Ty even finished. "It's simply too dangerous for it to remain in this world any longer. Humans have come too far, developed too much technology. You all have the power to create giant armies with weapons that can easily bring down even the mightiest warriors from my realm. Hecate won't stop until she gets that belt and overthrows me."

"So, this is really all about you?" Leo asked, disdain dripping from his words.

Hades's face darkened. "Careful, human. Unlike your friends, you are expendable."

Penny poked him. "Hey. Forget about him. Answer the question."

Hades glared down at her. "Do not touch me again."

Penny resisted the urge to roll her eyes. Despite seeing his power in action, she strangely wasn't as afraid of Hades as she should be. She was starting to believe he really didn't want to kill them. Oh, she knew that if provoked enough, he would indeed blast them into oblivion, but it wasn't his intention to do so. If it was, he would have done it when he killed Victor's men.

Still, feeling it wise not to anger him further, Penny dropped her hand. "Tell us. Is this really about keeping hold of the underworld?"

Hades glared a moment longer before answering. "Not entirely. Of course I want to hold on to my domain. Can you name any king who wants to lose his kingdom?"

He definitely had a point there.

"But it goes deeper than that," he continued. "If Hecate takes over my world, it will upset *all* the worlds. Things were divided the way they were after the Titan clash for a reason. It was the way to keep the peace. To keep a balance. If one of my brothers or I were to lose control, it would mean a war. One that would end this world and possibly mine. We saw that when we defeated our parents. My brothers and I vowed to keep that from happening ever again unless it was absolutely necessary to preserve the fabric of the universe.

"Even wielding the power she would take from me were she to defeat me, Hecate would have trouble controlling those who have been loyal to me for centuries. Fights would erupt. Demons and monsters the likes of which you have never seen would escape to terrorize both realms. My brothers would launch an attack on her to avenge me. *Everything* will come crumbling down."

"So why not kill Hecate?" Ty asked. "Eliminate her and the problem is solved."

Penny agreed. It seemed simple enough, and Hades was a *god*. This should be easy for him.

"Because I can't find her."

"What do you mean, you can't find her?" Penny demanded. "Track her however you tracked us. I'm assuming it has something to do with our god blood."

Hades nodded. "It does, but she's shielded herself. She *is* the goddess of witchcraft."

Keira stepped forward. "Maybe you need another witch to find her."

Penny grasped her friend's arm at the implications of what she was saying hit. "Keira, no."

"Wait." Ty laid a hand on her arm. "That's not a bad plan." He looked at Hades. "I'm no expert in how all this works, but it sounds plausible. Could Keira find her for you?"

Hades pressed his lips into a thin line, mulling over the idea. "It's possible, but Hecate is much stronger. Her magic older. You would have a difficult time of it, I fear." Then he waved his hand, dismissing the entire plan. "But it doesn't matter. You will give me the belt and the problem will be solved. With it in my possession, she will have lost and the balance will be safe."

"But what if she convinces someone close to you to steal the belt?" Leo asked.

"What?" A dark scowl marred Hades's features.

"Think about it," Leo continued. "She'll still be alive and in the underworld, right?"

Hades nodded.

"So, who's to say she won't one day convince someone to double cross you and steal it for her?"

"Because no one would dare," Hades declared darkly.

"Just like she didn't dare to cross you?" Keira asked.

Hades's glower darkened further as some uncertainty crossed his face. Penny felt victory surge. They had planted some seeds of doubt in his mind and finally seemed to have some leverage. She still didn't like the thought of Keira working with Hades, but if it saved them, kept the belt out of Hades's hands, and stopped Hecate, she supposed she could learn to live with it.

She stepped forward. "You need us, Hades. If you really want to keep the balance, you need us."

He scoffed. "I do not need a bunch of humans—demigod abilities or not—to help me stop Hecate. I just need that bloody belt!"

Penny stepped back out of his reach. She wouldn't put it past him to grab her and forcibly remove it. "And what about what Zeus and Poseidon will think if you have an artifact like that? I doubt they will be happy."

Hades looked down his nose. "They will be happy I have averted disaster."

Penny shrugged. "Maybe for a little while, but eventually they—especially Zeus—will come to resent the fact you have something that would make it impossible for them to best you in a fight."

"Do you really think Zeus—the head honcho god who has destroyed others for even looking at him funny—will allow you to keep such an artifact?" Ty asked.

Leo laughed, joining the argument. "You're definitely dreamin' if you think that's the case, Hades. We may not know as much about how your society works as you do, but if our history texts are even partly correct, Zeus will sneak in and steal it out from under you, stomp you like a bug, and then make your life miserable for the next who knows how many centuries."

Hades stared hard at them all. Penny could see the wheels turning as he thought over what they said. She knew they were right. She could feel it deep in her bones. Whatever fate she and Ty and Keira—and even Leo—were meant to have, she could feel it was this. This fight. Hecate had to be stopped, and they were all supposed to be a part of it.

Taking a leap of faith, and praying she was right—that Hades saw the truth as she did—Penny slid the belt from around her waist and held it out to Ty.

"Penny? What the hell are you doing?" he demanded.

She thrust the belt at him again. "Take this."

"No. Put it back on."

She shook her head. "In a minute. Take it." She stared at him hard, willing him to understand, or to at least cooperate.

After several seconds, he sighed and took it.

Penny immediately stepped forward until she was only a foot from Hades.

"What are you doing?" Hades looked at her, uncertainty making him frown.

"If you really believe taking the belt back with you will solve this, that you can keep the status quo, you can kill me now and have it. I give you my word it will be yours."

A dark grin spread across his face, and Penny felt the first glimmer of fear skate down her spine. Maybe making a bargain with the devil wasn't the best idea she'd ever had.

She squared her shoulders. Too late now, though. The words were out and there was no turning back.

"Why are you willing to die when you don't have to?" Hades asked, genuinely curious.

"Because we're right. For a while, your plan will work, and it will appease your brothers. But Zeus *will* very quickly become jealous. You know that, and I don't know why you're denying it. Unless you plan to freely give him the belt, you will start the very war you're right now trying to prevent."

"Maybe I want a war with Zeus. Did you ever think of that?" Hades bent down until his nose nearly touched hers.

Penny quirked a brow, refusing to let him intimidate her. He was blustering. The seriousness that should accompany such a claim was absent from his eyes. "You don't want a war with Zeus. Poseidon will take his side and you will lose. It's why you've never taken him on in the first place. It's why the three of you were split the way you were. You all want to rule, but neither you nor Poseidon can take the throne without the other, so neither of you ever does. It's all about the balance."

She raised a hand. "You. Need. Us." She poked him in the chest again with each word.

"Aargh!" he roared and spun away. He thrust his hands into his hair, gripping the strands before violently throwing his hands back to his sides. "I should have fucking stayed home and let it all come crashing down!"

Penny smiled, knowing she just won. Who knew it would be so much fun to make a god lose his cool?

He spun back to her. "I suppose you all have a plan?" Hades looked past her to Keira. "You. Witch. You said something about using your abilities to find Hecate. What do you intend to do?"

Keira looked at Leo and Ty before stepping forward to join Penny. "I'm not entirely sure yet."

She held out a hand in a placating gesture when Hades looked like he would erupt again. "This is all still very new to me, and I need to do some research first. I don't know what I'm doing. I don't even know how I managed to blast you across the clearing. It shouldn't have been possible, but I did. We need some time." She looked up at Penny. "I think the basic plan, though, is to find Hecate and then let you blast her into oblivion."

Hades's mouth quirked. "I do like that last part. How much time do you need?"

Keira shrugged. "I'm not sure. We know someone who can help us." She glanced back at Ty, and Penny knew she was thinking of Jack. "It's just a matter of how quickly I can find information and figure things out so Hecate doesn't kill me, or disappear—or both—when I track her down."

Hades nodded and looked up thoughtfully. "All right. But to make sure you don't dawdle, I'm going to give you some incentive." He brushed past the women, moving quickly toward Ty and Leo.

Before any of them could react, Hades touched his staff to Leo's chest. Instead of the fire that spread through Victor, a golden light flowed from Leo's chest and into the staff.

Leo gasped, trying to draw air into his lungs. His back arched and his muscles strained, tendons popping, while his eyes bulged wide as the staff pulled the light from him.

Within moments, the last of the light left him to seep into the staff. Scroll work on the staff, invisible before, now glowed brightly with the golden light. It pulsed angrily for a moment before it settled into the scroll lines.

Leo collapsed onto the ground on his hands and knees, sucking in great big gulps of air.

"Leo!" Keira pushed past Hades and dropped next to him, wrapping an arm around his back.

Leo looked up, more haggard than Penny thought anyone could look. "What... what did you do to me?"

Hades studied the glowing light on his staff, a thoughtful look on his face, before turning his gaze back to Leo. A self-satisfied smirk sat firmly on his lips. "I took your soul. You can have it back when you and your friends bring me Hecate."

The same breath Leo just sucked in began sawing in and out, his eyes wide in panic. "No. No, you can't!"

Hades grinned. "Oh, but I can. And I did."

He sobered and looked at them all. "You have ninety days to bring me Hecate, or Leo's soul is mine for all eternity."

Penny stared in disbelief at the evidence of his claim swirled along the scroll lines on his staff. She hadn't thought there was a fate worse than death, but she had been wrong. At least in death, there was rest for one's immortal soul. If they failed, Leo would be at Hades's mercy forever.

Ty rose from where he crouched next to his friend. "Wait. *Bring* her to you?"

Hades nodded. "Yes. I've decided this was all much more trouble than I expected. I have other matters to attend to, and I don't plan to be at your beck and call to destroy Hecate. You will bring her to me, and I will destroy her at my leisure."

"How?" Penny asked, stunned. "How are we supposed to get to her and bring her to you? She's in your world."

Hades pulled a handful of coins from his pocket. "When you figure out where she is hiding, go to the Necromanteion and enter the underworld. Give these to Charon and he will ferry you across the river so you may pass through the kingdom's gates. Find Hecate and bring her to my palace."

Penny took the coins. The gold gleamed in the glow from the fire, the intricate engravings seemed to dance across the surface of the coins.

"How do we know you'll release Leo's soul once we turn over Hecate? Or let us leave? You're not exactly known for releasing souls from the underworld," Ty asked, angrily.

"You have my word," Hades replied.

Ty scoffed. "Forgive me if I don't find that comforting."

Hades laughed. "I guess you'll just have to trust me."

With that, he backed up a few paces before striking the ground with his staff. The wind began to swirl as it had earlier. Dust and debris spun rapidly around Hades. Penny and the others watched, unease filling all their hearts at their new situation, as the cloud grew, removing Hades—and all the bodies—from their presence.

"Remember," Hades's voice boomed from the cloud. "Ninety days."

The cyclone reached a fevered pitch before shooting up into the sky to disappear, taking Hades—and Leo's soul—with it.

CHAPTER 49

Four weeks later...

"Are you ready for this?"

Penny nodded at Keira from where she sat in front of the mirror. Keira finished clipping Penny's veil to the bun wound at the back of her head and smoothed the fabric so it fell nicely down her back.

"Are you sure?" Keira's eyes caught Penny's in the mirror. "It's all happened so fast."

It had indeed. They had quickly learned that if they had any hope of trapping Hecate and bringing her to Hades, Penny and Ty needed to unite their powers, so they each had the other's abilities. Only a bonding ceremony would allow that.

They had decided to marry as well and make their union complete. A local judge would perform the marriage. Keira would perform the bonding tonight at the height of the full moon.

Penny nodded again. "I'm sure." She turned to face her friend. "It's fitting of the whirlwind that has been our lives lately. And I love him. He's everything I've ever wanted. And if we survive this—if we actually defeat Hecate and bring back the balance—I will have him by my side forever." She clasped Keira's hands to convey her earnestness.

"I truly want that. I could not ask for a better life mate than Tyreece Farris."

Keira pulled Penny in and hugged her, veil and all. "I'm so sorry about all of this."

Penny pulled back to look her friend in the eye. "Don't be. It's fate."

Keira scoffed and looked away pensively. "Well, fate has a nasty sense of humor and I'm not really happy with her right now."

Penny's heart ached for Keira. It had been nearly a month now since Hades took Leo's soul. She knew it weighed heavily on Keira's mind. It was up to Keira to save him. Penny and Ty were only along for the ride and to provide muscle. It would be Keira who would have to outwit the goddess to save the man Penny suspected Keira loved as much as she loved Ty.

But her friend was tenacious and tough. She would find a way to do it, and then she would get her own happily ever after.

There was a knock on the door before it cracked open. Jack poked his head in.

"You ladies ready?"

Penny quirked a brow at Keira. Keira sniffed softly and nodded.

"Yes. We are." Penny rose from her chair and stepped forward.

Jack opened the door fully to take her hand. "You look lovely, my dear. Come, let's go make my son a happy, happy man."

Penny grinned, delighted beyond words this man was going to be her family from this day forward. Jack was an unexpected blessing in all this turmoil.

"Yes. Let's."

Ty tugged at his suit collar as he waited for Penny and his dad to make their appearance. He and Leo stood under the small floral covered arch they had erected in the backyard of the Charleston estate for the wedding. He could hardly believe he was getting married today.

But he was ready for this. Penny meant the world to him, and he wanted to bind himself to her in every way possible.

The back door to the house opened, and Keira stepped out in a soft pink, tea-length strapless dress. Her riotous curls were tamed into a braid, hanging down her back, tiny flowers and ribbons woven amongst the strands of her hair. Leo's sharp inhale from where he stood next to Ty made him smile. He had a feeling Leo would follow him down the aisle soon if they made it through the next couple of months.

All thoughts of Leo, Keira, and their pursuit of Hecate fled Ty's mind as Penny stepped out behind Keira. His breath left him in a whoosh. She looked like a vision on his father's arm. They had gone with simplicity for their ceremony, both because of time constraints and because neither of them wanted a large, flashy wedding. Penny's dress reflected that. It was a simple white silk gown that draped her long curvy body to perfection. It was almost Grecian in design, but more modern, the bodice crisscrossing under her bust to wrap around her waist before the gauzy skirt flowed out from beneath to flutter around her ankles. Her dark hair was braided like Keira's, but then drawn up into a bun at the back of her head. A gauzy veil hung from a pearl comb tucked into the bun.

Leo nudged him from behind. "Breathe, man."

Ty took a deep breath, filling his lungs with much-needed oxygen. His bride was stunning. It was near agony, watching her walk the short distance through the yard to get to him. He wanted her to run. He needed to touch her. To feel the silk of her skin beneath his hands, the softness of her lips against his.

When she finally reached the arch, Ty was strung as tight as a bowstring. Jack handed her to him with a kiss on her cheek. Ty clasped her fingers in his and smiled.

"You look beautiful," he told her softly.

Penny beamed at him. "You don't look so bad yourself."

The judge greeted them, and they turned to face him.

The next few minutes were a near blur to Ty. They elected to use the traditional vows, and both quickly repeated the words. Ty's hands shook when he slid the platinum and diamond wedding band over Penny's finger, the significance of what they were doing hitting him. It was a scary yet thrilling prospect to be tying himself to this woman for the rest of eternity.

***

Penny's heart sang as she slid the platinum band onto Ty's finger. He looked devastatingly handsome in his navy suit and champagne-colored tie.

And he was all hers.

Forever.

It was such a heady feeling. She loved this man more than life itself. Never in her wildest dreams did she imagine her life would lead her here. That it would lead her to this man and this fate.

She couldn't help thinking, as the judge pronounced them husband and wife, that despite all the turmoil surrounding them and the trials to come, she felt blessed.

***

"By the powers that be, so let it be, that two become one and share all for eternity." Keira spoke the final words of the bonding ceremony over Ty and Penny and stepped back.

The now familiar glow of their powers rose to dust their skin. It flowed down their arms and over their clasped hands and into each other. Ty could feel Penny's powers sink into him this time. They buried themselves in his heart and took root.

He looked at her in surprise. He knew she was powerful, but the strength of her ability rivaled his physical strength. It was almost boundless. He wondered what she could do if fully pushed. He also prayed they would never have to find out.

"That is so cool," Leo intoned from his place outside the circle. He, Jack, and Colin had all wanted to observe the ceremony and sat on the ground nearby, watching the proceedings.

"Strange is more like it," Colin said with a laugh.

"You can see it too?" Penny asked.

Leo nodded. "It looks like flames, almost. And your eyes are just freaky."

"Now *that* I agree with," Colin stated.

"Same here," Jack agreed.

Ty laughed. He had thought the same thing the first time all the power-y stuff occurred. He leaned forward and touched his forehead to Penny's. "I guess this means we can't ever make love where someone can see us." They'd probably send someone to the loony bin if they did. Or have the fire department called on them.

Penny laughed softly.

"Ugh. TMI," Keira said, disgusted, then laughed.

Ty grinned at her. "Get used to the TMI *and* the PDA. Since you're going to be living with us, you'll be seeing and hearing a lot of it."

"Great," Leo groaned. "That means I will too." They had decided it would be best for Leo and Keira to stay with them on the estate until they found Hecate and retrieved Leo's soul. They all needed to study up on Hades and his kingdom. It was just easier if they were all together. Safer too.

Laughter flowed around the circle as they all took in Leo's look of utter disgust.

"Don't worry. We'll keep it PG-13 outside the bedroom."

Leo rolled his eyes. "Have you *seen* a PG-13 movie lately? That doesn't exactly fill me with joy."

Penny smiled at him. "We'll behave," she promised before turning back to her husband.

As the glow surrounding them faded with the completion of the power transfer, Ty could see the love shining bright and strong in Penny's eyes. He felt so lucky to have this woman as his wife, his everything, despite all the bad juju surrounding them right now.

Even with all the uncertainty in their lives, he was content.

EPILOGUE

Hecate waved away the image in the water and leaned on her hands on the well.

The first inklings of fear settled low in her gut. This was a troublesome development. The bonding of Thetis's and Hercules's heirs would make her plans harder to accomplish.

And her own great-granddaughter was a powerful, powerful witch.

She silently cursed Hades. *Why* did he have to go and take that man's soul? It had only energized her young descendant and her friends in their quest.

The pitcher next to the well went flying as she gave it a swift kick across the courtyard. She had waited centuries—*thousands of years*—to exact her revenge and take control of her own destiny. Four humans would *not* stop her, no matter what abilities they had inherited from their ancestors.

Jaw tight with determination, she began pulling items from her shelves. Family or not, her young great-granddaughter was about to discover what it really meant to be a witch and the power Hecate held.

***

Keep reading for a sneak peek at book 2 in the *Hecate's Rebellion* series, *The Chosen*.

PROLOGUE

Thick, choking smoke rose from the fire on the cavern floor. The gray swirl obscured much of the light from the flickering flames. Hecate stood to the side, surveying her work. Her laughter, gleefully evil, rang through the chamber and echoed off the walls. She watched as the smoke ascended to the ceiling and flowed through the cracks in the roof, on its way to wreak havoc in her great-granddaughter's life. The meddlesome young woman was in for a surprise she would never see coming. Keira's amateurish witchcraft would never detect the potent spells she just sent her way.

Hecate twirled her fingers through the wisps as they rose. She was done playing nice and biding her time. Victor was supposed to defeat that little twit, Penny, so Hecate could take possession of the belt, but he failed miserably. It was unfortunate Hades got involved, but Hecate wouldn't let that stop her plans. She had waited far too long to get what she wanted. The god of the underworld would not stop her, and neither would a troublesome band of gifted humans.

No. Hecate would get her revenge and show the world that she alone controlled her fate.

CHAPTER 1

A light breeze blew through the trees, making the leaves whisper a soft song. The hot September sun tried to penetrate the lush canopy, but only dappled sunlight fell over Leo Devereaux's face. Straddling a tree limb some twenty-feet off the ground, his thighs gripped the sturdy branch as he worked on the security camera, peering out from the tree's thick foliage. He was thankful for both the breeze and the thick leaf cover. He would roast without them. Changing camera batteries was hot, sweaty work. Today was no different, but at least up here, he got a bit of a break from the relentless Carolina sun.

He wouldn't be out of the heat at all if it weren't for the fact this tree offered an amazing view of the road running along the backside of the estate owned by his friends Ty and Penny Farris. Leo had been staying with them for the last couple months after the shit storm that went down at his home in Louisiana eighty days ago.

He was determined no one would sneak up on them here. Since he got his hands on the security, he'd locked the estate down like a gator's jaw on a chicken. A squirrel didn't eat a nut on the property without him knowing about it.

Despite all the security measures he put in place, he still felt vulnerable. He could ward the grounds against human invaders all day long. But it didn't do shit against the supernatural. For that, he had to rely on the still fledgling knowledge of all things magic held by their resident witch-slash-demigoddess, Keira Artherton. It irked him to no end he couldn't protect them all better. Protection was what he did. He had joined the Navy to protect his country. Had done unspeakable things in the name of protecting the world. Now, he couldn't even fully protect fifty acres of land in South Carolina. Some SEAL he was.

Jesus. Leo swiped a hand down his face. Could he be more of a Debbie Downer? Maudlin seemed to be his go to emotion nowadays.

He scoffed at himself. Having the Greek god of the dead steal your soul and threaten to keep it for all eternity tended to mess with one's emotional stability.

But he was still better than this. He had been trying so hard to go on as if nothing was wrong. But now, with only ten days remaining of their ninety-day limit, he was beginning to wonder if they would succeed. As far as he knew, Keira had made little headway in finding Hecate, even though she holed up with her books and herbs all day, every day. She hadn't told him anything about her progress.

He hadn't asked, though. Leo didn't figure she needed the added pressure of him nagging her about it.

So, here he was perched in a frickin' tree high off the ground, protecting the estate from an enemy they would never see coming, no matter how many cameras he put up.

Shaking his head to rid it of his depressing thoughts, Leo pried the cover off the back of the camera and popped out the batteries, quickly swapping them for the spares in his pocket.

He stretched his arms out to replace the cover, when the air around him took on an electric feel just before a fine gray linen covered his previously bare arms.

"What in the hell?" He stared down at himself in disbelief.

His eyes traveled the length of his arm before landing on the rest of his god-awful outfit. The gray linen was attached to the rest of a Victorian-era tailcoat. His t-shirt was gone, replaced by a soft, white silk shirt, its ruffled collar strangling him. The jeans he donned that morning were gone, too. Thin, fawn-colored, moleskin breeches, tucked into tall black boots, covered his legs now. Without the protection of the heavy denim, tree bark bit into his inner thighs.

Leo shifted his weight and blew out a harsh breath. He was going to kill Keira. The little witch had left him alone lately. He couldn't help but wonder what he did to piss her off now.

It couldn't have been anything too terrible. He usually remembered stoking her fire. It was fun to watch the annoyance flash in her eyes and her spine go ramrod straight. She reminded him of a pissed off kitten. Teasing her was a pleasant distraction from his own problems.

Doing his best to stretch in the restrictive coat, Leo put the cover back on the camera. The tree bit into his legs once again as he shifted his weight to climb down.

As gracefully as his clothing allowed, he swung down off the branch into a fork made by two lower branches. He straddled the sturdier of the two and swung down, dangling six feet from the ground, and let go. His brand new, tall riding boots did little to absorb the shock of his landing.

His dog, Clyde, stood up from his resting spot at the base of the tree. He looked up at his master and whined.

"I know, Clyde. I look ridiculous. Let's go find Keira and get my normal clothes back." Straightening the coat, Leo strode determinedly toward the house and the demigoddess responsible for his wardrobe.

AFTERWORD

Thank you for reading *The Shifter*! I hope you enjoyed it. Please consider leaving a rating or review. It would be greatly appreciated!